I0669214

The Witches of Wells

By

Cheryl Kennedy

W & B Publishers
USA

W & B Publishers

For information:
W & B Publishers
Post Office Box 193
Colfax, NC 27235
www.a-argusbooks.com

ISBN: 978-0-6159448-9-0
ISBN: 0-6159448-9-2

Book Cover designed by Cheryl Davis

Printed in the United States of America

Salem Massachusetts
Gallows Hill
July 22, 1994

Cloaked in darkness, with only the light of the full moon to guide them, the candidate and her sponsor move silently up the embankment. The air was thick with thousands of unseen insects swarming the hillside, drowning out the sounds of modern day life and transporting them back in time. What was once a grassy slope was now a steep ledge of bedrock unearthed to make way for the railroad built in the early 19th century. Beyond the rock they ascended a recently cleared path through a cluster of twisted vines and thorny bushes where another member of the coven meets them, wielding a sword.

"Who comes to this sacred place?"

"I am Ingrid, spawn of the earth and heavens."

"Who speaks for you?"

"It is I, Radiance, who vouches for her."

"You are entering a place of power, a place beyond imagining. As you step between the worlds, you stand on the threshold of the eternal life, are you strong enough?"

"I am."

"Then prepare for your rebirth."

Stepping forward, the challenger draws her sword, cutting the tie that connects Ingrid's robe. As her sponsor removes the robe, exposing her naked body, the challenger steps closer, placing a blindfold over her eyes. From the darkness, the remaining members of the coven move forward to surround the candidate. Truly at the mercy of those around her, she allows them to lead her down the path in silence. Without her sight, she relies on her other senses to comfort her. The smell of burning wood permeates the air, though she isn't close enough to feel its heat. As they come to a stop she hears the sound of liquid being poured into a vessel and she remains still. Guided by the others, she steps into a shallow basin where she is bathed in preparation of the ceremony. One at a time, each member of the coven steps forward to participate in the bathing ritual until she is believed to be cleansed of her previous life before being dried off. Once dry, a long white robe, representing her purity is draped over her body and she is led to the fire circle.

Stepping out of the darkness, dressed in a long black cloak, the High Priestess approached the candidate.

"Have you come to us of your own free will?"

"I have."

"Are you willing to suffer to prove your commitment?"

"I am."

Removing her blindfold, the High Priestess takes her hand, directing her to kneel before her. Stepping forward, the challenger bows before their leader as she presents the sword. Accepting the instrument, the Priestess turns the candidates palm upward, pressing the blade into the heel of her hand to extract a small amount of blood before pressing it against her heart.

"Repeat after me...I solemnly swear to protect and defend my sisters of the coven. I vow to never reveal any secrets within the coven. I swear on my mother's womb and my eternal life, and in the presence of those before me."

Repeating the vow, Ingrid rose with the help of her sponsor.

"Come and be anointed."

Without hesitation, Ingrid stepped forward. Removing a vial from the pocket of her robe, the Priestess spills the oil into a waiting vessel. Dipping her finger into the oil, she traces the sign of the pentacle upon Ingrid's forehead.

"You have been accepted into the coven. I name you Summer in honor of this sacred season."

With that, the women of the coven clasp their hands as a sign to unity and rebirth. Making a circle around the fire they began to chant.

Just beyond the rocky slope, where the path branched out, leading to the plateau and the ceremony playing out before him, a young boy crouches behind a bush.

Like so many nights before, the pretty lady didn't arrive until well after his mother had thought him asleep. It started a few weeks before school ended. His bedtime had always been eight o'clock, then without even telling him why, his mother told him he had to go to bed at seven. Not only did all his friends get to stay up much later, but it was way too light out to fall asleep. Although she told him he could read in bed until he got tired, that wasn't the point. While he was stuck in bed, his friends were all playing outside just down the street. He knew they were probably laughing at him, calling him a baby. It wasn't long before they were making plans without him and by the time school was out, they had their summer already planned and their plans didn't include him.

He tried to explain to his mother that he was too old for such a baby bedtime, but she wouldn't listen so he decided he would just stay awake until she went to bed just to show her how grown up he was. Most nights he fell asleep before she came in to check on him around eight, but the nights the pretty lady came over she forgot all about him. On those nights, he was too curious to fall asleep.

Before the lady came over he could hear his mother pacing the floors. Some nights he could hear her pray, asking God for guidance. The fear in her voice scared him. He wasn't sure what she was so afraid of because as soon as the pretty lady arrived she seemed to be fine.

Most nights he would lie on the floor, peering under the door to see down the hall into the living room. That's how he knew what the lady looked like. She always wore long dresses and sandals on her feet. They sat on the floor instead of the couch, which he thought was funny. He had never seen grownups sit on the floor like that. While his mother's purse only had boring stuff aside from the occasional pack of gum, the pretty lady's bag seemed to be filled with all sorts of interesting things. Every time she came, she seemed to have something different in her bag. There were candles that she lit and placed on the floor between her and his mother as well as small bags filled with what looked like dead grass. She had a bunch of weeds that she would light and then blow out before dancing around the room with them. He hated that one. It smelt really gross and he had to cover his mouth and nose so he wouldn't cough and give himself away. His favorite thing was a cool purple crystal that hung from a chain. When she took that out of her bag, he simply had to get a closer look at it.

Pulling himself off the floor, he carefully opened his bedroom door; listening to make sure they hadn't heard him. Silently he made his way down the dark hallway toward the living room on his tiptoes. Dropping to his hands and knees behind the back of the sofa, he watched as the lady dangled the chain over a drawing of a star. While his mother's eyes were closed, the lady looked down at the drawing and whispered a rhyme he wasn't familiar with. Every nerve in his body tingled in anticipation. He had never seen anything like this and he wondered if all grownups played this game when their kids went to bed. When the crystal stopped spinning, the lady told his mother they were done. While she gathered her things and his mother walked her to the door, he slipped back into his room and into his bed.

He thought about asking his mother who the lady was and why he couldn't stay up and play with them, but he was afraid if he admitted he was awake she would only put him to bed earlier. He was almost eight and a half and she still treated him like a baby. If he had a dad he was sure he would let him stay up later. Sometimes, when he was mad at his mother, he told her he wished he had a dad like his friends. He knew it hurt her feelings and he always said he was sorry later. She never got mad at him when he said it, she would only cry, promising him that when he was older she would tell him about his father.

As the weeks passed, the lady came more and more. Each time she came, his mother seemed more and more nervous. Finally, his mother told him they would be going on a trip. He was so excited. Every summer his friends went on family vacations while he was stuck at home. His mother always promised they would go away someday, but it never happened. Maybe he was finally going to get to go to the big amusement park he had heard his friends talk about, the one with the big roller coasters and scary rides.

Finally, on the day they were set to leave, she explained they were going to Massachusetts. At first he was disappointed but then she explained that they would visit some of the museums he had heard about and go on a boat ride, so he was more excited. They had spent the last three days, doing just that and he was even allowed to stay up as late as he wanted. He had almost forgotten about the pretty lady and her games when his mother suddenly announced he had to go to bed early their final night in town. Despite arguing that he could sleep in the car the following day, she insisted he turn in at eight o'clock. Although it was an hour later than she allowed at home, it was still too early and he struggled to fall asleep while she sat outside their motel room on a plastic chair, writing in her journal.

Occasionally he would sneak out of bed and peek through the big window to see what she was doing, but her head remained bent while she wrote in the leather book. He was just starting to doze off when a car pulled into the lot shining its bright headlights into the room. Moments later, his mother and the pretty lady entered the room and he watched through squinted eyes across the darkened room as his mother removed her clothes and wrapped herself in a long robe. As she approached the bed, he closed his eyes and held his breath while she leaned in to kiss his forehead.

As quietly as she'd come the pretty lady, followed by his mother, slipped out the door and got into her waiting car. Jumping out of the bed, he peered through the curtains as he watched the car disappear down the road. Stripping off his pajamas, he quickly dressed in a t-shirt and shorts before pulling his sneakers onto his bare feet. Peeking out the window once more to make sure no one was watching, he opened the door and sprinted for the road.

He ran until his stomach hurt and had nearly given up hope of finding them, when he spotted the familiar car. Stopping long enough to catch his breath, he scanned the area for any sign of movement. Other than the moon, there was no light in the immediate area and he nervously considered turning around and heading back to the motel. Steadying his breath he listened for any other sounds besides the chirping crickets and humming insects.

Across the dark street, beyond an embankment, he could smell burning wood. Cautiously he crossed the street, making sure to look both ways like his mother had taught him. The hill was more difficult to climb than he expected and it took him several minutes to reach the top. Moving quickly down the path, he stumbled on roots and rocks, scrapping his hands and knees in the process. Finally he arrived at the stage where several women, including his mother were dancing around a fire.

Ducking behind a large rock, he watched in fascination while the women moved around the crackling fire. Coming to an abrupt stop, all but one woman knelt down with their backs to the flames. While the woman in the black robe disappeared into the darkness, the women swayed back in forth with their eyes closed. Finally the woman returned with a bowl in her hands. As he watched from afar, she dipped her fingers into the bowl and wrote something on each of the women's foreheads. As she did so, one at a time the women began to rise until only his mother remained kneeling. With the help of two women, one on each side, she was helped to her feet while her eyes remained closed.

Unable to hear what was being said, he moved in closer, careful not to give himself away. He watched as his mother leaned her head backward toward the fire and the remaining liquid was poured over her forehead. In an instant, flames shot up, causing the two women to let go of his mother as they stepped out of harm's way. Unable to steady herself, she stumbled backward into the flames and he watched in horror as the white gown ignited, engulfing her in flames. While the women scrambled to free her from the fire, she screamed in agony as the oils she was anointed with only fueled the fire.

Powerless, he stood, unable to move, as he watched his mother be consumed by the fire. A warm stream of release spread across the front of his shorts and down his legs as he looked on in horror.

Removing their cloaks, the women surrounded Ingrid and quickly began smothering the flames. When they finally stepped back, removing the last cloak from her blistered body, all that remained was the look of terror on her melted face. Someone began to scream and it wasn't until the group moved in his direction that he realized it was him.

Unable to cope with what he had witnessed, he withdrew from reality into a world of his own making. It would be several years before he would be able to rejoin society without the paralyzing fear that held him captive in his self-imposed prison.

Chapter One

The final bell, signifying not only the end of the school day, but also the school year; was drowned out by the cheers of more than two hundred elementary school students scrambling for the exits. Squeaky sneakers and the sounds of small chair's metal footings scrapping against the waxed floors made it impossible for the staff to hear themselves let alone instruct their students to fall in line and exit in an orderly fashion.

Anticipating such a reaction, Thena—or Miss Burnor as her students called her—positioned herself in front of her classroom door minutes before the bell was scheduled to ring. Advising her students to follow fire drill protocol and form a single line, she waited for them to quiet down before proceeding with her annual speech encouraging them to seek out learning experiences while they enjoyed their summer vacation and not to waste it away sitting inside playing video games and watching TV. Of course, as soon as the bell rang, chaos ensued and she stepped aside, as not to be trampled, shaking her head and yelling at them to walk and not run.

Watching from the doorway until the last student exited the building and the hallways echoed with the sound of the slamming door, Thena took a deep breath, letting it out slowly before returning to her classroom for a final walk-through and clean up. Although she had only been teaching for five years and was still considered green by her fellow colleagues, it didn't change the fact that she welcomed the summer break as much as those that had been in the game since she, herself, had walked the halls of Chester A. Arthur Elementary School. It had only been two years since her own fourth grade teacher had retired. Still, like many of her colleagues, she had anxiously waited for this day to arrive, counting down the days every since spring break. Now that it was finally here, she felt a brief moment of sadness, realizing that her class had moved on and September would arrive all too soon with a brand new batch of eager minds to mold.

When Thena decided to become a teacher she knew immediately that she wanted to teach at the Elementary level. She wanted to re-experience the enthusiasm that she remembered from her own childhood before boys and fashion took the place of reading and writing. Even though home gaming systems were just becoming a household staple and television was catering to a hipper generation, Thena's own childhood was a world apart from today's virtual world. She still remembered playing jump rope and hopscotch during recess, of reading Swiss Family Robinson and Tom Sawyer. Just this year the PTA had insisted that the school remove any old copies of the latter and replace them with the revised version minus the N word.

Tossing the last of classroom's artwork into the trash, Thena sighed before heading in the direction of the wall of windows facing out to the school's tiny play yard. Where there was usually a handful of students, who lived within walking distance of the school; hanging around to play on the swings and monkey bars after school, there was now only a couple of birds perched on the top of the swing set. As if sensing they were being watched, the pair flew off, leaving the play yard barren and somehow sad.

"Hey! Earth to Thena…" Ethan called from the doorway.

Thena jumped at the sound of her colleague's voice, knocking over a planter with the remains of a failed science experiment. Grabbing the planter before it fell to the floor, Thena cursed as dirt and plant debris cascaded down the front of her pants.

"Jesus, Ethan…you nearly gave me a heart attack."

Ethan chuckled, making his way over to her as she knelt down to pick up the clumps of soil that had escaped from the planter and were scattered across the floor.

"Sorry about that, what had you so distracted anyway?"

Helping her up from the floor, Ethan took the planter from her hand and placed it back on the window ledge.

"Ah, just reminiscing. Remember when kids used to play outside until their mothers called them in for the night? When kids played jacks and hopscotch on the sidewalks and playgrounds like this meant endless hours of fun?" She said, pointing to the empty playground.

"Or when kicking a can could entertain you for hours?" Ethan joked, prompting Thena to punch him in the arm.

"Very funny. You know what I mean. Kids don't enjoy the simple things anymore. All they care about is the latest video game, the newest tech gadget or the coolest pair of sneakers. It wasn't that long ago that I was a kid, for Christ's sake; but so much has changed…and not for the better."

"Okay…well all this is a little heavy for the last day of school. I stopped by to let you know a bunch of us are headed over to O'Brien's Pub for a couple of drinks. Want' a join us?"

"As appealing as that sounds, I've got packing to do before I head to Maine."

"One drink isn't going to kill you. Come on…besides Gavin's buying. As cheap as the old man is, we might not ever have this opportunity again."

Thena sighed, defeated. "Okay but only one, I have a hundred things to do."

"That-a-girl." Ethan stated, patting her on the back before turning on his heels and disappearing down the hallway.

Giving the classroom one final look, Thena brushed the remaining soil from her hands into the wastebasket and collected the remaining papers left behind by students eager to begin their summer vacation. Satisfied she hadn't forgotten anything; she reached into her bag and pulled out her car keys before making her way out of the building and into the sunny parking lot. Noting that the only other car in the lot besides from her own belonged to the school custodian, Thena quickened her pace to catch up with the rest of the gang.

By the time she joined her colleagues at O'Brien's they were well into their second round and barely noticed as she pulled up a stool and sat down. Only Ethan winked as acknowledgement to her late arrival. Although there were several conversations going on at once, Thena concentrated on the one that seemed to be on everyone's mind lately; the announcement of the discovery of yet another young woman that seemed to be the victim of some sort of ritualistic sacrifice. This latest victim was the fourth in as many months and according to news sources, seemed to point to some sort of cult, although there didn't appear to be anything connecting the murders and was more than likely the work of more than one copycat.

"I heard she was visiting relatives out of state when she simply disappeared." Janet argued.

"I'm telling you, they said she had already left her relatives and was back home when she went missing." Paul insisted.

"Whatever…all I know is you'd have to be out of your mind to travel alone until they figure out who's responsible." Janet shrugged, taking a long sip from her drink.

Thena shook her head and rolled her eyes, drawing the attention of those involved in the conversation. Realizing that at least Janet looked annoyed by the fact she seemed to be taking the situation lightly, she spoke up.

"Just because four women disappeared in New England and turned up dead doesn't mean that the cases are related or that it's the same person's killing them. For all they know it could be four different guys taking advantage of the first guy's sick fantasy. What better way to get rid of someone you have it out for than to pin it on one deranged individual and make him look like a serial killer? Either way, I for one am not altering my plans on the chance there's a killer or killers on the loose."

This time it was Janet that shook her head and rolled her eyes.

"That's the problem with your generation…you don't take anything seriously." Janet clucked, pushing her glasses up her nose with her index finger before looking to her colleagues for agreement.

Stepping in to redirect the conversation to something less heated, Ethan suggested a game of pool. While several of the men jumped at the proposition, the women seemed content to linger at the bar. When the conversation split off into several less intense subjects including gardening, local shoe sales and the latest gossip about a newly single father of one of the students, Thena used the diversion to slip out unnoticed and return to her original plan of packing for her trip.

As she made her way through the busy streets of Essex Junction in route to her townhouse, Thena couldn't help but wonder if there might be some validity to what Janet had said. Until now she hadn't considered altering her plans, not that her family hadn't tried to convince her otherwise. At the time she had brushed it off, arguing that they needed to stop treating her like a child and come to grips with the fact that she was an adult. While she appreciated their love and concern, she also insisted on boundaries and expected them to respect her decisions whether they agreed with them or not.

"You're just letting them get into your head." She scolded herself, shaking her head as if she could physically rid herself of the voices imbedded in her mind.

By the time she pulled into the driveway, her mind had drifted to thoughts of what to pack and whether or not she should stop for a quick oil change before she left in the morning. Although it was only a four-hour drive at most from her condo to Wells Beach, it had been several months since her last oil change and the old Volkswagen was becoming less and less reliable as it neared the two hundred thousand mile mark. Still, it would be nice to just get up and go. Ultimately realizing if she did break down and had to call her father for help she would never hear the end of it, she decided it wasn't worth risking it and called her mechanic for an early morning appointment.

Wells Beach had been a family get-away for as long as she could remember, though it wasn't until she graduated from college and moved into her own place that she began spending time there alone. For the past four years she had rented a tiny cottage directly on the beach. The couple that owned the property preferred to use it off-season when the summer tourists were gone and the small town was a quiet get-away from their noisy city life. Meeting the couple through a mutual acquaintance, the three of them had formed an instant bond and they had quickly agreed to rent Thena the cottage exclusively every summer for as long as she liked.

The first summer she had spent four weeks at the beach but quickly realized it wasn't long enough. By happenstance she had overheard one of her colleagues attempting to find an affordable summer rental for her grandson who attended college in their neighboring city of Burlington and had quickly proposed that he rent her condo for the summer, giving him a place to stay and her peace of mind that her home was being looked after. Of course she did have to jump through a few hoops with the Condo Association who wasn't originally thrilled with the prospect of having a college student in their midst. All that changed once the Association had a chance to meet the young man, who was anything but the stereotypical frat boy they expected. Without the additional expense of a mortgage payment, Thena was able to swing the cottage rental for the entire summer. This arrangement was mutually beneficial for the cottage owners who were able to avoid the hassle of seeking out renters who may or may not be respectful of their property.

This was now the third year that Thena had signed on for the entire summer and she couldn't wait to get there. Over the years she had become friendly with a number of the local business owners as well as a handful of regulars at some of the establishments she frequented. What had begun as a vacation of sunbathing, reading and beachcombing had quickly turned into days and evenings filled with countless social events and more than a few summer romances. Though her teaching contract required her to attend various conferences and educational events during the summer months, she was close enough to home to make the trip there and back and only spend the night in the case of a two-day conference, in which case she would simply spend the night at her parents' home.

Stuffing the last swimsuit into her bulging bag, she made her way to the condo's only bathroom where she rounded up the rest of the things she would need for the summer. Since she made it her personal rule that Maine was a makeup-free zone, she only gathered the essentials necessary for her personal hygiene, ignoring the drawers dedicated solely to foundation, blusher, eye shadows and lipsticks, opting instead for sunscreen, lotion and lip balm. Thena smiled to herself realizing that the more years that passed, the fewer things she packed. What had seemed essential even last year had sat on the shelf of the cottage's tiny bathroom untouched until it was repacked at the end of the summer. Still, as many things that had been crossed off her packing list over the years had also been added. She learned early on that it was cheaper to bring anything she may need rather than pay tourist prices at the IGA.

By the time she finished packing it was nearly eight o'clock and she was feeling the effects of the drink she had earlier on an empty stomach. Having nearly emptied her cupboards and refrigerator in anticipation of leaving town, she had no choice but to call for take-out. Grabbing the stack of menus from a drawer in the kitchen, she shuffled through them before settling on a local Italian restaurant. Phoning in an order for a small pizza, Thena went about the condo emptying wastebaskets and gathering fresh linens for her tenant. Having done a thorough housecleaning the previous night, she only needed to tidy things up a bit and remove any remaining items from the refrigerator to go out with the trash.

She had just sat down in front of the TV with the pizza and a glass of wine and was flicking through the channels when her phone rang.

"It figures." She grumbled, scrambling for the handset that was just out of reach.

By the time she reached the phone, the answering machine had already picked up and she waited for the outgoing message to play and the caller to identify him or herself.

"Thena? It's Mom." The caller announced.

"Hi, Mom." Thena answered, knowing before she spoke why she was calling.

"I just wanted to check in with you before you left. Are you sure you wouldn't like some company to come along?"

"Mom...we've been over this before. I'll be fine. I'm a big girl; I can take care of myself. Besides...it's not like I'm a completely alone. I have plenty of friends at the beach."

"So you've said, but your father and I were just thinking that it might not be a good idea for you to go alone this year."

"Oh my God! Is this about the girls on the news? Look, Mom…I appreciate your concern, I really do; but I'll be fine. Now if that's the only reason you called, I have a pizza that I'd like to eat before it gets cold."

There was a moment of silence on the other end of the phone and Thena realized immediately she had hurt her mother's feelings.

"I promise I'll call as soon as I get there tomorrow and will check in at least once a week. Oh and you can tell Dad I've scheduled an oil change for the morning before I head out of town."

"Okay Dear…well you be careful and if you change your mind you just give us a call."

"I will. Love you, Mom."

"I love you too. Bye Dear."

Chapter Two

By the time her oil change was completed and she had gassed up the old bug, it was nearly eleven o'clock and Thena debated about whether or not she should grab some lunch before getting on the Interstate. Opting instead for a Diet Coke and a bag of chips from the Minimart at the gas station, she made her way onto 89 S, settling in for the long drive. Traffic had picked up slightly and it looked like she would be lucky to make it to Wells by five when she hit the tolls on 93 S.

Although she didn't have any plans for the evening, she preferred to arrive much earlier, giving her plenty of time to air out the cottage, unpack and pick up groceries before the crowds started coming out for the evening. Considering her likely late arrival, it was probably smarter to drop off her bags and go directly to the store, saving the unpacking for later.

As it turned out, whatever was causing the slowdown, cleared as quickly as it began and she was easily able to make up time by going slightly over the posted speed limit. Pulling into the crushed shell driveway that she shared with the cottage next door, Thena checked her watch and smiled; realizing she had made it in a little over four hours. She removed her suitcases from the back seat of the car before making her way around to the front of the cottage.

As usual, the owners had left a welcome note for her on the small dining table along with this year's calendar of events from the Chamber of Commerce and the latest take-out menus. Little had changed in the cottage over the past few years, giving Thena a sense of coming home. The tiny kitchen opened up into the living area of the cottage, which doubled as both a living room and bedroom with a pullout couch for sleeping. Besides from the small dining table and sofa, the room contained two end tables, a coffee table and a small bookcase, always stocked with the latest collection of romance novels. If she didn't know better, she would think her mother had somehow influenced the property owners on the genre in hopes to coax her into producing the grandchildren she constantly reminded Thena she hoped to have in the near future.

The cottage's only closet contained a small bureau, which Thena promptly emptied the contents of her suitcases into, only hanging the handful of sundresses she had brought on the rod above it. Stashing the suitcases, one inside the other on the shelf above the clothes rod, she grabbed the remaining tote bag and made her way to the tiny bathroom. Not much larger than her bedroom closet at home, the bathroom consisted of a pedestal sink, toilet and shower stall. Above the sink was a small medicine cabinet where she placed the toiletries she had packed. Moving to the shower, she pulled back the curtain and deposited her shampoo, conditioner and facial scrub. hanging a couple of towels on the empty hooks on the inside of the bathroom door.

Before making her run to the local grocery store, Thena made a quick call to her mother to announce her safe arrival and promised to stay in touch. Gathering her pocketbook and heading for the door, she pulled it open, nearly stumbling into the unexpected guest. Sucking in the salty air, she stepped back slightly bending down to greet the tiny visitor.

"Well hello there little guy…where did you come from?" She asked, petting the sandy-colored terrier.

Thrilled with the enthusiastic greeting, the dog jumped up, placing his front paws on her bent knee and was rewarded with a more vigorous petting.

"Shane! Shane! Down, boy." His owner called out, approaching from the cottage next door. "I'm so sorry…don't worry, he doesn't bite. Come. Shane!" He ordered, patting the side of his leg.

"He's adorable, I think we're going to be great friends." Thena announced, standing up to greet her new neighbor. Extending her hand, she introduced herself.

"Hi…I'm Thena. Are you renting the cottage next door?"

"Nice to meet you Thena, I'm Mason and, yes, I'll be your next-door neighbor. Will you be here for long?" He asked, bending down to scoop up his dog before returning his attention to her.

"The whole summer, how about you?"

"Same here. Can I offer you a cold drink?"

"Maybe another time, I need to pick up some supplies at the grocery store before I get settled in."

"I understand…well it's an open invitation, drop by any time." He called back as he headed toward his cottage, "It was nice to meet you, Thena."

"You too." Thena responded, smiling as she watched Shane wiggle free of his owner and sprint toward a couple of children playing on the beach.

As she made her way through town to the IGA, she couldn't help but wonder if her neighbor might be single. Whether it was her mother's less than subtle hints or the fact that it had been far too long since she was involved in a long-term relationship, she couldn't be sure. Either way, she couldn't dismiss her immediate attraction to the man next door. He didn't possess what one might classify as obvious good looks, with a nose that was perhaps a tiny bit crooked and his dark brown hair a tad unruly; but there was something in his dark eyes that gave him a kind of mystery that intrigued her on some level. At roughly six feet tall and approximately one hundred eighty pounds, though not overly muscular, he had a rugged yet gentle air about him that invited her in. He appeared to be self-confident without coming off as arrogant, which was an appealing trait.

Cursing herself for becoming so enthralled by this man she had only exchanged pleasantries with, Thena pulled into the parking lot of the market determined to distract herself with the task at hand. Her familiarity with the market allowed her to breeze through the aisles quickly, gathering a week's worth of groceries in record time. Selecting her favorite wine, she paused briefly; considering whether or not she should pick up a six-pack of beer or some hard lemonade in the event she might have some unexpected company. Scolding herself once again for reverting back to thoughts of her new neighbor, she ignored her reservations and reached for the lemonade, confident that she would drink it herself at some point regardless.

Too exhausted from her long drive to consider cooking, she made a quick stop at Billy's Chowder House for an order of fish and chips to go. By the time she arrived back at the cottage and unpacked her groceries, she was famished and she sat down at the small table to eat, opting for one of the lemonade's she had earlier debated about to wash down the meal. A half hour later, with her stomach full and the craziness of the day behind her, Thena opened a second bottle of lemonade and took it out to the cottage's small porch, which looked out onto the beach.

Kicking off her flip flops and resting the back of her ankles on the sun-bleached railing, Thena leaned her head back against the wooden rocker she sat in and closed her eyes, allowing her senses to take in all that the beach had to offer. The scent of the ocean saturated the air and she breathed deep, taking the salty mist into her lungs. Shrieks and laughter could be heard from down the beach where a group of teenagers still remained long after most of the beachgoers had called it a day. The faint sound of an acoustical guitar drew her attention and she lifted her head and peered into the distance in an attempt to locate the source. Spotting a small group of people sitting in a circle down the beach, she could just make out the silhouette of a young man, perched atop a large rock in the center of the group, with a guitar. While he strummed the instrument, the small group swayed in response as if hypnotized by the melody.

The enthusiastic yelp of a dog broke her trance and she refocused her attention just in time to see her neighbor's dog bound up her porch steps and jump up onto her lap.

"Shane!" Mason yelled, quickly sprinting the distance between the two cottages. "I'm sorry...I swear this dog will be the death of me someday." Mason climbed the steps two at a time, shaking his head and pointing sternly at the dog.

"Oh, I think he's adorable." Thena smiled, wrapping her arm around the small dog in a hug. Shane responded with a slew of wet kisses, aggravating his owner even more.

"Get down. The lady is trying to relax, she doesn't need you bothering her." Mason grumbled, lifting the dog from her lap and directing him to the steps.

"Nonsense...he's no bother at all. Can I offer you both a drink?" She asked, silently cursing herself for sounding too eager.

"If you're sure we're not intruding." Mason responded; keeping a watchful eye on the dog to make sure he wasn't about to run off again.

"Not at all, please...have a seat." Thena insisted before disappearing into the cottage and returning a short time later carrying a bowl of water for Shane and a bottle of hard lemonade for Mason.

"So tell me, Mason...how did you manage to snag the cottage for the summer? It's not like the Millers to miss a season on the beach." She said, petting Shane who had returned to her lap and settled in.

"The who?" Mason asked absently while reaching over to tousle the shaggy dog's coat.

"The Millers...the old couple that own the cottage. I just assumed you rented it directly from them."

"No...wait...I'm confused. I rented it from my boss. As far as I know, he's the owner." Mason stated, scratching the dog's head.

"Who's your boss?" Thena asked, wondering if perhaps she was the one that was confused.

"Clayton Parrish. Do you know him?" Mason asked, settling back into his chair and taking a sip of his drink.

"Yes, he's the man I'm renting from as well. I wonder what happened to the Millers."

"I couldn't say. All I know is he mentioned that he had purchased the place this spring and was looking for someone to rent it out for the summer."

"Hmmm, well they were getting up there in age, maybe they just decided to sell and move south. I'll have to give Celeste a call to find out what happened. They were an adorable couple, I hope they're okay."

Eager to find out as much as she could about her new neighbor, Thena directed the conversation toward him.

"So I know Clay is involved in redevelopment, what is it that you do?"

"Yes, he's the Director for Planning and Policy Development and I work under him as the Senior Planner for Special Initiatives. Basically I identify and develop funding resources and design plans for new initiatives. It sounds a lot more exciting than it is." He teased. "How about you?"

"I'm a fourth-grade teacher and it's every bit as exciting as it sounds." Thena laughed.

By the time they had polished off the remainder of the six pack it was nearly midnight and although Mason offered to make a quick run to the store to pick up some more, Thena insisted she really needed to get some sleep.

Promising the next drinks were on him, Mason scooped up the sleeping dog that was comfortably lying on Thena's lap and made his way across the cool sand to the cottage next door. Thena stayed where she was until her new friend disappeared through the door before pulling herself out of the rocker and heading back into her own cottage, making sure to securely lock the door behind her. Any hesitations she might have had about being alone with a possible killer on the loose had vanished as soon as she had met Mason. With a strong man next door she felt confident that she was protected from any potential intruder.

Placing the empty bottles in the recycle bin under the kitchen sink, she smiled to herself thinking how easily they had fallen into a rhythm in their conversation. In only five hours she felt like she knew him better than co-workers she had known for years and considered friends. The instant chemistry between them couldn't be fabricated and was truly unexpected. As she brushed her teeth and changed into a long t-shirt she used as pajamas, she made a mental note to call Celeste in the morning, not only to find out what happened to the Millers, but also to thank her and Clay for renting the cottage next door to such a nice guy.

It was nearly nine o'clock when she woke up to the sound of her cell phone ringing. Reaching over the arm of the sofa to the end table, Thena grabbed the phone and cleared her throat before answering.

"Hello?" She responded in her scratchy morning voice.

"Thena? I'm sorry…did I wake you?" Celeste asked apologetically.

"No…well, yes, but I need to get up anyway. We must be on the same wave length, I was going to call you this morning." She responded, sitting up and sliding her legs over the edge of the sofa bed.

"Oh…is everything okay?" Celeste asked, suddenly worried.

"Yes, everything's fine. I met Mason yesterday and he mentioned you had purchased the cottage next door so I was just going to call to see what happened to the Millers." She explained.

"Oh, that's actually why I was calling. I know you've grown close to them and I wanted to let you know they're okay. Millie called us back in January and told us that Joe had a stroke back in November. He's recovering well, but they needed to sell the cottage to help pay for medical bills and she wanted to offer it to us before they officially put it on the market. Of course we couldn't pass up on the deal. It's nice to have control of who lives in the cottage next door."

"Well I'm glad he's going to be okay, but I'm going to miss them. It was like having my grandparents living next door. I might have to actually use the stove this summer. Millie was always conveniently making too much food and inviting me over for dinner." She laughed recalling how obvious it was that they were simply worried she might fade away if they didn't feed her.

At five foot three and just under a hundred pounds, the Millers weren't the only ones that worried about her health. Thena was under constant scrutiny from her parents and co-workers who accused her of being too thin. The truth was, that despite the fact that she ate every meal like she hadn't eaten in days, her high metabolism kept her from gaining any weight. Her doctor told her she had nothing to worry about and insisted they were just jealous that she was able to eat whatever she wanted to and not gain a pound. He also warned her that eventually her metabolism would slow down and she would have to adjust her diet accordingly.

"So you met Mason. How did you get on?" Celeste probed.

"Careful Celeste…you're starting to sound like my mother." Thena teased.

"Am I that obvious? I'm going to have to work on that." Celeste joked.

"Yes, you must be terrible at poker. Anyway, to answer your question...we got on just fine. We hung out last night and talked for hours and I just love his dog Shane. We bonded immediately."

"Well, Clay is going to be thrilled to hear it. He wasn't certain you would appreciate our selection. Our families go way back, which is why Clay hired him in the first place, but Clay was afraid you might think we were trying to play matchmaker."

"Oh jeez, it's not like we're picking out china patterns, we just met. Besides, I never said it was love at first sight. I only said we got along fine." Thena insisted.

"Neither did I, so I think it's you who's showing her poker hand now." Celeste laughed, leaving Thena speechless for a moment.

Embarrassed by the fact that she might have revealed something she hadn't intended, that she had felt an instant attraction to the man next door; Thena changed the subject.

"If you have the Miller's address I would love to send them a note just to let them know how much I'll miss spending my summers with them and wish Joe a speedy recovery."

Jotting down the address and catching up on the latest beach gossip, Thena hung up the phone and wandered into the tiny kitchen to brew a pot of coffee. It was nearly eleven o'clock by the time she had eaten and drank her coffee and she realized she had better hurry if she wanted to get a good spot on the beach. Shuffling through her bathing suit drawer, she selected a red bikini along with a red and white paisley sarong. Quickly dressing, she returned to the bathroom where she tied her long dark hair up in a high ponytail to keep it off her neck. Like makeup, she refused to use a hair dryer in the summer, instead preferring it to dry naturally, which didn't always pan out very well.

Selecting a steamy romance from the bookshelf and grabbing the beach chair she kept by the cottage door, she made her way out into the hot summer sun, silently hoping she might spot her neighbor outside as well. While there were several groups of sunbathers on the beach, it wasn't as packed as she expected and she was easily able to find a spot directly in front of her cottage, close to the water. Placing her chair inches away from the shore so that she might sink her feet into the wet sand and allow the waves to splash at her ankles, Thena settled in, opened her book and began reading.

Although the story was engaging, Thena found herself reading the same passage over and over without really digesting it and realized she was far too distracted to concentrate. Standing up and setting the book on the chair, she casually looked around the beach for a familiar face—his face—before deciding to go for a quick swim. She only made it in as far as her knees before she decided it was a little too cold and she returned to her chair, picked up the romance novel and gave it another shot.

It was nearly one-thirty when she returned to the cottage, thirsty and drained from the sun. While she prepared a light lunch, she peered out the kitchen window at the cottage next door, wondering where Mason might be. With the blinds closed to the small window she knew to be in the main room of the cottage, she shrugged, assuming he was probably still sleeping. While the beach was now buzzing with the sounds of children's laughter, radios tuned in to various stations and a vigorous volleyball game not too far down the stretch of sand; she knew from her years of summering on the beach that it was possible to sleep through just about anything. The sounds of the waves along with the cries of the seagulls had a way of drowning out nearly every other sound and had a somewhat hypnotic effect on the mind.

Placing the cucumber sandwich she made in a plastic baggy and filling a travel mug with sweet ice tea, Thena returned to her spot on the beach determined to enjoy her first day of vacation without another thought of her handsome neighbor. She was nearly half way through the romance novel when the clouds began to move in and the distant rumble of thunder along with, a too close for comfort bolt of lightning; brought a sudden hush to the beach crowd followed by a frenzy of activity as everyone began frantically gathering their belongings, shoving them into beach bags and heading for their cars. Fascinated by the unexpected change in weather, Thena remained seated with her feet in the water until the wind picked up and the rain moved in. By the time she made it back up the beach to her cottage, the wind was so strong she struggled to hang onto her chair, which was acting as a parachute, pulling her back two steps for every step she moved forward. Pulling open the door to the cottage, she stumbled inside, using the weight of her body to close it behind her.

Grateful to be inside, she made her way to the closet, selected a t-shirt, underwear and a pair of yoga pants before heading into the bathroom for a hot shower. She had just finished shampooing her hair when a loud rumble of thunder shook the small cottage and the lights went out. Jumping out of the shower and grabbing a nearby towel, Thena quickly dried off and dressed, making her way out of the bathroom just as another round of thunder shook the cottage. As she ran a brush through her wet hair, she stood in front of the large picture window that looked out onto the beach, mesmerized by the huge waves and the lightening that danced in the sky. Eventually making her way to the sofa, she wrapped herself in a warm blanket and laid down to wait out the storm.

Chapter Three

A loud knock at the cottage door followed by a brief pause and the calling out of her name, roused Thena from her midday slumber and she rubbed the blurriness from her eyes before rolling off the couch. Before she had time to fully awake there was another, more aggressive round of knocking, promptly her to stumble toward the door.

"Just a minute!" She called, cursing as she slammed her knee into the end table on her way to the door. "Damn it...this had better be important."

Flinging open the door without checking to see who it was, as she would normally do; her expression softened as she saw her neighbor.

"Oh, hey...it's you. What's so urgent? I nearly killed myself getting over here." She exaggerated, reaching down to rub her throbbing knee.

"Sorry, I just wanted to make sure you were okay." He apologized, looking beyond her into the cottage.

Confused, Thena opened the door wider to allow him passage and motioned toward the living room area.

"Why wouldn't I be?" She questioned, stifling a yawn and moving in the direction of the couch.

"Why? You do realize we just survived a hurricane?" Mason asked in dismay, wondering if perhaps her knee wasn't the only thing she'd injured.

Thena spun around, suddenly alert and rushed to the window to examine the beach.

"Oh my God!"

Outside the beach was littered with debris. Metal trashcans had been pried from their cement footings and were scattered up and down the beach. Lifeguard chairs were shattered and bits of wood were floating near the shore. Several loose items, apparently belonging to the cottage dwellers along the beach were scattered across the sand making it appear as though beach goers had simply walked away and left their belongings behind.

"It's a mess, huh?" Mason said, coming up behind her. "We're lucky our places are still standing."

"I can't believe I slept through it. Is it safe to go out now?" She asked, eager to go outside and investigate.

"Yeah, it's passed us now. I was afraid you might be out there somewhere when you didn't come outside with everyone else when it cleared up."

Whether she was still foggy from her nap or in shock over the fact that she might have been killed without ever realizing she was in danger, she wasn't sure, but Thena stood motionless in front of the picture window in stunned silence until Mason reached out and placed his hand on her shoulder.

"Are you okay?" He asked, genuinely concerned by her far-away gaze.

"Hmm? Yeah…yeah I'm fine. I had no idea a hurricane was predicted. Don't they usually announce those things in advance?"

Leading her toward the couch and sitting down next to her, he responded.

"It was supposed to hit the Cape and lose speed, but it veered off coast and then took an unexpected turn for us.

The good news is it was only a category one so there was no structural damage. If the winds had been any stronger this cottage would be floating right now…that is, if it was still standing."

Getting up from the couch, Mason looked around.

"Where are your shoes? If you want to go outside to look around you'll want to have something on your feet. There's a lot of broken glass and splintered wood out there."

Thena absently pointed in the direction of the closet before getting up herself. Snapping out of her stupor she realized she must look a mess and wasn't even wearing a bra. Making her way to the door while Mason retrieved her flip flops, she pulled the elastic from her hair and ran her fingers through the still damp tangled mess before pulling it back up into a sloppy bun. Hoping she didn't look as bad as she imagined, she thanked him as she tossed the sandals on the floor in front of her and stepped into them before heading out onto the porch.

Though unbroken, the porch chairs had been tossed about and were turned over on their sides and shoved up against the railing. They each grabbed a chair and placed them back in their original position before stepping down onto the wet sand. Seagulls circled the shore, diving to scavenge crabs and fish that had washed up from the storm. A warm light breeze intensified the odor of the fish as well as the clumps of seaweed scattered about the beach, making the air difficult to breath. Cupping her nose and mouth with the palm of her hand, Thena walked alongside her neighbor as he gathered pieces of splintered wood from the sand and placed them in a pile.

"At least we'll have a nice bonfire tonight." He reasoned, placing the last of the lifeguard chair remnants on the nearly five-foot mound.

By now there were more than a dozen people—some of whom Thena recognized as her neighbors—wandering up and down the beach, gathering their belonging that had been swept away by the heavy winds. A large beach umbrella turned inside out was giving an elderly woman some problems and Thena rushed over to assist. The lifeguards that would normally be sitting atop their perches monitoring the swimmers were out in full force, armed with rakes and trash bags in an attempt to expedite the cleanup.

After seeing the elderly woman back to her cottage, insisting she allow her to carry the ruined umbrella, Thena returned to where Mason and a handful of able-bodied men were dragging a dingy—or what was left of it—back to shore. Thena stepped aside to allow a jeep driven by one of the lifeguards to pass. Stopping just beyond the men, he shifted into park and hopped out, grabbing a rope from the back and attaching it to the front of the boat. With nothing left but the mound of wood and large clumps of seaweed, the beach cleaner came through, raking the sand and picking up any remaining debris.

Although bonfires were normally not allowed without a town permit, the caretaker informed the residents they would make an exception in order to clear the large volume of wood fragments rather than bring in a truck to haul it away.

Mason wiped his sweaty brow with the bottom of his t-shirt before turning his attention to Thena who had returned to her cottage and was seated on the bottom step. Making his way over, he pulled off his damp shirt, tucking it into the back of his shorts.

"I don't know about you, but I could use a cold one. Would you like to join me?"

"Absolutely." Rising from the steps, Thena followed as Mason led the way to the cottage next door.

Mason opened the screen door and stepped aside to allow her to enter first before heading to the refrigerator to retrieve a couple of cold beers. Thena looked around the cottage at the familiar layout, surprised by the fact that nothing had changed and that apparently the Millers had left all their furnishings behind. The décor transported her back in time with a '60s vibe. Bright floral prints, somewhat faded by age and sunlight, covered the upholstered sofa and chair. Reproduced Pop Art decorated the walls and lacquered tables in bright yellow and orange completed the look. Thena smiled recalling the first time she had visited the Miller's summer cottage and the stories they had told her about their lively youth.

Lost in thought, she didn't hear Mason approach.

"Pretty groovy huh?" He teased, startling her from her reverie.

"Yeah...you would have loved the Millers. Even at their age they're cool. I loved coming over here and listening to their stories about their youth. They were Dead Heads, hitchhiking their way across the country and back again following the Grateful Dead. Even I would blush at some of their stories of what went on during their travels. They had no regrets, only fond memories, some of which they were pretty foggy on."

Mason smiled, imagining what it must have been like to live in that time. Suggesting they take their drinks outside while he warmed up the grill, he once again stepped aside to allow her to pass before him. The gentlemanly gesture was not lost on her and Thena lead the way back onto the small porch where she sat down on the hanging swing. Sipping her beer, she watched as Mason dumped half a bag of charcoal into the firebox of the park-style post grill that was permanently secured by a cement base buried into the ground. Dousing the coals with lighter fluid and igniting a flame, he stepped back, allowing the flames to settle down before flipping down the grate. While they waited for the coals to turn white, Mason joined Thena on the wooden swing where they discussed the earlier storm.

"I still can't believe I slept through that." Thena stated, though she admitted to being a heavy sleeper.

"It actually woke me up. I'm not really a morning person...more of a night owl. At first I thought someone was knocking at my door and I ignored it, but then I heard the rain pounding on the roof and got up to look outside."

While Mason grilled a couple of burgers, Thena ran next door and tossed a salad, returning just as he removed the juicy patties from the grill. As they ate in silence, washing down their meals with a second beer, their neighbors made their way out of their cottages armed with blankets, beach chairs and coolers filled with cold beer.

Returning to her own cottage, Thena changed into a comfortable sundress and brushed out her hair before pulling it up into a high ponytail. Grabbing a beach blanket from the closet and the bottle of wine she had purchased on her arrival, she returned next door to find Mason talking to a young couple she recalled seeing earlier during the clean-up.

"Here she is." Mason said, as she approached. "Thena this is Autumn and Bryce. They're from the yellow cottage down the beach."

Thena smiled, shifting the blanket and wine in her arm to shake their hands. Somewhat disappointed that it appeared she'd would be spending the evening with a couple she'd just met rather than enjoying the bonfire getting to know her handsome neighbor more intimately, Thena put on a happy face and followed the trio toward the gathering encircling the large mound of wood.

Realizing she hadn't opened the wine or brought glasses, Thena excused herself to retrieve the items, but Mason insisted she stay put and took the bottle from her hands, returning to his cottage. Although he couldn't have been gone more than five minutes, Thena was relieved when he returned having spent the time awkwardly sitting next to the young couple as they fondled each other in plain view of everyone around them.

While two of the men whom Thena recognized as the same men that had assisted Mason with the boat earlier doused the wood with lighter fluid, another young man strummed on an acoustic guitar while the girl he was with hummed a Spanish lullaby. Several matches were tossed into the woodpile and seconds later it erupted into flames. A round of whistles and cheers broke out in response before the small gathering settled in, mesmerized by the beautiful colors in varying shades of orange. The lighter fluid quickly burned off and smoke billowed out from the wet wood. Bundles of dry wood were added to the pile to keep the fire burning.

Mason poured two glasses of wine, handing one to Thena before leaning back on his elbows. Nodding his head toward the couple next to them who seemed oblivious to the crowd, Thena looked over, blushing as she saw Bryce's hand disappear between Autumn's thighs and she let out a soft moan. Quickly looking away, Thena ignored

Mason as he chuckled at her obvious discomfort. A shift in the light breeze sent a shiver up her spine and she twitched in response. As the flames licked the splintered wood, which popped and hissed in response, the young man with the guitar stopped playing long enough to take a drag from the joint the girl next to him held up to his lips.

The familiar odor of weed made its way toward them as the joint was passed around the circle. Mason took a long drag, offering it to Thena who shook her head in response.

"You don't smoke?" Mason asked, passing the joint to the young lovers next to him.

"A little in college." Thena admitted.

"Oh it's much better now. It'll give you an amazing high."

Thena shrugged, on the fence about possibly losing control, but intrigued all the same. Sipping her wine she watched as the joint made its way around the circle, silently hoping someone would take the last drag and toss it into the flames allowing her to avoid confronting it again. Looking over at Mason she furrowed her brow at the amusement he prominently displayed on his face.

"One drag isn't going to kill you, I promise." He winked, prompting Thena to backhand him on the arm.

When the butt made its way back around to her, Thena debated with herself only briefly before taking a long drag, sucking the toxins deep into her lungs before releasing a puff of smoke in a fit of coughing. Mason roared with laughter as he patted her on the back and lifted his wine glass up to her lips.

"Are you happy now?" Thena choked, taking a gulp of wine and clearing her throat.

"Extremely." Mason responded through gritted teeth as he inhaled another drag before handing the butt over to Bryce.

As the effects of the marijuana took hold, Thena swayed with the music, her eyes fixed on the fire in front of her. The rhythm of the guitar along with the hypnotic sounds of the surf lulled her into a peaceful trance. To her right she could see the young lovers intertwined in a passionate embrace, oblivious to those around them. Another couple rose from the circle, stripping down to their underwear before making their way into the cold water. Thena's heartbeat quickened as—encouraged by the others--another couple disrobed completely, joining the first couple waist-deep in the water. Following her vision, Mason looked toward the naked couples, elbowing her to get her attention.

"Now that's what I'm talking about." He whispered slyly.

Blushing, Thena quickly looked away taking a long sip of her wine before reaching for the bottle to refill her glass.

"Careful now, you don't want to drink away your inhibitions." Mason teased.

By now the pile of debris had burned down enough so that she could see the other side of the circle that had previously been obstructed from her view and she focused her attention on a couple of middle-aged women who were dancing to the music. Another joint was lit and made its way around the circle. This time Thena took a drag without hesitation, breathing it deep into her lungs before slowly releasing it. The two couples returned from their swim and wrapped themselves in their blankets before partaking in the shared drug.

Lying back on the blanket, Thena crossed her legs at her ankles, placing her wine glass in the sand before raising her arms up and placing her hands behind her head. Mason joined her, moving in closer without being obvious. Closing her eyes, Thena let her senses carry her away. The strumming of the guitar in unison with the crackling fire and lapping waves compounded the effects of the wine and drugs and she drifted into a semi-conscience state of euphoria. With all of her senses magnified she could taste the salty air on her lips while she was all too aware of the musky scent of the man who lay next to her.

The young musician picked away at his guitar, playing something familiar but beyond recognition in her current state and Thena rose, struggling to recall the name of the tune. Looking around the circle she realized only a half dozen couples remained and wondered how long she had been lost in her daze.

Mason sat up, sensing her confusion. "You ready to call it a night?"

"I think that's a good idea." She responded, standing too quickly and nearly falling face first into the hot embers that were all that remained of the fire.

Mason grabbed her, pulling her away from the glowing heat and wrapping his strong arm around her waist.

"Whoa...careful...I got you."

"Thanks, I guess I had a little too much to drink. I'm a little light headed." Thena responded, adjusting her dress and steadying herself.

"Let's get you back to your cottage" Mason insisted, holding onto her with one hand while gathering the blanket, bottle and glasses with the other.

Thena giggled as she stumbled her way up the beach toward the little cottage, while Mason struggled to keep her upright. The four steps up to the front door were particularly difficult to maneuver and he was forced to drop the things he was carrying on the sand to assist her up the steps. Once inside he deposited her into a chair while he pulled out the sofa bed. To his amusement he watched as she struggled to figure out how to remove her flip-flops.

"Let's get you in your PJs and put you to bed before you hurt yourself." Mason teased, heading in the direction of the closet.

"I like to sleep like this." Thena announced, prompting Mason to turn around.

Standing naked with her arms outstretched and her dress and panties carelessly tossed on the floor, Thena—no longer bound by her inhibitions—invited her handsome neighbor into her bed.

Chapter Four

A pounding headache as well as an upset stomach stirred Thena from her sleep and she shielded her eyes from the blinding sunlight filtering through the sheer curtains. The lingering effects of over-indulgence confused her senses and it took several minutes for her to realize she lay naked beneath the sheets. Upon realization of her state, a flood of memories rushed to the surface of her mind and she groaned, clutching the covers tighter around her.

She hadn't intended on taking things so far with Mason and she was both embarrassed and ashamed of her behavior, perhaps more so because she wasn't clear on the details. Looking around to be certain she was alone, she rose from the bed, steadying her wobbly legs before making her way to the bathroom. A hot shower was just what she needed to wash away her shame and help clear her head. Unfortunately, the hot water tank was far too small to rid herself of her lingering regret and the water turned cold forcing her to abandon the shower for the warmth of a towel.

Dressing quickly in a tank top and cut-offs, she stripped the bed and changed the sheets before folding it back into the base of the sofa. Anxious to rid herself of the pounding headache she made her way to the kitchen for a tall glass of orange juice and a couple of Tylenol. It was there that she found the note Mason had left.

Had to go back to Boston to check up on a project. Thanks for a great night. See you in a couple days.
   M

Thena stared at the note, her mind searching for hidden meaning in his words. Had she scared him away? Did he really have work to do or was he just trying to distance himself from her? Refusing to let herself read more into the words than was actually there, she crumpled the note and tossed it in the trash before popping a couple pieces of wheat bread into the toaster and taking a gulp of her juice. This was actually a good thing, she reasoned. She needed a couple of days to free herself from her embarrassment and hopefully by the time he returned things would be back to normal. The last thing she wanted was any sort of awkwardness between them.

In order to get her mind off things, Thena decided to spend the day browsing through the antique shops along Route 1. There was one in particular that she had grown fond of over the years and had become quite friendly with its owner. Grabbing her bag, she left her self-loathing behind and headed out. Nothing helped bring her out of a funk quicker than a little retail therapy.

While she browsed the shelves, she eavesdropped on a conversation between the shopkeeper and an elderly woman who was insisting that she had purchased fabric there just a couple of weeks before.

"I'm sorry, you must have us confused with another shop. We sell antiques here."

"I'm not confused…I was in here just last week." The old lady insisted.

"Okay, well we don't sell fabric any longer. Is there something else I can help you find?" The shopkeeper relented, hoping to appease the woman who was becoming more and more agitated.

"Never mind." The woman snapped, storming out of the shop.

The shopkeeper watched as the old woman got into the passenger seat of an old Buick where an elderly man was waiting behind the wheel. Thena approached her friend, following her gaze.

"The poor thing." Thena commented, watching as the car slowly backed out of the lot and drove away.

"I know, that was Mae Pritchett. She was the Librarian at the Wells Public Library up until last year. She knew exactly where to find every book they had without looking through the card catalog. It's so sad how quickly the dementia took over."

Annabel shook her head, turning toward Thena.

"Enough about Mrs. Pritchett, it's so nice to see you. How's the family? What's new?"

Thena smiled, eager to talk about happier things. Allowing Annabel to lead her by the hand to a small Victorian sofa in the center of the shop where they sat down, she filled her old friend in on the latest family drama and the impact the storm had on the beach. When another customer came into the shop that appeared to need assistance, Annabel excused herself encouraging Thena to browse through a recent acquisition bought at an estate sale. Amongst the vast assortment of bric-a-brac she located a bronze statue of a beautifully detailed prancing stallion atop a rectangular base and she quickly snatched it up to add to her collection.

"I've been looking for one of these forever. Now I can cross it off my list and move on to another one."

"Oh I'm so glad you got it. It just came in from the Wheelwright estate. I don't know if you're familiar with the name. I forgot you collect horse figurines, I'll have to keep my eye out for them."

Insisting that they get together for dinner and drinks to catch up, Annabel walked Thena to the door just as a tour bus pulled up with a group of elderly passengers. Thena smiled, winking at Annabel before heading to her car.

"Have fun." She called back, amused as she watched a parade of walkers and canes make their way into her friend's shop.

Thena visited a couple of new shops that had opened up since the last time she was in town before stopping at the local sandwich shop to grab a bite to take back to the beach. When she arrived back at the cottage she was surprised to see only a handful of sunbathers scattered on the beach and wondered if perhaps vacationers were scared away by the aggressive waves that often followed a hurricane. Though there were half a dozen brave surfers enjoying the aftermath, there were no swimmers in the water and red-warning flags had been posted up and down the beach. Lifeguards that would normally be perched atop their tall white chairs were busy picking up newly deposited storm debris that continued to wash ashore.

Excited by the prospect of enjoying a quiet day reading on the beach without having to dodge Frisbees and kids kicking up sand as they ran in and out of the water, Thena unloaded her purchases from her car and headed for her cottage for a quick change of clothes. Armed with her beach chair, book, sandwich and a cold can of soda, she made her way onto the sand, settling for a spot midway between the cottage and the shore. The waves were too rough to consider setting up any closer.

Opting to eat her sandwich before getting back into the romance novel she was currently reading, Thena watched the surfers as they rode the ten-foot waves toward the shore, only to paddle back out and do it all over again. It hardly seemed worth the effort to her, though it was thrilling to watch. By the time she finished her sandwich and settled in to read, the blue skies were dotted with white puffy clouds and a warm breeze gently caressed her skin, lulling her into the relaxed state she so badly desired. She had been reading for nearly an hour and was deeply engrossed in the novel when the couple approached her; casting a shadow on the page she was reading and forcing her to look up.

"Thena, right?" Autumn asked, plopping down on the sand next to her and dragging Bryce down with her.

"Yup." Thena confirmed, folding back the corner of the page she was reading to mark her spot before setting it on her lap.

"What are you two up to today?" She asked, secretly hoping their plans didn't involve another public make-out session she would be forced to endure.

"We were planning on hosting a small get-together later and wanted to invite you to join us. Unless you have other plans?" Autumn winked, implying she was aware of what had transpired between her and Mason after the previous evening's bonfire.

Blushing, Thena quickly agreed to join them hoping to dispel any rumors that may be making the rounds. Although she was aware that Mason had returned to Boston for work, she feigned ignorance as to his whereabouts to reinforce her indifference to the man she had spent the night with. Although she didn't challenge her, it was obvious that Autumn wasn't buying it though she merely smiled, dropping the subject and continuing on with the details.

"It'll be very informal so dress for comfort. We're asking everyone to bring a side dish; we'll provide the burgers and the alcohol. Oh and you might want to bring a chair or blanket to sit on."

Thena agreed, watching as the couple made their way back down the beach, stopping occasionally to chat with other residents who were most likely being invited to the gathering as well. As she watched the carefree couple, she couldn't help but envy their obvious affection for each other. It had been far too long since she was involved in a long-term relationship and she yearned for that kind of comfortable companionship. Whether it was the romance novel she was reading or the lingering effects of a night of passion, she couldn't be sure, but despite her earlier shame she couldn't deny that she hoped it was the beginning of a budding romance and not just a one-night stand.

Too distracted to continue reading, she picked up her things and made her way back to the cottage, hoping to get in an afternoon nap before joining the others. Glancing at her neighbor's cottage as she made her way up her porch steps, she wondered whether or not Mason was also preoccupied with memories of the previous night and she smiled to herself hoping he was.

After a quick shower to wash away the sunscreen and sand that somehow always managed to find its way into her hair; she threw on an over-sized t-shirt and a comfortable pair of panties before making her way to the sofa to take a nap. Apparently more exhausted than she realized from the previous night's over-indulgence, she quickly fell asleep.

She awoke two hours later, fully rested and eager to join the others for an evening of relaxation under the stars. After selecting a floral print cotton sundress in shades of orange and red that complimented her dark hair and olive complexion, Thena brushed through her tangled, slightly damp hair before pulling it up and wrapping it in a neat bun, which she secured with a handful of bobby pins. Slipping on a pair of strappy wedges made of brown leather and cork to complete the look, she wondered if perhaps she might be a bit overdressed for the get-together. Rather than worry about sticking out as opposed to blending in with the crowd, she slipped off the dress and pulled on the cut-offs she had worn earlier in the day and selected a cute peasant shirt in white gauze. Satisfied that she had made the right choice, she made her way to the kitchen to prepare a tray of cheese and crackers to bring with her.

Armed with her beach blanket and tray of snacks, she made her way down the beach toward the sounds of laughter and smell of charcoal and lighter fluid. Autumn spotted her first and rushed up to relieve her of the tray and pull her by the arm.

"I'm so glad you made it. Come on…let me introduce you to everyone."

Thena smiled, instantly glad she had accepted the invitation. As Autumn pulled her through the small crowd, she introduced her to the other guests before dragging her over to the makeshift bar that had been made out of a plastic kiddy pool filled with ice. Reaching down and grabbing a bottle of hard lemonade, Autumn shoved it into Thena's hand.

"Come on, drink up, you have some catching up to do."

Thena accepted the beverage, though it didn't seem she had a choice in the matter and took a long drink. Satisfied with her compliance, Autumn excused herself to help prepare the food, encouraging Thena to mingle before skipping her way over to Bryce, who was busy tending the grill.

Thena looked around at the other guests, spotting a small group of women who appeared to be in the middle of a deep discussion. She was about to head their way when the young man she recognized as the musician from the previous night approached her.

"You don't want to go over there." He whispered.

"No?" Thena asked, trying to figure out whether or not he was teasing.

"No…they'll eat you alive."

"Is that so?" Now she was intrigued. "What makes you say that?"

"Well I can't say for certain, but suffice it to say, they have a reputation for bringing grown men to their knees. They're known as "The Vultures" around town and if you rub them the wrong way, they won't think twice about gouging your eyes out."

Thena laughed as he plunged the stick he was holding into the sand in dramatic fashion, twisting it about while gritting his teeth to emphasize the force.

"Oh my, well I will certainly steer clear of them then. I'm so glad you warned me."

"No problem." He bowed in a grand gesture just as his girlfriend approached with two plates of food, handing one to him.

"Is this guy bothering you?" The girl teased, nudging him in the belly with her elbow.

"Not at all, in fact; he may have just spared my life." Thena winked, nodding toward the gaggle of women who now seemed to be studying the crowd.

"Oh, I see... well, in that case you have done well, Victor. By the way, my name is Adara. I saw you last night with Mason right?"

"Um...yes, well not with him exactly." Thena stuttered, not wanting to give the wrong impression.

"That's not what it looked like to me." Victor teased, winking at his girlfriend.

"What I mean is, we came together, but we're not a couple...just neighbors. I only met him a couple of days ago."

Victor and Adara smiled at each other, causing Thena to blush and look away before changing the subject.

"You're quite the musician. Do you play as a profession or is it just a hobby?"

"A little of both. Adara and I work at coffee house in town and I play there a couple nights a week. You should come by sometime."

"That's wonderful...I definitely will. I'm amazed at all the new faces around here. I've been coming here every summer for the past few years and I don't recognize anyone."

The couple followed her line of vision as she looked through the crowd for a familiar face. While everyone else seemed to know one another, she seemed to be the odd man, or woman as it was; out.

"A lot of the old residents sold off their summer homes over the past few years. I think there is only one or two besides from yours that still have the original owners. You can blame that on the banking industry. Even towns like this have been affected by the recession."

"I guess you're right." Thena agreed, shrugging off the uncomfortable feeling she briefly felt in a sea of strangers.

By the time she'd had her second drink, which she was careful to absorb with a plate of food; she had gotten to know the young musician and his girlfriend well enough to join them in a sing-along. Though she couldn't carry a tune if her life depended on it, the alcohol aided in her confidence and she enjoyed herself despite her earlier discomfort.

By midnight only the three of them remained beside the hosts themselves and Victor pulled out a joint to pass around between them. No longer apprehensive about indulging, Thena partook in the drug without hesitation. While she had felt uncomfortable the previous night by the groping and fondling of the other couples, Thena now secretly wished Mason was there so that she too, might participate in a little PDA. While the two couples were distracted, Thena slipped away, returning to her cottage to spend the night alone.

Chapter Five

Mason discreetly checked the time on his watch for at least the fourth time during the seemingly endless meeting. Although he hated to admit it to himself, it had been difficult leaving the warm comfort of his neighbor's arms for the long drive to the city and the even longer meeting he was suffering through with the investors. What would normally have been the perfect excuse to escape the clutches of a one-night stand was now hindering his desire to spend a relaxing day in bed with an incredible woman.

By the time the meeting broke for lunch, Mason was wishing he had thought to ask Thena for her number so that he could at least check in with her. He considered asking Clay for the digits, but quickly changed his mind thinking she might be embarrassed that they had hooked up so quickly and might not appreciate him advertising the fact. While Clay led the group toward the building's elevator, Mason hung back; checking his cell phone for missed messages in hopes that she might have contacted Celeste for his number. Disappointed, he took the next car down to the lobby where the rest of the group was waiting and was greeted by a stern look of disapproval on Clay's face telling him he'd better get his head in the game.

Although Clay was only fifteen years his senior, he had taken Mason under his wing as an intern during his senior year at BU. With the encouragement of Celeste, an old family friend, while other interns had moved on to other challenges, Mason had stayed behind, eager to learn from the best and confident in the mission they strived for. Now, nearly five years later, he continued to look to Clay for guidance and approval.

As they made their way on foot to a popular Bistro a block and a half away from the office, Mason discussed the odds of the Red Sox making it to the playoffs this season with a well-known entrepreneur. Clay nodded his approval from across the table as they took their seats at a large booth in the back of the restaurant, which was reserved for business luncheons. While Clay generally preferred to keep business in the office and direct the conversation to less important matters during lunch, there were always one or two investors who insisted on keeping the conversation going over food and drinks.

By the time they made it back to the conference room, it was nearly three o'clock and it was obvious that they wouldn't get any more accomplished that day. Handing out a modified proposal Clay's secretary had put together while they were out, they agreed to resume the meeting a nine o'clock the next morning.

After shaking hands and saying goodbye to the investors, Clay invited Mason into his office to go over their strategy for the next day.

"So, Celeste tells me you met Thena."

"Yeah, actually it was Shane that forced the introduction. He took an instant liking to her."

"And you?" Clay pried, looking up over the wire-rimmed glasses perched on the end of his nose.

"Yeah, she's a nice girl." Mason mumbled, downplaying his attraction to the girl next door.

"Celeste thought you might think so." Clay responded, smiling to himself as he returned his attention to the papers in front of him.

Eager to change the subject, Mason went over his notes from the day, emphasizing their need to lock down firm commitments at the follow-up meeting. Ignoring his employee's discomfort, Clay pressed on.

"Celeste thought you might like to know that Thena has a fondness for history. Perhaps you could invite her to join you at the Historical Society's fundraising event this weekend. I just happen to have a couple of tickets we aren't going to use."

"The what?" Mason asked, feigning disinterest as he flipped through his notes.

"The Historical Society holds an annual fundraiser each year to kick off the summer tourist season. It's a walking tour of some of the town's historical sites followed by a cocktail party at the museum. I've never been, but Celeste tells me it's a good time"

"Yeah, maybe." Mason responded, not wanting to commit to anything until he got back to Maine and saw how things felt.

"Well here...take them, if you decide not to go you can just give them to someone else."

In his experience, it could go either way. Either things would be awkward between he and Thena and they would avoid each other as much as possible or she would eagerly await his return so that they could continue where they left off.

Clay knew Mason too well not to know when it was time to back off, so he dropped the subject and invited him to join them for a sail and a late dinner back on land. Although the offer was tempting, Mason declined explaining that he needed to go over his notes before the next day and didn't like to leave Shane alone too long.

"If I don't take him out for his nightly stroll, he'll tear the place apart. The last time I left him alone he tore through the trash and pissed on every piece of furniture in the apartment."

Clay laughed, agreeing that it probably wasn't a good idea to leave the dog alone and confirmed that they would meet back up at eight o'clock the next morning to strategize before the others arrived.

Chapter Six

Thena woke to the sound of heavy rain and thunder and quickly realized she had left all the windows in the cottage open the previous night. Stumbling out of bed, she hastily ran around closing the windows before grabbing the bath towel draped over the shower curtain to soak up the small puddles of rainwater that had formed throughout the bungalow. Satisfied with everything now under control, she made her way back to the bathroom to relieve herself and to take a quick shower while she tried to figure out what she should do with herself for the day.

Under normal circumstances she would have simply crawled back into bed and enjoyed a lazy day of napping and reading, only leaving her bed to eat and use the bathroom, but after a night filled with dreams involving her next door neighbor, she needed to distance herself from the premises and the reminder of their night together.

Stepping out of the shower, she quickly dried off, wrapping the towel around her body and grabbing another for her hair. Selecting a pair of black and pink compression capris and a matching pink tee, she dressed for comfort as well as the gloomy weather. After brushing out her damp hair and pulling it up into a ponytail, she made her way to the kitchen where she poured herself a glass of orange juice and popped a bagel into the toaster. While she waited for her bagel to toast, she thumbed through the pile of local listings and the event calendar Celeste had left for her, hoping something would catch her interest. Although there didn't appear to be anything going on until later in the week, there was a listing of some of the new shops that had opened up in the area since the previous summer.

Ignoring the large number of gift and souvenir shops that always topped the list, Thena scrolled her finger down until she found a listing of several thrift and antique shops throughout the area. Circling half a dozen places that she didn't recall seeing on her previous visits, she folded the paper and tossed it in her pocketbook before retrieving her bagel from the toaster. The dark skies had allowed her to sleep later than she normally would have and by the time she finished eating her breakfast and quickly straightened up the place, it was nearly eleven o'clock.

Stepping out of the cottage onto the small porch, she looked up and down the beach that was eerily desolate. Although the rain had died down to a drizzle, the distant rumble of thunder promised more to come and perhaps still shaken from the recent hurricane, any tourists that might still be in the area, had chosen to stay away from the beach. A warm breeze carried the scent of low tide as well as the overwhelming smell of rotting seaweed and dead fish that had washed ashore as a result of the recent storm.

Thena hurried toward her car, unconsciously holding her breath until she was safely inside. Pulling the listing out of her bag she formulated a strategy based on the location of the various shops, selecting the one furthest away from the beach to begin with intending on eventually making her way back home. Excited by the prospect of what she might find, she tuned the radio to a local country station and hummed along to the latest hit by Carrie Underwood, determined to rid her mind of anything but the possibility of a successful shopping day.

The first shop was little more than an unorganized display of used clothing, packed so tightly together they were impossible to separate from the racks let alone browse through. Thena made her way through the tight aisles feigning mild interest only because she was the sole patron in the shop and didn't want to rudely walk out as soon as she entered, although that was her immediate reaction.

The next shop was more interesting and she spent nearly an hour exploring shelves filled with everything from antique linens to toys she recalling having as a child. Although there was only a small collection of knickknacks scattered amongst a large display of milk glass vases, candy dishes, lamps and plates, there were a pair of equestrian bookends and she snatched them up along with a wooden plague with a famous quote she thought would like nice on her bookcase at home.

The next two shops were next door to each other and she could see from the large front window displays that they promised to be interesting. The first shop catered to the nautical enthusiasts and carried a wide variety of antique brass compasses, lanterns and bells of assorted styles and sizes as well as weather instruments, porthole mirrors and a display case filled with scrimshaw art. The storekeeper was an elderly man who looked as though he had just stepped out of the pages of a Melville novel with his long gray beard and wavy hair tucked inside a sailor's cap.

"Let me know if I can help you with anything." He muttered without looking up from the pocket watch he was repairing.

Thena responded with a polite "will do" and continued to browse the shop. Although she wasn't particularly fond of brass, she found the scrimshaw art fascinating and spent several minutes studying the intricate details engraved into pocketknives, belt buckles, tie clips and everything in between. When she turned around to ask him a question about the artist, she saw he had fallen asleep in his chair with his arms across his chest and his head bobbing up and down with the rhythm of his heavy breathing. Smiling to herself, she exited the shop, clutching the brass bells hanging on the door as she slowly pulled it shut so as not to wake him.

The smoky scent of incense encircled her as she entered the shop next door, which was dimly lit with twinkling clear Christmas lights, lamps with orange bulbs and numerous LED tea lights throughout the shop. Tapestries in multiple colors draped the walls depicting phases of the moon, pentacles and female goddesses in various positions. A Celtic flute played in the background along with soothing sounds of the ocean to add to the overall calming effect of the incense.

Thena slowly browsed through the esthetically pleasing arrangement of stones, crystals, oils and herbs displayed in rustic baskets throughout the shop. Along the far wall exhibited on open shelving were a number of amulets, talismans, scrying bowls and incense burners as well as an assortment of statues. On the right wall was a long glass display case which contained crystal balls, jewelry and fairy figurines. Several spinning wire display racks were scattered throughout the center of the shop containing everything from books and calendars to CDs and note cards. Old wine barrels were filled with lotions, soaps and bath beads as well as herbal teas and novelty gifts. To the left were several tables piled with alter cloths, bags, pouches and several interesting pieces of clothing.

Tucked into the far corner, just beyond the counter where the cash register sat; surrounded by small baskets filled with smudge sticks, candles and small wooden boxes, was a doorway, covered by a purple beaded curtain and topped with a wooden sign that read "Tarot Card Readings".

A woman in her early forties sat perched on a stool behind the cash register humming along to the music while she absently flipped through the pages of what appeared to be some sort of spell book. While Thena assumed the woman was aware she had entered the shop, she didn't appear to be interested in pushing any sales on her. In her opinion there was nothing worse than being relentlessly pursued by a sales clerk who commented on every item she picked up and followed her around like she was a common thief that couldn't be trusted to browse the store unchaperoned.

Tucking a shopping basket inside her elbow, Thena slowly made her way through the store selecting several candles and packages of incense. She had just set her basket down to sample some of the lotions when a couple of woman exited the back room deep in whispered discussion. Glancing quickly in their direction she recognized one of the women as Adara and smiled to herself thinking she was just the type to get sucked into a tarot card reading. Although amused, she wouldn't have given the sighting anymore thought except that she overheard the other woman mention Autumn. Placing the lotion bottle back with the others, she picked up her basket and quietly made her way toward a rack of long gauzy skirts where she could remain out of sight, but would still be close enough to the women to hear what was being said. Fingering through the skirts as not to appear suspicious, she listened as the women discussed some sort of ritual having something to do with the Summer Solstice.

While she personally felt such beliefs and practices were a bunch of hogwash, she found it interesting that her two new friends might be involved in something of that nature. She was debating whether or not she should step forward and announce her presence, when Adara hugged the other woman and made her way to the exit, making the decision a moot point. Selecting a skirt with an ombre of blue shades, she added it to her basket before making her way to the counter as the other woman disappeared behind the beaded curtain.

"Hi, did you find everything okay?" The clerk asked, setting down her book and hopping off her stool.

"Yes, thank you. You have a beautiful shop. I could spend days in here and still not see everything."

"Well you're welcome to come back as often as you'd like. Do you live around here or are you just visiting?" The clerk asked, looking Thena over with a keen eye.

"I'm renting a cottage on the beach for the summer. I'm sure I'll be back."

The clerk nodded, appearing as though she was about to say something but changing her mind. Out of the corner of her eye, Thena could see a slight movement of the beaded curtain and felt the uncomfortable sensation of being watched. Slightly unnerved by the feeling as well as the bits of conversation she had overheard, Thena paid the clerk, smiling nervously as she accepted the bag containing her purchases and exited the shop making a beeline for her car.

Too freaked out to continue her day of shopping, she decided to head in the direction of Annabel's antique shop in hopes of convincing her friend to join her for a late lunch. Although she was certain she was letting her overactive imagination get the best of her, there was definitely something peculiar about the tarot card reader and the fact that she seemed to spy on her rather than simply approach the counter and introduce herself.

By now the rain had stopped and only a few distant clouds remained in the sky. Although the AC was cranked up as high as it could go, the intense humidity of the outside air made the beetle a virtual oven and Thena reached into her glove box and retrieved a handful of napkins to wipe the back of her neck where she was dripping with sweat. When she finally pulled into the lot of the tiny shop, she breathed a huge sigh of relief seeing her friend sitting out front on an antique rot iron bench sipping sweet tea from a tall glass. Recognizing her friend's car, she jumped up, waved and approached the car as Thena opened the door.

"Hey girlfriend, I didn't expect to see you again so soon. What brings you out on this dreadful day?"

Thena greeted her friend with a quick hug before gesturing toward her glass. "May I?" She asked, taking the glass from her hand without waiting for a response. After taking a quick sip from the straw, she handed Annabel back the glass and followed her back to the bench.

"I decided to do a little shopping and I thought you might be interested in joining me for a late lunch. That is, unless you've already eaten."

"That sounds lovely. Actually this was the first break I've taken all day. I think everyone had the same idea as you. The shop was buzzing all morning. Now that the sun's come out, everyone seems to have made other plans. Let me just close up quickly."

Following her inside Thena was hit immediately by the heavy hot air. Throughout the shop, several fans were spinning the hot air without actually cooling the place down at all.

"Don't you have an AC?" Thena asked, wiping her brow.

"I did, but it conked out this morning. I was hoping the fans would circulate the cool air that was in here before it broke, but so many people came in and out that it didn't last long. Hopefully they'll have some left over at the hardware store and I can put it in later. If I let it run all night, I should be good by tomorrow."

Annabel moved about the shop switching off the fans and table lamps while Thena stood by deep in thought. As she approached her friend, Annabel immediately saw the distant look in her eyes and reached out to take her hands.

"Okay...what's really going on? You didn't just happen to be in the area and decide to invite me to lunch did you?"

"No, I guess not. It's kind of a long story, let's figure out where we're going to eat and head out and then I'll fill you in."

"Okay, it's a deal. I'll drive." Annabel insisted, locking the shop's door and digging into her bag for her car keys.

"Thank God, my AC's shit. I nearly died on the way over here."

"I'm not surprised," Annabel teased, "I'm amazed she's still running at all."

Nodding rather than defending the old girl, Thena climbed into the passenger seat of her friend's 2012 Jeep Cherokee that somehow seemed to still possess that new car smell. Setting their sights on Lord's Harborside for lobster rolls and iced tea, they drove in silence listening to the local country station and enjoying the cool air blasting from the dashboard. Although she could feel her friend's eyes shifting from the road over to her and back again, Thena kept her eyes fixed on the road ahead, choosing to wait until they arrived at the restaurant and she had her full attention before unloading.

The restaurant was nearly empty of patrons due to their late arrival and they were quickly seated. After placing their orders and receiving their drinks Annabel leaned across the table and placed a gentle hand on Thena's arm.

"Okay, let me have it? What has you so distressed?"

Thena took a deep breath in preparation before confiding in her friend that she had done the unthinkable and slept with her handsome neighbor and was now suffering from Catholic guilt.

Annabel laughed, "Is that all? Why didn't you mention it when I saw you yesterday? You had me worried for a minute. Good for you girlfriend. So? Come on...details. How was it?"

Thena sighed, relieved that her friend didn't share her disgust with her actions while at the same time disappointed that she was making light of her predicament.

"You don't think things are going to be awkward now that we've slept together? You don't think it's a bad sign that he slipped away while I was sleeping and I haven't seen him for a couple of days?"

"I'm sure he would have preferred spending the day in bed with a beautiful woman to driving back to Boston for a boring meeting. You're over thinking it. I say enjoy your youth while you have it. We're only young once."

"You're probably right." Thena considered, swirling her straw along the inside of her glass.

"I know I'm right. Just take your cues from him. Wait for him to come over, feign indifference and you'll have him begging at your feet."

Thena smiled, "I knew you'd make me feel better. I should have told you yesterday instead of continuing to punish myself."

Pausing their conversation while the waitress delivered their lobster rolls, the women thanked her and took a couple of bites before Annabel asked which shops she had visited and whether or not she had found anything interesting. Thena listed off the shops, detailing her impressions before ending with her final stop at Mystical Treasures.

"It was the oddest thing. I didn't know whether I should announce myself or scurry into a corner and hide. There was definitely something strange about the way they were talking and what they were talking about. Then after she left I could have sworn I saw the card reader peering at me through the beaded curtain."

Thena waited for her friend to respond, hoping she might once again tell her she was being foolish, but she remained quiet, concentrating on her sandwich and avoiding eye contact.

"Annabel?"

"Huh?"

"Don't you think that was weird?"

"I don't know. People around here take the summer solstice and all that pretty seriously. I doubt it was anything more than the two of them making plans for a party to celebrate the beginning of summer."

Again Annabel picked up her lobster roll and took a big bite, washing it down with a sip of iced tea.

"Okay but that doesn't explain why the other woman was staring at me through the curtain. If she was curious about me why wouldn't she just come out and introduce herself?"

"Yeah...I don't know. Like I said, you have to stop looking for trouble and just enjoy the summer and your handsome neighbor. Lord knows there's a shortage of good guys out there."

Flagging down the waitress, Annabel requested the check and insisted on buying despite Thena's protest. While Thena had hoped they might drive over to Stutesy's Pub for a couple of drinks, Annabel maintained she needed to get to the hardware store to pick up a new air conditioner and drove Thena back to her shop where she had left her car. Promising to catch up with her in a few days, Annabel insisted once again that Thena stop dwelling on the small stuff and enjoy her summer vacation.

Watching as her friend drove away Thena couldn't help but wonder what Annabel might have meant by "trouble" and despite her friend's insistence that she ignore her predisposition to over think everything, she found herself doing just that as she drove back to the beach.

By the time she pulled into the driveway it was nearly six o'clock and she noticed Mason had returned from his trip to Boston. Avoiding looking in the direction of his cottage, in case he might glance out the window, she quickly made her way around the corner and up the porch steps to her front door. With her arms loaded down with her pocketbook and purchases, she struggled to get her key in the door without dropping anything.

"Let me give you a hand." Mason called out, taking the steps in a single bound.

"Oh hey...thanks." Thena responded, handing over her keys and stepping back to give him room.

"How was your trip?" She nervously asked, hoping she sounded casual and not at all as anxious as she felt.

"It was okay, good I guess. I accomplished what I needed to so I won't need to go back for at least a couple of weeks."

Stepping aside to let her enter first, he relieved her of some of her packages and followed her into the cottage where he placed them on the table.

"Looks like you've been busy." He commented.

"Yes well it wasn't exactly a beach day today. I figured I'd take advantage of the lousy weather and check out some of the new shops in town."

Making her way to the refrigerator she pulled out a couple of beers and handed one to Mason assuming he was planning on sticking around for a while. Suggesting they sit outside on the porch, Thena led the way detailing her evening spent down the beach with an emphasis on the highlights.

"So...you're a regular pothead now are you?" Mason laughed, winking as Thena blushed. "Did I miss out on any good make-out sessions between Autumn and Bryce?"

"Actually it wasn't just them, Victor and Adara got in on the action too."

"And you?" Mason raised an eyebrow and smirked.

"That's when I called it a night and came back here."

"Too bad I wasn't here to take the edge off." Mason teased causing Thena to blush once again.

Thena ignored the comment and focused on a couple of teenagers tossing around a football down the beach while she sipped her beer. Mason took the hint and switched the conversation to a more mundane topic bringing Thena's attention back to him. As he attempted to explain the nature of his current project in layman's terms,

Thena listened politely, understanding little, but trying nonetheless. They had just finished their beer and were discussing the upcoming fundraiser at the Historical Society, when Victor, followed by Adara; approached the cottage, guitar in hand.

"Hey...we're having a clambake tonight over at our place. We'd love it if you would join us. It will just be us, Autumn and Bryce." Victor announced.

"What do you say?" Mason asked, nudging Thena's arm.

"Yeah...sounds great. Can we bring anything?"

"We've got you covered. See you around eight." Victor waved, heading back down the beach with Adara struggling to keep pace.

"Well I guess I should probably take a shower then. Why don't you come back in about an hour and we'll have another beer before we go?" Thena suggested, hoping she wasn't being too presumptuous.

Mason agreed, handing her his empty beer bottle before skipping down the steps and heading in the direction of the cottage next door. Thena waited, watching until he disappeared inside before rising from her chair and making her way inside.

Stopping in the kitchen long enough to toss the empty bottles in the recycle bin before unloading her purchases and heading for the shower, Thena smiled, realizing she had been foolish to think things would be awkward between her and Mason. His comment that he would have been willing to "take the edge off" the previous night suggested he didn't consider their encounter a one-night stand and that somehow comforted her earlier feelings of guilt and shame.

After a quick shower, Thena selected a fuchsia sundress with spaghetti straps along with a pair of nude colored gladiator sandals. Pulling her long hair up off her neck and pinning it into a French Twist, she stood on her tiptoes and turned sideways to inspect her reflection in the mirror. Satisfied with the results, she returned to the living room of the cottage and picked up the book she was currently reading to wait for Mason to return.

Chapter Seven

Mason arrived promptly at seven o'clock toting a six-pack of beer and a freshly-shaven face. Dressed in a loose-checkered button down shirt and a pair of cargo shorts he looked every bit the tourist and Thena couldn't help but smile at his eagerness to please. Unlike her, Mason was bare-footed.

"Aren't you afraid you might step on something and cut your feet?" Thena asked, pointing to his bare feet.

"It's not likely anything could penetrate these bad boys. The bottom of my feet are as tough as leather. Besides…it wouldn't be so bad if I hurt myself, every man needs a little nursing now and then." Mason winked.

Handing Thena a beer and setting another on the counter for himself, he placed the remaining four in the refrigerator before joining her back on the sofa. While they drank their beer they discussed Thena's fondness for literature and the books she felt were most relevant in today's society. They had finished their beer and were working on their second one when Mason glanced at his watch and announced it was a quarter past eight. Somewhat disappointed that they had accepted the invitation to attend the clambake when she would rather spend the evening alone with Mason, Thena agreed they should head over to the others and continue their discussion at a later time.

As they made their way down the beach, the familiar aroma of clams, lobsters, potatoes and corn on the cob filled the air. A gentle breeze tickled the back of Thena's neck where loose wisps of hair, too short to stay in the twist; danced against her skin. Appearing larger than normal, the moon was displayed prominently in the clear night sky and the waves kissed the shore in a soothing hypnotic rhythm. Everything about the night screamed romance and Thena wondered if Mason was also feeling the effects of the elements.

As they approached the others they were met with a round of enthusiastic greetings and "what took you so long?" questions. Patting Mason on the back and escorting him toward a keg of beer, Bryce asked him where he had been the past couple of days. Autumn and Adara each grabbed one of Thena's hands and pulled her toward the small fire encircled by a grouping of stacked rocks, apparently collected from the beach. Tugging her down to a beach blanket positioned a few feet from the fire, the women immediately began grilling her about her relationship with Mason. No topic seemed to be off-limits as they bombarded her with questions covering everything from how she rated his kissing to the size of his manhood.

Thena threw her hands up in the air to stop the questioning.

"Hey, what makes you think I know? It's only been a few days since I got here."

The women stared at her with their mouths hanging open for a moment, considering her denial before looking at each other and rolling over in laughter. Thena shook her head.

"Whatever…think what you want. I'm going to get a beer, do either of you want one?"

They stopped laughing long enough to shake their heads before leaning into each other and giggling once again. Thena rose from the blanket and headed in the direction of the three men who were deep in discussion about the latest ball game. Working her way in between them, she grabbed a red solo cup from the stack on top of the keg and filled it before returning to the blanket where she was certain to be the target of another round of pokes at her love life.

To her surprise, when she returned the women seemed to have gotten themselves together and they each apologized for giving her a hard time. Due to the fact they were on point with their questioning, Thena couldn't stay mad so she accepted their apologies and changed the subject.

"So I did a little shopping today. There's a bunch of new stores that opened up this season. Have either of you been out?" Thena asked, paying close attention to Adara.

Autumn shook her head. "Bryce and I spent the whole day in bed. We only got up to eat and use the bathroom. Besides, we live here year round so what's new to you is old news to us."

Thena smiled wondering how they had the energy to have sex given the copious amount of pot they smoked.

"Actually I was out earlier." Adara interrupted. "I picked up a few things at my Aunt's shop in town."

"Which shop is that?" Thena asked, knowing full well the answer.

"Mystical Treasures...you should check it out. She has the best incense and candles. It used to be in Ogunquit, but she moved this spring. She figured she'd get more business here in Wells."

Thena could have sworn she saw something pass between Adara and Autumn, some meaningful glance, but it happened so quickly she couldn't be certain.

"Actually, that was one of the shops I visited today. I picked up several things. I told the clerk I would definitely be back to look around some more."

"Oh that's great. I'll have to tell my Aunt, she likes to keep track of her repeat customers, to send out sale fliers and such."

She was about to ask if her Aunt was the card reader when the men approached, carrying plates for the women weighed down with the spoils of the clambake. While they ate in near silence, Thena was plagued with the memory of the strange conversation between Adara and the card reader and couldn't help but wonder what it was all about. When they finished eating and tossed their paper plates into the fire, Bryce lit a joint while Victor retrieved his guitar and began strumming a melody. Bryce passed the joint to Autumn who took a toke before handing it off to Mason. Taking a drag, Mason motioned for Thena to open her mouth and he leaned in to share the powerful weed, sealing it with a kiss while it burned inside her lungs. Releasing her, Mason passed the joint to Adara who offered up the same method of transfer to Victor as he plucked away at the strings of his guitar without missing a beat.

Again the joint made its way around the circle only stopping when it burned the fingers of its last victim and was tossed into the fire. While Victor continued to strum on the guitar, Adara and Autumn walked hand and hand to the water's edge, dipping their toes in the cool ocean before agreeing to take a swim. Wiggling out of their dresses, the women, wearing only thongs, made their way into the surf, shrieking and laughing as the cool water caressed their bodies.

"Aren't you going to join them?" Mason teased, elbowing Thena who was watching the pair in stoned fascination.

"I'm not that brave." Thena admitted, wishing she could rid herself of her inhibitions.

"Come on...I'll go with you." Mason insisted, standing up and pulling Thena up off the blanket.

Resisting at first, Thena gave in and allowed Mason to pull her toward the water. As they approached the shore, Mason stopped and disrobed as Thena shyly looked away.

"Do you need help with that?" Mason asked, pointing to her dress.

"Thanks, but I think I'll keep it on." Thena insisted.

Mason shrugged, feigning indifference though it was obvious by his expression he was disappointed. Unlacing and kicking off her sandals, she followed him into the surf, cringing as the cold water lapped at her legs and then higher until she was chest deep in the ocean. Clearly confident in his own skin, Mason did the backstroke catching up with the other women who were frolicking in the waves. Watching from a distance as Mason lifted the naked women one at a time out of the water and tossed them into the surf, Thena envied their free spirit. Although she was aware of her naturally good looks and toned body and wasn't normally self-conscious, amongst this group of nonconformists she felt like an outsider. As she watched, Adara playfully latched onto Mason's back as he swam with the tide, allowing the waves to carry them closer to her.

Autumn shrieked and called out, "My turn, my turn."

Without looking in Thena's direction, he eased Adara off his back and swam back toward Autumn who eagerly climbed on. While he didn't appear to be doing anything more than enjoying some fun in the surf, Thena felt her blood boiling as both women surrounded Mason, giggling and flirting as their hands disappeared beneath the water. Disgusted by what she saw, Thena turned from the trio and headed back to shore where she gathered her sandals and headed in the direction of her cottage.

Muttering profanities to herself, she quickly pulled off her wet clothes and wrapped herself in a towel while she waited for the water in the shower to warm. By the time she stepped out of the shower, having rid herself of the sand and seaweed that clung to every crevice of her body, she was bound and determined not to let a couple of promiscuous women come between her and a good thing. Pulling on a pair of cut-offs and a tank top, she made her way back across the sand where the trio had returned to shore and we drying off in front of the fire.

"Hey, where did you disappear to?" Mason asked innocently.

"I went back to the cottage to shower and change." She responded, hoping he picked up on her annoyance.

Stepping up to the keg, she poured herself another beer before joining the women who were now wrapped in towels discreetly covering what was previously on display. While she sipped her beer she sat quietly as Mason asked the two couples whether they were from the area or just vacationing. Explaining that she and Autumn grew up in the Wells-Ogunquit area and went to high school together, Adara described how the two women hooked up with the men and had been inseparable every since. Eventually the conversation drifted to the upcoming fundraising event.

Adara turned her attention to Thena. "You're planning on going, right?"

Thena shrugged. "Mason and I were talking about it earlier. We haven't really decided one way or the other."

"Nonsense!" Autumn interrupted. "Everyone will be there. You have to come. We'll make it a triple date."

"Maybe," Thena replied noncommittally, "We'll see how things go."

Looking over her shoulder at Mason who was now preoccupied with the men, she wondered whether or not his behavior with the women was his way of saying he wasn't a one-woman man. As if he sensed he was being watched, he looked up, making eye contact with her and winked, raising his cup up in salute. Thena gave a slight nod before returning her attention to the women and their current discussion about fashion.

The remainder of the evening went by without incident and it was a little past midnight when they all decided to call it a night. As they made their way back toward their cottages, Mason draped his arm around Thena's shoulder.

"You were pretty quiet tonight." Mason commented, watching for her reaction.

"I guess." Thena responded, stiffening at the memory of his water aerobics. "Actually, if I'm going to be honest, I was a little shocked by what appeared to be happening between you and the girls. At least from my prospective anyway."

Mason stopped walking and faced her. "What exactly did you think you saw?"

Thena blushed with embarrassment, not certain how to put it into words. Mason waited, his brows creased in defense.

"It looked…well it seemed to me…that is…hell, it looked like something more intimate was going on under water. Don't make me say it, you know what I mean."

Thena turned away, ashamed that she was letting jealousy get the best of her. Mason sighed, turning her around to face him.

"Look, I admit it wasn't awful having a couple of naked women riding my back. That's my bad, but what you think you saw them doing to me they were actually doing to each other. I was just an innocent bystander."

"That's disgusting." Thena spat, breaking away from his hold and stomping away.

Mason ran to catch up with her.

"Hey, listen…nothing is going on between me and either of those girls. I promise…I'm not that kind of a guy. I'm sorry if I made you feel uncomfortable. I never should have put you in that situation. I knew you didn't want to go in, I shouldn't have pressured you. Will you forgive me?" Mason batted his lashes.

"Ugh…fine, you're forgiven, but just so you know, I'm not that kind of girl. I'm not a prude by any means and I'm certainly not naïve, but I'm not willing to put my goods on display either. At least not around a bunch of people I barely know."

"I understand and to be honest I'm not so sure I wouldn't have felt the same if the roles had been reversed. Actually I am sure. Please don't take your clothes off in front of Bryce and Victor."

Thena swatted him then, rolling her eyes. "The good ole double-standard. It figures. Well you don't have to worry about that, because I'm fairly certain the occasion will never arise that I feel the need to strip down naked in front of those two potheads."

At that they both laughed, continuing their stroll toward their cottages. While Mason tried to convince Thena he should spend the night, Thena steered him in the direction of his own cottage.

"You're forgiven for you bad behavior but that doesn't mean I'm willing to invite you into my bed either. Go home and sleep it off."

When Mason realized his whining was falling on deaf ears, he kissed her goodnight and stumbled next-door leaving Thena muttering "Idiot" from the porch.

Chapter Eight

The next couple of days passed without incident while the summer residents of Wells Beach settled into their vacation rhythm. Both Mason and Thena agreed it was probably a good idea to slow things down a bit and get to know each other on an intellectual level rather than a physical one. Although they continued to spend the better part of their days and evenings together, they stayed away from temptation by avoiding the party scene down the beach.

When the day of the Historical Society's fundraiser arrived Thena splurged on a spa day in Kennebunkport, getting a facial as well as a manicure and pedicure. While she refused to break her no makeup rule, she did purchase a tube of pink lip-gloss, convincing herself that she was merely protecting her lips from the sun. Stopping at a small boutique a couple doors down from the day spa, she selected a vintage-inspired ivory beaded cocktail dress with straight lines and cut just above the knee. Although the price was a bit higher than what she was accustomed to spending, she rationalized that it was a timeless piece that could be worn for an infinite number of occasions. Satisfied, she headed back to Wells Beach, confident and excited about what was certain to be a memorable night.

Having already decided they would skip the walking tour and go directly to the cocktail party, Mason and Thena decided to have a light dinner beforehand at The Steakhouse. At five o'clock sharp, Mason rapped at her screen door before letting himself in. Thena was just coming out of the bathroom, her hands around her neck struggling to clasp a strand of pearls.

"Wow...you look amazing. Can I help you with that?" Mason asked, crossing the room and taking the necklace from her hands.

"Yes, thank you. I'd about given up hope of ever getting this thing on. The clasp is so small it kept slipping out of my fingers."

Thena turned around, lifting her hair away from her neck. Mason easily connected the piece, stepping back to admire the completed look.

"I'm nearly ready, I just need to do my hair." Thena apologized.

"Leave it down, it looks great just the way it is." Mason assured her.

"Really, you don't think I should put it up?" Thena fidgeted with her long strands, tucking a stray piece behind her ear.

"It's perfect, I promise." Taking her by the hand he led her out of the cottage, stopping long enough for her to lock her door before escorting her to his waiting car that was idling in the driveway with the AC blasting to cool down the interior. Walking her over to the passenger-side door, he opened the door for her and waited for her to swing her legs inside before closing it and making his way over to the drivers-side.

As they drove the short distance to the restaurant they discussed the probability that either Autumn or Adara would behave inappropriately at the fundraiser that was certain to bring out the wealthier, more sophisticated residents of Wells. By the time they pulled into the parking lot of The Steakhouse, they were both roaring with laughter at the image of women dressed in eveningwear more appropriate for a tawdry nightclub than a stylish cocktail party. Mason envisioned Bryce and Victor donning surfer shorts and wife-beaters, neither wearing shoes. Dabbing her eyes to wipe away the tears of laughter, Thena waited for Mason to once again make his way around the car and open her door for her.

Although the place was buzzing with groups of diners both small and large, they were quickly seated and selected a bottle of wine. Avoiding the heavy entrees they ordered crab cakes and shrimp cocktail to share from the appetizer portion of the menu.

When the wine arrived, Mason raised his glass. "Here's to our first real date and the hope that many more will follow."

Thena gently leaned her glass into his, "Cheers." Taking a sip and placing her glass back on the table she nodded toward him in approval.

"By the way, you're looking very handsome tonight. You clean up well."

Mason beamed, nodding his head in agreement. Sporting a crisp light blue button-down long sleeve dress shirt with the cuffs rolled up and topped with a navy blue tie dotted with white anchors, he looked like he had just stepped off a yacht. The look was completed with tan slacks and a pair of dock shoes in dark brown leather.

"I know a thing or two about fashion. I'm not exactly a caveman, you know."

"Don't get defensive, it's just that up until now I've only seen you in beach attire. It's nice to see you all dressed up."

Mason put away his hurt puppy eyes and raised his eyebrows, appeased by her clarification. The food arrived and they ate while discussing the lousy weather that had plagued the area and whether or not the upcoming weeks would be any better. Thena explained that in all the years she had been coming to Wells, she had never seen such inclement weather.

"Well at least we have each other's company." Mason reasoned. "It's not as bad as spending vacation alone on a rainy beach. I can think of lots of ways we could spend our time that doesn't involve the outdoors."

Thena shook her head. "I'll bet you can."

They finished their appetizers and poured the rest of the wine into their glasses while they waited for the check to arrive. Thena excused herself and went to the restroom where she reapplied her lip-gloss and ran a brush through her hair. Satisfied, she returned to the table just as Mason signed the receipt and handed it to the waitress.

Making their way on foot to The Meetinghouse Museum, they stepped in line with several other couples that were just returning from the walking tour. Thena looked around to see if she could spot any familiar faces in the crowd when she heard a yell from the back of the line.

"Thena! Mason!" Adara screamed.

Turning around, they waved hello quickly before facing forward once again.

"Well, that didn't take long. We aren't even in the door and I'm already humiliated." Thena whispered.

Mason squeezed her hand to show his support, keeping his eyes on the front of the line in hopes that their neighbors would at least wait their turn and not try to cut the line to go in with them. Thena snuck a peek back, quickly assessing the situation.

"All four of them are back there." She whispered.

"Can you see what they're wearing?" Mason asked, wondering if his or Thena's predictions were closer.

"No, I can only make out their faces. I don't want them to see me looking."

By now they had made their way into the museum where Mason handed over their tickets and signed the guest book placing a check into the donation box. As the museum's historian thanked him for his contribution and handed him a button, which he tucked into his pants pocket, Thena placed her own donation in the box and signed the registry. Taking two glasses of champagne from the caterer's tray and handing one to her, Mason led her toward the back of the room where they could blend in with the other guests and have a perfect view of the entry. Thena was sipping her champagne and taking in the assembly of beautifully dressed women when Mason nudged her, nodding toward the entrance. Thena nearly choked on her drink as she spotted the two couples enter the premises, avoiding the donation box and heading directly to the makeshift bar.

Both Adara and Autumn were dressed in long flowing skirts and peasant shirts, reminding her of clothing worn at renaissance fairs. As predicted, their feet were bare besides from toe rings attached to fine chains that clasped around their ankles. Each woman wore a headpiece adorning their foreheads made of silver and beads and depicting some sort of symbol in the middle and wrapping around the back of their heads where they were fastened with a clasp atop their hair. Around their necks they wore golden stones hanging from silver chains. Victor and Bryce were dressed head to toe in black, wearing t-shirts and jeans. Black boots completed the look.

Although both Thena and Mason stared at the couples in shock, neither able to put into words what they were thinking; no one else in the room seemed to pay them any attention. As she looked around the room, Thena noticed several other women dressed similar to the girls. Moving seamlessly from the bar to a table filled with a bounty of hot and cold hors d'oeuvres, the foursome chatted loudly drawing the attention of a couple of middle-aged women. As the women approached the couples, Mason elbowed Thena.

"Here we go, get ready for a scene."

Thena followed Mason's line of vision and watched as the two older women spoke softly yet intensely to the girls. Although both Mason and Thena assumed the women were requesting the couples leave the premises without incident, neither was prepared for what followed. As they watched in stunned silence Victor and Bryce stepped back as the four women joined hands in what appeared to be some kind of prayer circle. As nearly everyone in attendance stopped what they were doing and directed their attention to the circle, the women closed their eyes and began to sway back and forth as they recited what seemed to be some form of prayer.

While Mason and Thena stood by in shock, several other women in the crowd began making their way through the crowd handing all those present a candle. Accepting the offering, Thena turned to Mason.

"This must be some sort of performance piece." She whispered. "I had no idea they were involved with the local theater."

"Me either." Mason responded keeping his eyes glued on the scene playing out before them.

Several uncomfortable minutes passed while the circle continued to sway back and forth and Thena wondered what the point of it all was. She noticed for the first time that someone had lowered the lights and other than the candlelight and the full moon shining outside through the windows, the room was eerily dark. The scent of incense filled the crowded room and an occasional cough was the only sound that interrupted the circle's faint chanting. With their hands still connected, they raised their arms toward the sky as they made a tighter circle. Then, as if they were familiar with the performance; the entire crowd besides from Mason, Thena, Bryce and Victor; formed a circle around the women. No one appeared to notice their absence as they moved clockwise around the women.

The performance or whatever it was, ended as abruptly as it began and the circle broke off into small groups, picking up conversations previously interrupted as if nothing had happened. Neither Thena nor Mason spoke as they watched the room transition from a spiritual gathering to a typical cocktail party, only breaking their silence as Bryce approached.

"What was all that about?" Thena asked, nodding in the direction of the women.

"Autumn said it's a local tradition, a shout out to the witches that brought notoriety to the town. They will end the evening with a fire ritual to honor the summer solstice."

Thena laughed. "Seriously? Do people around here still believe in that stuff or is it just for fun?"

A look of unease passed over Bryce's face and Thena looked down as Mason's grip on her hand tightened.

"Not everyone believes in it, but these people do. Every since 1692 when a local clergyman was arrested and executed for witchcraft during the Salem Witch Trials these people and their ancestors have been holding an annual candlelight ritual where they pray for the souls of those accused to find peace in the afterlife. Nearly everyone here tonight lost an ancestor as a result of the craft. The town council is made up entirely of direct descendants of those accused and executed. They have been for over 300 years."

Again Bryce looked over his shoulder, obviously nervous about being overheard discussing local politics. Over at the bar, Autumn waved and motioned for them to join her and the others. Following Bryce's lead, Mason and Thena made their way over to the bar, handing off their glasses to a waiter carrying a tray of empties.

"Did you enjoy the circle?" Adara asked, beaming with pride.

"It was beautiful." Thena responded, hoping she sounded sincere.

"After everyone has enough to cat and drink we will make our way back to the beach for a big bonfire. I've taken the liberty of preparing herb pouches for both of you to toss into the fire."

"What's the significance of that?" Thena asked curiously.

"It's symbolic...a way of tossing away your troubles or pain. The herbs are a combination of vervain, sage, rosemary and lavender."

Although Mason seemed somewhat reluctant, Thena agreed to meet the others back on the beach after returning to their cottages to freshen up. Victor pulled Mason aside to invite them to join the others back at his cottage before the bonfire to get high.

"I'll run it by Thena, thanks." Mason responded, without committing to the invitation.

Thena and Mason walked back to his car in silence, each mulling over what they had seen and heard. Opening her door for her before making his way over to the driver's side, Mason looked back at the Museum where several couples were mingling outside.

"Well that certainly turned out to be more interesting than I anticipated." Thena chuckled.

"You've got that right. I'm not surprised Clay stays away during the summer. I don't think it would be very good for his reputation to be involved with something as strange as that, although…now that I think about it… it was him that encouraged me to attend."

"He probably doesn't know what goes on there. As far as I know, he hasn't lived here since he finished college. He and Celeste only come to town during off-season. If he did know, I'm sure he wouldn't have suggested it."

"You're probably right. Anyway…Victor invited us to join them for a pre-bonfire smoke. I told him I'd run it by you."

Thena considered the offer, wondering if they would be offended if she refused and feel it had something to do with the ceremony she had just witnessed.

"What do you want to do?" Thena asked, deflecting the offer back to him.

"I never refuse an offer to get high, but if you'd rather not, I'm cool with that."

"Okay then, it's settled, we'll go. Let's stop at my place first to use the bathroom and then we can head over."

Minutes later Mason pulled into their shared drive, telling her to go ahead in while he retrieved Shane who would join them on their quest. While they waited for the others to return, they sat on the porch and drank a beer while Shane lay on the floor and she massaged his back with her bare feet. Shane closed his eyes and let out a breath, enjoying the attention.

"You're spoiling him." Mason commented, frowning at the dog. "He's going to be hell to live with when the summer's over."

"Oh hush, everyone need a little pampering now and then, even dogs. You're just jealous it's him and not you."

"Well that goes without saying, but it doesn't change the fact that he's going to be following me around my apartment, whining and nudging me to scratch his neck and rub his belly."

"Would it make you feel any better if I offered to scratch behind your ears?" Thena teased.

"Not the ears but perhaps a little lower." Mason winked and laughed as Thena shook her head in feigned disgust.

By the time they finished their beer, they could hear the laughter and shouts of the others as they returned to the beach along with a caravan of cars belonging to the other fundraiser attendees. Making their way toward the party with Shane pulling at his leash in an attempt to get there faster, Mason and Thena watched as car after car arrived and people began unloading armfuls of wood for the bonfire.

Victor waited for them on the porch and ushered them inside along with Shane. Offering them each a pillow to sit on, Victor leaned over a large wooden spool that was used as a makeshift table and retrieved a joint from an old cigar box. Sitting down next to Adara, he lit the joint and inhaled deeply before passing it over to his girlfriend.

While they waited their turn, Mason spoke to Victor.

"So is this your place or Adara's?"

"It actually belongs to her mother but they don't ever use it so technically it's hers. They bought a place down in Florida a few years ago and sold their house here in Wells. She convinced them to keep the cottage and let her live here year-round."

"Nice." Mason said, nodding his head while he looked around the cottage. Although it was basically the same design as both his and Thena's cottages, there was a screened in porch on the front and a small addition that appeared to be an actual bedroom. While some of the furnishings appeared to be remnants of the 80's, perhaps belonging to her parents; the majority of the décor seemed to be made up of flea market finds and warehouse cast-offs. Not only was there the wooden spool that originally held wire or cable, but there were also several other pieces that appeared to be made from pallets and crates. There was an old couch against one wall that was covered in an old blanket, most likely to hide stains or rips in the fabric. Large floor pillows surrounded the wooden spool for additional seating as well as a heavily worn wooden rocker. Old sheets covered the windows in place of curtains and a bookcase made out of pallets held a number of bongs and pipes as well as an assortment of candles, jars filled with herbs, wooden bowls and incense.

Thena handed the joint to Mason drawing his attention back to the group who were discussing their favorite bands and what concerts they had recently attended. Mason took a long drag from the joint before passing it over to Autumn and joining in on the conversation. As the effects of the marijuana took hold, the dialogue steadily declined until there were more giggles and sighs than actual words spoken.

A roar of applause from the beach informed the circle that the bonfire had been lit and the group made their way out of the cottage and onto the sand to join the others. Thena noticed that the others had abandoned their candles and were now holding small pouches, which they rubbed between their hands while silently praying. One by one they tossed the pouches into the flames causing the flames to rise and saturating the air with the overwhelming scent of herbs. The combination of the heat from the flames and the scent of the herbs in her stoned state was almost too much to bear and she found herself struggling to stand. Thena reached over and grabbed Mason's arm to steady herself, afraid she might pass out and fall into the fire. Entranced by the flames, Mason barely noticed Thena's struggles until she stumbled, nearly dragging him down with her.

"Hey, you okay?" He asked, pulling her up and away from the circle.

"I feel a little light-headed. I need some fresh air." Thena panted.

Taking her by the arm, Mason directed her toward the shore and into the cool water.

"You're probably just over-heated. The water should cool you down."

Easily lifting her up, he cradled her in his arms as he made his way into the water until he was waist deep before easing her down. As the cool water saturated her expensive dress and instantly lowered her body temperature, she sucked in the salty air while allowing her senses to be stimulated. Holding her at the waist, Mason waited until she seemed steady on her feet before suggesting she ease onto her back and allow herself to float on the surface of the water. Agreeing, she leaned back against his outstretched arms until the cool water soaked her hair, sending a refreshing chill through her body. Once again confident in her condition, she rolled over in the water, hiking her dress up to her waist and plunging under the surface of the water before coming back up for air.

"Feeling better?" Mason asked, swimming out toward her.

"Much better, thank you." Thena called, as she swam quickly away, forcing him to pursue her.

She was no match for him and Mason quickly caught up with her, grabbing her by the waist and pulling her on top of him. Wrapping her arms around his neck, Thena clung to him as he swam effortlessly through the water and away from the activity on the beach. When he finally stopped and gently eased her off his back, they were in front of their own cottages and he held her by the hand as they made their way to the shore.

"You're a great swimmer." Thena acknowledged.

"Why thank you. I've had a lot of practice." He boasted.

"Oh I see. So I'm not the first girl you've rescued then?"

"I think I'll plead the fifth on that one." Mason winked, dragging her up the beach in the direction of his cottage. "I will say you're by far the prettiest."

"Men never seem to realize they reveal more by what they don't say than what they do." Thena countered.

Dropping her hand so that he might open the door, Mason stepped back allowing her to enter first.

"You do realize we left Shane back at Victor's right?"

"I know…I thought we could shower and change before heading back over. Besides, I'm a little jealous of the attention you give him." Mason admitted.

"Well in that case I should probably go next door and take that shower." Thena suggested.

"Actually, I thought it would be must more efficient if we took a shower together. You know, to conserve water and all." Mason smirked, pulling her by the hand toward the bathroom.

"I'm not sure we can both fit in there, it's a little small." Thena argued while Mason turned on the water and waited for the temperature to adjust.

"I'm sure we can make it work. It might be a little tight but I think we can manage." Mason insisted.

"You say that like you speak from experience." Thena teased, raising her eyebrows while she allowed Mason to peel her wet clothes from her body.

"Not at all, it's merely a matter of space and body mass." Mason replied, stepping back to remove his own wet clothing.

Despite his claim to be concerned about water conservation, Mason took his time bathing Thena while she in turn washed him, only stepping out when the water turned cold. Slowing drying her off with a towel before tending to himself, he suggested she head back to her place while he went down the beach to retrieve Shane.

"I thought we were both going back over there?" Thena reminded him.

"I changed my mind. I decided I'd like to have you to myself tonight rather than share your attention. That is, unless you'd rather go back?"

"No, I think I've seen all I need to see for one night." Thena responded, recalling the strange events she had witnessed.

Mason dropped his towel and walked over to a pile of clean clothes sitting on the floor and selected a pair of board shorts, slipping them on before returning to her.

"Okay then, let's get you next door and I'll head over to get Shane. After I drop him off here, I'll come over."

Wrapped only in a towel, Thena collected her wet clothes from the bathroom floor before following Mason outside and over to her cottage.

Chapter Nine

Adara stepped inside the inner sanctum of Mystical Treasures where she found her Aunt filling small jars with herbs, the combination of which was intoxicating.

"Good morning, Auntie."

"Ah, so my beautiful enchantress awakes finally. Tell me, how did everything go last night?"

Eliza stepped away from her mixing table and took her niece by the hand, directing her to the small settee opposite the card reading table.

"Tea?" She offered.

Adara nodded and waited while her Aunt poured two cups from a porcelain pot, which was ever present in the event an unexpected patron might wish to have their tea leaves read.

" It's hard to say. She didn't participate in the circle, but I didn't really think she would. On the other hand, she didn't seem fazed by it either. I think we might have overdone it by offering such a powerful strain of weed. At one point she looked a little green and then Mason took her out into the water. After that we didn't see her again. Mason came back to get his dog and said they were going to call it a night."

Eliza sipped her tea, silently considering their next move. As Adara anxiously waited for her Aunt's instructions, she bit her lower lip while attempting to keep her shaking hands from rattling the cup against the saucer.

"Auntie?"

"Hmmm?"

"What do you want me to do now?" Adara asked nervously.

"Why don't you and Autumn invite her for a girls' day out. Do a little shopping, go out to lunch. Let her see you are just a couple of normal girls."

"What if she asks us about the circle?" Adara pressed.

"Brush it off. Let her think you don't take it seriously. Tell her it's just for fun."

Adara nodded, though she wasn't convinced she would be able to pull it off. She wasn't a good liar. She had too many tells. Her nerves always got the best of her and Autumn was never any help. She always took a back seat, going along but never fully committed to recruitment or whatever else the assignment might be. If it wasn't for the fact that she was Eliza's niece, she might also be able to take on a more secondary role, but since her Aunt had no daughters of her own, it fell to Adara to fill that position.

Thanking her Aunt for the tea, Adara promised to be in touch and left the shop. As she peddled her way back to the beach on her mint green Schwinn, Adara practiced her invitation hoping to perfect it. By the time she arrived, steering her bike into the shared driveway of Mason and Thena, she was more or less confident in her delivery. Pushing down the kickstand and hopping off the bike, she made her way between the cottages and onto the porch of Thena's bungalow. Rapping lightly on the screen door, she waited for a response, shaking off her nervousness.

After waiting a half-minute she peaked inside the cottage before calling out.

"Thena? Hello…it's Adara." Again she waited, but there was no response.

She was about to head next door, knowing she couldn't be far if she left her door unlocked; when she spotted the couple walking hand-in-hand on the beach with Shane in toe, heading back her way. Waving with both arms high above her head, Adara called out their names from the steps of Thena's porch. From their position on the beach, Thena was the first to notice the wild motions of their neighbor.

"Looks like we have a visitor." She announced, nudging Mason who had bent down to untangle Shane from his leash.

Looking up, Mason followed her line of vision to the animated Adara who was now hopping up and down while still waving her arms like she was trying to get the attention of a search plane. They waved to acknowledge her presence and continued to head in her direction. Shane reached Adara first, jumped up enthusiastically and was rewarded with a kiss and a round of "who's a good boy?"

"What's up?" Thena asked, wondering what brought her neighbor out so early in the day. Normally she didn't see any of her neighbors, including Mason until well after noon.

"I was hoping I could talk you into joining Autumn and me for a girls' day tomorrow."

"What did you have in mind?" Thena asked, unwilling to commit until she was certain of the plan.

"The usual, shopping, lunch maybe a pedicure. What do you say? It will be fun." Adara kept her eyes focused on Shane, afraid she might give herself away.

"Actually that sounds great. There's still a few new shops I haven't checked out."

"Great…so we'll pick up you around ten then? None of the shops open until then."

"Sounds good to me. Thanks."

Adara gave Shane one more kiss and a quick scratch before saying goodbye and skipping around the corner of the cottage to retrieve her bike. Mason watched in silent amusement until she was out of earshot.

"Well, isn't that sweet of her to invite you out for a girls' day." Mason teased.

"If nothing else, it should make for an interesting day." Thena shrugged. With a long list of chores to do, she said goodbye to Mason and Shane, promising to stop by later in the day. While she gathered her dirty laundry and her more than likely ruined cocktail dress, she balanced the basket on her hip and reached for her purse and car keys with her free hand. She made it as far as the door when her cell phone rang and she paused to consider whether or not she should stop to answer it or just let it go to voicemail. Opting for the latter she pulled the door open and stepped back outside into the hot sun.

Stopping at the bank first for a roll of quarters, Thena stood in line behind a couple of older women who were discussing the recent inclement weather's affect on their roses. Amused by the serious manner in which they discussed nature's fury as though it was a personal affront directed only at them, Thena chuckled. The women turned toward her, both furrowing their brows in disgust before turning back around to face the tellers. Thena cleared her throat and looked past the women as though her outburst had nothing at all to do with their conversation.

By the time she left the bank and deposited her soiled clothes into a couple of washers at the Laundromat, it was nearly one o'clock and she was famished. Dropping off the dress at the dry cleaners where she was scolded for getting the garment wet, Thena made her way to a small coffee shop where she ordered an iced coffee and bagel. Settling in at a small outside table, she finally checked her voicemail. To her surprise she had not one but two missed called and she listened to them in succession. The first call was from her mother and had been from the night before. She was calling to remind Thena that she had promised to stay in touch and that she hadn't heard from her since she arrived. The second call was from Celeste, who stated she was just calling to say hi and to give her a call when she had a minute.

Eager to get the first call out of the way, Thena took a bite of her bagel and called her mother.

"Well it's about time."

"Hello to you, too." Thena responded.

"Yes, well, your Father is quite upset with you, young lady. We have been worried sick."

"Yeah, I'm sure Dad has been sitting by the phone anxiously awaiting my call. Give me a break, Mom. I'm not a child."

"Well you certainly aren't acting like a responsible adult. For all we knew you were lying in a gutter some-place breathing your last breath."

"Oh for God's sake, Mom, stop being so dramatic. I'm sure if that were the case, you would have heard something on the news."

"That's not the least bit funny."

"Okay, I'm sorry. So anyway...everything is fine here. I've been busy making new friends, hanging out with old friends and relaxing. I haven't seen anything sinister going on unless you take into account a couple of old ladies that gave me the stink eye at the bank this morning."

"Well if you were as disrespectful to them as you are to me, they probably had good reason."

Thena related the discussion she had overheard and that seemed to sidetrack her mother long enough to calm her down. Avoiding mentioning anything related to Mason and the possibility of the beginning of a serious relationship, Thena filled her mother in on the new shops in town as well as the sad news about the Millers.

"I'm really going to miss them. I hope I get to see them again sometime." Thena said, pausing in thought.

Promising to call her mother back later with the Millers' address, Thena ended the call and took a couple more bites of her bagel before calling Celeste. Unlike her mother, Celeste answered the call with an actual greeting.

"Hello, Sweetie, I'm so glad you called me back."

"Hi...I was surprised you called. What's up?" Thena asked curiously.

"I was just checking in...oh who am I kidding? How are things going with you and Mason? Clay told me he seemed somewhat anxious to get back to the beach."

"I should have known, I swear you're in cahoots with my mother." Thena feigned annoyance even though she was dying to find out more about him.

"I cross my heart, I would never interfere with your love life. That being said however, I wasn't opposed to Clay renting out to him."

"Yes, I'm sure it never crossed your mind that we might hook up."

Celeste squealed, "So it's true. Details, girl, and don't leave anything out."

Thena smiled, eager to share her good fortune with someone, even if it was an edited version of the facts. While she left out the names of their new friends down the beach and the fact that they were all getting high on a fairly regular basis, she did mention that they spent time with two other couples and had attended the fundraiser.

"I had no idea people around here were into that kind of stuff. It's a little odd, but whatever floats your boat I guess. It seems harmless."

Although Celeste didn't elaborate, she did confirm that the town had a history of witchcraft going back more than three hundred years and that it was common knowledge that there was a large number still practicing the craft. While Celeste didn't go as far as to assure her she had nothing to be concerned about, she didn't seem to be overly concerned either.

By the time Thena ended the call and finished her bagel, nearly an hour had passed and she returned to the Laundromat to move her clothes to the dryers before heading out to the grocery store to stock up on food and alcohol. Taking her time so that her checkout would coincide with the completion of her laundry, Thena walked the aisles slowing, browsing the magazine racks and ready-made meals.

It was nearly three o'clock when she returned to the cottage and, with the help of Mason, quickly unloaded her groceries and clean laundry. While Mason put the groceries away, Thena folded and hung her clothes. Shane lay on the sofa watching her every move. When she closed the closet, he hopped off the couch and joined her as she made her way into the bathroom to put away the clean towels.

"So…what's the plan for tonight?" Thena asked as she made her way into the kitchen, accepting the beer Mason offered her.

"Well, I thought, since you'll be spending all day tomorrow with the girls; it might be nice to have a quiet evening with just the two of us. What do you say to pizza and beer on the beach around sunset?"

"Sounds very romantic, doesn't it, Shane?" Thena responded, scratching the dog behind the ear.

"Sorry, Shane, you're not invited." Mason insisted, prompting the terrier to tilt his head in recognition of his name and jump up on his owner's leg. "You have no idea what I just said, do you, boy?"

"Oh you're so mean. Come here, Shane; he's a meanie isn't he?" Again Shane perked up his ears and returned to Thena, who was rewarded with a slew of wet kisses.

The couple took their beer out onto the porch, followed by Shane who immediately jumped up on Thena's lap and closed his eyes. While they relaxed and drank their beer, Thena recounted her conversation with Celeste, leaving out the parts concerning Mason and focusing solely on the brief history lesson about the town.

"Celeste didn't seem surprised at all, but she also didn't seem to take any of it too seriously. Now I kind of wish we had gone on the walking tour. That's probably why we were the only ones surprised by the ceremony. I'll bet they talked about it and explained everything on the tour."

Mason considered her words. "We could always explore on our own…do a little online research or visit some of the historical sites. I'm sure the Chamber of Commerce has all that information."

Thena nodded, sipping her beer and watching as a toddler ran back and forth to the shore, filing her pail with water and returning to where her father was helping her build a sand castle.

"You know it's kind of funny that this is the first that I'm hearing about all this." Thena said absently.

"What do you mean?" Mason asked, glancing over briefly before returning his gaze to a couple of teenage girls walking down the beach wearing bikini tops that barely covered their nipples let alone the rest of their breasts and thongs that left little to the imagination.

"I mean, my family's been coming here for years and no one has ever mentioned the town's history, at least not that I remember. For all I know, I might have ancestors that came from here. I've never really thought about it before."

"I thought you said all of your family lives in Vermont?" Mason asked, not taking his eyes off the two girls who were now spreading out a blanket in front of the cottage a couple feet away.

"As far as I know, both my mother and father's side of the family have lived in Vermont for several generations, but who knows where they lived three hundred years ago."

When Mason didn't offer up a response, Thena followed his gaze to the two girls who were now busy applying suntan lotion to themselves.

"For all I know, I could be related to those two." Thena said, nodding toward the girls.

"Hmmm, maybe....wait...what?" Mason snapped out of it, blushing as he realized he'd been caught ogling the girls who were probably no older than sixteen.

Thena simply rolled her eyes and shook her head in disgust. Taking the last sip of her beer, she lifted Shane off her lap and onto the porch floor before rising from her chair.

"I have a few things I need to do." She stated, extending her hand to relieve him of his empty bottle.

"Oh, okay…we're still on for dinner right?" Mason stammered.

"Yeah come back over around seven. I have a conference on Monday I need to get organized for and I have no idea what the topic of discussion is, so I need to go over the agenda and see if I need to prepare anything. I don't want to wait until the eleventh hour."

"No problem, see you later." Mason leaned in for a quick kiss before scooping up his dog and heading back to his own cottage, careful to keep his eyes from wandering back to the attractive girls on the beach.

Chapter Ten

A rap at the door announced the arrival of Adara and Autumn and Thena glanced over at her alarm clock confirming it was ten o'clock on the dot. Shoving her feet into a comfortable pair of flip-flops, she made her way to the door just in time to avoid another round of anxious knocking.

"Good morning ladies, come on in. I just have to get my bag." Thena stepped aside to allow her guests entry before retreating to the couch to grab her purse and sunglasses. Calling over her shoulder she asked, "So what's the plan?"

Autumn took the lead excitedly counting down a list of shops they thought might interest their new friend.

"We thought we'd have lunch at Billy's and then end the day at the Post Road Tavern for a couple of drinks." Adara interrupted.

Thena joined the women, "Sounds good."

With Autumn driving and Adara riding shotgun, Thena sat in the middle of the backseat where she could easily hear the front seat chatter. While she had originally had doubts concerning whether or not the day would be filled with awkward silences and inappropriate conversations, she was pleased to admit to herself that she had more in common with the women than she realized.

Adara explained that while she worked at the little coffee shop with Victor as a barista she intended to go to night school, ultimately hoping to receive a bachelor's degree in business management so she could open her own shop some day. Autumn, on the other hand, had no interest in attending college and survived solely on an allowance given to her by her parents and a substantial trust fund left to her by her grandparents.

"So you both grew up in Wells, then?" Thena asked, curious how the two, who seemed to come from different social circles; had become friends.

"I did, Autumn grew up in Ogunquit." Adara explained.

"We went to the same high school though."

Pulling into a small plaza, Autumn parked her car in front of what could only be called a "head shop" and announced they had arrived at their first stop. Amused, but not surprised; by her choice of retail therapy, Thena followed her with Adara bringing up the rear. The shop was dimly lit with black lights and spinning lampshades that cast colorful waves upon the walls. The store's sound system was blasting The Grateful Dead while the shopkeeper kept rhythm on a set of bongos as he sat cross-legged on an orange shag rug in the middle of the shop. Nodding to acknowledge their presence, he continued to sway with the music as the trio looked around the tiny shop.

Pulling Thena by the arm to a collection of hand-blown glass pipes, Autumn explained that a local artisan made the one-of-a-kind pipes out of his studio across town. Although she wasn't interested in purchasing a pipe, Thena was impressed by the work and asked whether or not he made anything other than smoking apparatuses.

"Oh yes, he makes all kinds of things. Several of the shops in town carry his work. He makes vases, Christmas ornaments, decorative pieces; you name it he makes it. It just depends on the type of store for what you're going to find."

The trio browsed for several more minutes before Adara selected a small dark wooden bowl with a lid stained in a lighter shade and half a dozen packs of rolling papers. After depositing her purchases into the trunk of Autumn's car, the women made their way over to the next shop in the plaza. Catering to a more sophisticated clientele, this shop carried collections from Vera Bradley and Brighton as well as jewelry from Periwinkle and Pandora. In a separate room a display of gourmet chocolates; homemade jams and specialty teas filled the shelves. An elderly woman carrying a small silver tray offered them samples of the chocolates, explaining that they were having a sale on select boxes. All three eagerly snatched up a box and were rewarded with a second sample. Making their way back out to the main room of the shop, the group split up, each focusing their attention on a different collection. Nearly an hour later they left the shop, arms loaded with bags and their wallets a little emptier.

Heading out of town in the direction of Kennebunkport, the women excitedly discussed the deals they had found, confident in their choices and certain they were unlikely to find better deals anywhere in town. Arriving in Kennebunkport, Autumn passed through the streets lined with shops catering to tourists and headed off the beaten path to a small bookstore tucked amongst a row of 19th century Victorian-style homes.

The outside of the shop blended in with the homes in the area and only announced itself with a small wooden plague hanging above the door which read "Old and Rare Books". If you weren't aware of the shop's existence you might not even notice the plague that was weathered and faded, rendering it virtually unreadable. Pulling open the door, the women were immediately taken aback with the smell of musty old books and period furniture. Large plank wooden floors squeaked with every step they took, announcing their arrival to the handful of patrons browsing the shelves. Each of the half dozen customers turned to look at the women as they passed by as if wondering how they had come to find their private library. Their false smiles and nods did little to conceal their displeasure with the intrusion.

"How did you even find this place?" Thena asked curiously. It didn't seem like the sort of place either one of the women would frequent.

"My mother told me about it. I've been meaning to check it out for a while." Autumn explained.

Ignoring stares, the women slowly made their way through the rooms first familiarizing themselves with the layout before splitting off for a closer look. While both Adara and Autumn headed back to the room catering to books on plants, gardening and home remedies, Thena focused on a selection of books pertaining to local history.

Slowly making her way through the room, she removed several titles from the shelves for closer inspection. Satisfied she placed them on a long library table and sat down to examine them. Nearly all the books were in pristine condition with their jackets intact. As she flipped each cover to confirm whether or not they were first editions, she was surprised to see the same stamp in nearly every book. In elegant script the books were each inscribed, Belonging to the library of Prudence Putnam.

Returning the books that didn't appear interesting to the shelves where she had found them, Thena gathered the remaining volumes and went in search of Autumn and Adara. Finding the two bent over a large leather manuscript that appeared to be extremely old, the pair didn't notice her approach until she spoke.

"That looks interesting." Thena said, motioning to the book.

Adara quickly slammed the book shut, placing it back on the shelf while Autumn distracted Thena with feigned interest in her selections. Returning from the shelves, Adara suggested they check out and make their way back to Wells for lunch.

"I don't know about you two, but I'm starving."

Although she didn't press the issue, Thena couldn't help but wonder what it was the women had been looking at and she strained her eyes past Adara to try to read the title of the book. Unable to see that far away without being obvious, she smiled and agreed that she too could go for a cold drink and some fried clams. Making a mental note to return to the shop on her own at a later date, Thena brushed off the startled response of the women and followed them to the front room where an adorable old woman with lavender hair wrapped her purchases in kraft paper and tied them with string in keeping with the 19th century feel of the establishment.

While Autumn and Adara chatted endlessly in the front seat about the shop's abundant stock of books on botany,

Thena's mind wandered back to the large leather-bond volume convinced that there was indeed something odd about the way they reacted when she approached them. In the front seat, neither Adara nor Autumn seemed to notice her distant stare out the window or the fact that she didn't contribute to the conversation.

By the time they arrived at Billy's Chowder House, it was after one o'clock and the restaurant was packed. After nearly a half hour's wait, they were finally seated and all being familiar with the menu, they ordered before the waitress was able to pass out the menus. Parched, the women gulped down large glasses of ice tea, flagging down their waitress, who had just returned from the kitchen, for refills.

While they waited for their meals to arrive, Adara asked Thena about her life back in Vermont as a teacher. Expressing her love for the work as well as the luxury of having the summers off, Thena spoke fondly of her students, regaling them with funny stories about young crushes, over-involved parents and the occasional student prone to mischief.

"It's a thankless job really, but I love it and most of the kids are great."

"Do you want to have kids of your own or do you get your fill at work?" Adara asked.

"It depends on the day. Some days I envy the parents whose kids are a joy to be around, but then there are days that I can't wait to get home for some peace and quiet. I suppose if I were in a serious relationship I would give it more thought, but right now it's on the backburner. What about you two?"

Autumn perked up. "I can't wait to have kids. I swear if Bryce doesn't pop the question soon I might just have to dump his ass."

Both Adara and Thena laughed. "What about you?" Thena asked, nodding to Adara.

"I'm not ready for that kind of commitment. I like my freedom too much. Besides, I've only known Victor for a few months"

Their meals arrived and the women ate in silence, finishing in less than fifteen minutes. Splitting the bill three ways, they paid the tab and hopped back in Autumn's car and made their way over to the tavern. As they pulled into the lot, Thena immediately recognized Mason's car.

"Looks like Mason's here." She pointed out.

"I told Bryce we would end up here so I'm sure they're all inside." Autumn announced.

Making their way through the noisy crowd in search of the men, Adara lead the way saying "excuse me" at least a dozen times before reaching the table where the men were seated.

"Wow this place is really hopping." Thena commented, dropping into the seat next to Mason.

While the women gave their significant others a detailed account of their shopping excursion, Victor motioned for the waiter to bring another pitcher of beer and glasses for the ladies.

Leaving out the parts she planned to tell him about in private, Thena described the amazing bookstore they had visited and encouraged him to check it out. Before the next pitcher of beer arrived, Thena asked Autumn if she would mind dropping her off at the cottage so that she could prepare for her conference the following day. Mason insisted however that he needed to get back himself before Shane tore his place apart and so, after retrieving her purchases from Autumn's car, Mason drove her back home.

Sensing something was on her mind other than the conference, Mason pressed Thena for details.

"I really did have a good time. The shopping was great and they were on their best behavior. Not at all embarrassing to be with. There was something weird though."

"Here it comes." Mason teased.

"I'm probably just overreacting, but at the bookstore I found them studying a book that looked really old and when I approached them Adara slammed the book shut and put it back on the shelf before I could see what it was."

"Maybe it was a book of nudes." Mason suggested slyly.

"I doubt they would have been embarrassed by that. I swear it was as if I caught them with their hands in the cookie jar. They couldn't have changed the subject quicker. When I get back from Vermont I plan on going back there and seeing what it is for myself."

"It's probably nothing, those two are a little odd, but they're harmless. I would like to check out the shop though. Let me know when you're going and I'll tag along."

Thena nodded again, deep in thought. Although Mason offered to grill burgers, Thena declined, still full from the late lunch and eager to prepare for the next day. Grabbing her packages from the backseat of his car, Thena thanked him for the ride and gave him a quick kiss before disappearing into her cottage.

Chapter Eleven

It was nearly five o'clock by the time Thena got on the road early the next morning and she prayed she wouldn't run into any traffic delays. Her original plan was to get up no later than three, shower and dress and be on the road by four, but a night filled with strange dreams had kept her tossing and turning into the wee hours of the morning resulting in a later than expected wake time.

Making a quick pit stop at the gas station to fill her tank and procure a much needed large coffee, Thena stretched the limits of the posted speed to just under ten miles over the legal limit, hoping it was enough to make up time without being reckless. With a sign-in time of nine o'clock, the odds were against her making it in time and she found herself clutching the wheel as if the intensity of her concentration would somehow make the traffic in front of her move aside to allow her smooth passage. The first summer she had spent at the beach she had simply left a day ahead, taking her time driving back and spending a leisurely evening with her parents, but the more friends she made in Wells, the more of a social life she had and she very quickly decided to risk being late and drive in the morning of the meetings. For the most part it hadn't been a problem and she managed to get there early or at least on time. Only twice had she run into either roadwork or an accident, she was never quite sure which it was; and arrived more than an hour late. Basically she had missed the introduction of the panel of speakers, something that was clearly transcribed on the meeting's agenda. Still, because the sign-in table was only manned until the opening of the meeting, she had to work her way through the crowd during the breaks to find the person in charge of collecting the signatures in order to get credit for her attendance.

Thankfully she arrived at the hotel with twenty minutes to spare and signed in before locating several of her colleagues who were chatting amongst themselves. The conference was a complete snore-fest and Thena found it difficult to stay awake. Several times Ethan had to elbow her when she started to nod off, whispering to her that she might want to have another cup of coffee at the next break. By the end of day not only were her teeth floating, but she was feeling the effects of too much caffeine and not enough sleep.

While the rest of her colleagues made plans to have dinner and drinks at the Italian restaurant next door to the hotel, Thena declined; anxious to get back to Wells for a good night's sleep.

Grabbing a sandwich and a bottle of water at the local sub shop, Thena fell in line with the rush hour traffic, taking bites of her sandwich whenever she was stuck in slow-moving traffic. Driving on autopilot, so to speak, she allowed her mind to wander considering what Mason might be doing in her absence. Assuming he had slept in until at least noon, she imagined he was most likely now in the company of their friends down the beach.

By the time she pulled into their shared driveway it was nearly ten o'clock and she noticed that the lights were out in the cottage next door. Gathering the remnants of her dinner, her purse and conference folder, she made her way up the driveway to her porch. Pinned to her front door was a note from Mason.

If you're not too tired, join us over at Bryce's.
M

Removing the note, she smiled at the thoughtful invitation and opened the door to her cottage. Inside she quickly realized that she had forgotten to open the windows before she had left and she was immediately struck with the thick humid air trapped inside. Dropping her things on the kitchen table, she made her way through the cottage, opening the windows and turning on the fans. Too exhausted to shower, she slipped off her clothes and pulled on a long t-shirt before heading to the bathroom to relieve herself and brush her teeth. Thankfully she hadn't stopped to fold up the sofa bed before heading out, so she simply switched off the lights and went to bed.

It was just after nine the following morning when Thena awoke. Drenched in sweat from the humidity she took a quick shower and threw on a cotton sundress with spaghetti straps and a pair of flip-flops. Pulling her hair up into a high ponytail, allowing her neck to breath, she stepped out of the bathroom and into the stuffy air of the main room of the cottage. Despite the two large pedestal fans cranked up to high and rotating back and forth, the cottage was a virtual oven. Tossing a bagel into the toaster and pouring herself a tall glass of orange juice, she stepped out onto the porch hoping for even a slight ocean breeze to relieve her already perspiring body.

Despite the early hour, the beach was bustling with tourists and locals trying to keep cool. Whether conscious of the early hour or simply too hot to participate in physical games, the crowd was more subdued than they normally might be. While there was typically a volleyball game and a few small groups tossing around a football or Frisbee, there were only dozens of beach umbrellas shading their owners from the blazing sun. At least a hundred swimmers and waders cooled off in the calm waters. Returning inside to retrieve her bagel, Thena was immediately assaulted by the heavy air. Quickly spreading a thin layer of cream cheese on the bagel, she returned to the porch to eat.

The familiar bark of Shane drew her attention next door and she smiled as she saw his little face peeking out the window. Having spotted her, he continued to bark until Mason was forced out of bed at least two hours before his normal wake time. Scratching his chin and yawning widely, Mason stumbled outside with the anxious dog oblivious to everyone around him and calling for the dog to hurry up and relieve himself so he could go back to bed. With something else in mind, Shane continued to pull at his leash in the direction of Thena's cottage.

Thena watched, amused by the dog's insistence while Mason was obviously still half asleep. Standing up, Thena called out to Mason.

"If you'd like I can watch him while you go back to bed."

Mason looked up for the first time, raising his arm to wave. Letting go of Shane's leash, he allowed the dog to run to Thena, following behind as he tip-toed across the hot sand.

"Thanks but I guess I'm up now. How was your conference?"

"Wish I knew, I was so exhausted I think I slept through most of it." Scratching Shane behind the ears, she returned to her rocking chair, motioning for Mason to join her.

"Mind if I use your bathroom? Shane didn't give me a chance to go before I let him out."

Thena laughed. "Go ahead...feel free to pour yourself some juice. There's bagels in the fridge if you want one."

Mason thanked her, disappearing into the cottage and returning minutes later with a glass of juice.

"So what did you do while I was gone? I got your note about going to Bryce's but I was too exhausted."

"That was about it. I slept the better part of the day and ran into him while I was walking Shane. He mentioned that he had some mussels he was going to steam and invited me to join Victor and him. Apparently the girls had something else going on so it was just the three of us"

While they drank their juice, Thena invited Mason to accompany her on her trip out to Kennebunkport where she intended to find out what the mysterious book was that Adara and Autumn had seemed so interested in.

"Sounds good, anything to get away from this heat. Let me just take a quick shower and put some food out for Shane. Give me a half hour."

Thena agreed, suggesting Shane sit with her while he got ready. Resting comfortably on her lap, Shane closed his eyes, content to stay where he was. Reminding her once again that she was making him difficult to live with, Mason returned to his cottage leaving his dog behind.

Insisting that he drive for fear of melting in her Beetle, Mason took the wheel while Thena directed him toward their destination. Unlike her previous visit to the bookstore, they appeared to be the only patrons and the same adorable old woman with the lavender hair welcomed them.

"Let me know if there's anything I can help you with." She called out as Thena directed Mason to the room where she had seen the leather-bond manuscript.

Confident in her memory, Thena went directly to the shelf and scanned its contents. Not seeing it immediately, she ran her fingers over the volumes one at a time, certain her eyes were deceiving her.

"Are you sure this is the right room?" Mason asked, noticing Thena's frustration.

"I'm positive, it should be right here."

"Maybe someone else was looking at it and it hasn't been returned to the shelf yet." Mason suggested.

"That seems unlikely, don't you think?"

Mason shrugged, "Mind if I look around while you try to find it?"

"No...go ahead...I'll keep looking." Thena waved him away focusing her attention on a lower shelf. Stepping back to examine the shelf as a whole, Thena jumped when the old woman approached.

"Can I help you find something dear?"

"Yeah...I was in here a few days ago with some friends and they were looking at a book. I thought I might buy it for them as a surprise, but I can't seem to locate it." She lied.

"Do you remember the title?"

"No, that is, I didn't see the title. It was a large brown leather book. I believe it had gold lettering on the front and some sort of symbol or picture."

"Oh that sounds like a book someone purchased yesterday. If you'll follow me I can check my receipts."

"Thank you, that would be wonderful."

Hoping she was mistaken, Thena followed the old woman back to her desk and waited patiently while she thumbed through her receipts.

"Yes, here it is. Oh my...perhaps this isn't the book your friends were looking at."

"Why, what's the title?" Thena asked, a sudden shiver running down her spine.

"Demonology and Devil-Lure." The old woman recited in a near whisper. Looking up to meet Thena's eyes, a frightened look crossed her wrinkled face.

"Can you tell me who purchased the book?" Thena asked, confident she knew the answer.

"Let me see...yes it was Autumn Putnam. Is she your friend?"

"No." Thena quickly lied. "Putnam you said? I purchased several books the other day that came from the library of Prudence Putnam. I wonder if there's any relation."

"Considering the subject matter, I would have to say yes."

"Why do you say that?" Thena asked, curious about what connection the woman was referring to.

The old woman looked around the shop nervously as if she were afraid someone might be listening, despite the fact Thena was fairly certain she and Mason were the only customers in the shop.

"Well, the Putnam family has somewhat of a reputation around here. Back in the 1600s young Ann Putnam accused a local clergyman of being involved in witchcraft and he was hung for his crimes during the Salem Witch

Trials. It only makes sense that a descendent of Ms. Putnam might be curious about such things."

Thena nodded. "That's interesting, I wonder if you have any other books from Prudence's library here."

"Well I can certainly check. It might take me a couple days to locate the donation log from her estate. If you'd like you can leave your name and number and I can give you a call."

Thena agreed jotting down her name and number on a small pad of paper the elderly woman provided her with. Thanking her again, she went in search of Mason who she found browsing through a collection of books on architecture. Selecting an old volume pertaining to Boston, Mason placed the remaining books back on the shelf.

"Hey, how did you make out?" He asked, returning his attention to Thena.

Thena repeated what the shopkeeper told her ending with her own interpretation of the information she was provided with.

"I'm telling you, I think there's more going on here than just a couple of free-spirited hippies. I think they're involved in something much more serious and I'm fairly certain Adara's Aunt is involved as well."

Although he appeared to briefly consider it, Mason shrugged. "I wouldn't take any of it too serious. It's all a bunch of nonsense. Leave it to those two to think they can conjure up some sort of 17th century spell and become modern day witches."

Mason returned his attention to the shelves, tilting his head sideways to read the titles of a series of map books, selecting one depicting cities and towns of early New England.

"You don't think there's anything dangerous about what they might be doing?"

"Hmmm? No...my guess is they're simply trying to relive their family's past for lack of anything better to do. Don't tell me you actually believe in that stuff?"

If Mason had looked up from the pages he was flipping through he might have seen the brief hesitation as Thena considered the question.

"No...of course not, but if they do Lord only knows what they might be involved with."

"You could always ask them." Mason suggested, collecting the volumes he intended to purchase and heading in the direction of the front desk.

"I don't think that's a good idea. If they wanted me to know, don't you think they would have told me already? The way they hid the book from me and then came back to buy it when I was out of town speaks volumes."

"I guess. Anyway...I wouldn't worry about. Like I said, it's all a bunch of hogwash, even if they do believe in that stuff it's not like it's real."

"I suppose you're right, but it still gives me the creeps."

Ending their conversation as they reached the front desk, Thena stood by deep in thought as Mason chatted with the lavender-haired woman about his love of early American architecture. When they finally left the shop it was nearly noon and Mason suggested they get a bit to eat at one of the waterfront restaurants where they could sit outside and enjoy the ocean breeze.

Although she smiled and laughed as Mason pointed out people on the beach with inappropriate swimwear as they ate their lunch, her mind was reeling with images of Autumn and Adara donning black-hooded robes while praising Satan. When Mason asked her a question and she responded with a fake smile, he realized she wasn't listening to a word he had said.

"Thena? You aren't still thinking about Autumn and Adara and all this witch stuff are you?"

"I'm sorry. I just can't stop worrying that they might be involved in something more sinister than love potions and spiritual guidance."

"I seriously doubt it. Look...they probably didn't tell you because they were afraid you'd laugh at them. Honestly, neither one of them is bright enough to do any harm."

"You're probably right...I'm being silly. I'm sure they just do it for fun." Less convinced than she sounded, Thena brushed the matter aside and concentrated on her lunch, enjoying Mason's narration of what he believed a fat man in a Speedo was saying to an attractive woman lying on the beach. His routine was so comical he had her wiping tears from her eyes and holding her stomach from laughter.

By the time they made it back to the beach the crowd had thinned significantly and Mason suggested they go for a late afternoon swim. Thena returned to her cottage to change into a swimsuit while Mason walked his dog and tied him to the porch next to a bowl of cool water to enjoy the fresh salty air. Lying in the shade under the porch swing, Shane sighed before resting his head on his front paws and dozing off to sleep. After quickly changing into board shorts, Mason made his way next door just as Thena emerged from the cottage. Mason whistled his approval of her choice of swimwear and Thena accepted the compliment with a twirl and a curtsy. Making their way into the water, Thena was uncomfortably aware of several eyes on her and she quickened her pace to sink beneath the surface of the water. Mason laughed, chasing after her and pulling her up and onto his back where she wrapped her arms around his neck and rode the waves with him. What were earlier calm waters were now intense waves and they quickly tired, making their way back to shore. As they made their way up the beach toward the towels Thena had left on her porch, they both turned as the familiar voice called out their names.

"Thena! Mason!" Autumn called, running to meet up with them as they wrapped themselves in towels.

"Hey, what's up?" Thena asked, looking beyond her for Adara, who was never far behind.

"There's going to be another bonfire on the beach tonight. The trucks came by earlier and dumped off a bunch of debris from the storm, downed branches, and wooden shingles...that sort of stuff. Bryce wanted me to let you guys know and invite you to join us for a pre-fire cookout. Just burgers and hot dogs, nothing fancy."

"What do you say?" Mason asked, deferring to Thena.

"Sounds good. What time? I can make a pasta salad if you'd like."

"Great, seven o'clock. Oh and Adara's making margaritas so you don't need to bring anything to drink." Skipping off, Autumn didn't wait for a response.

"Okay then, I guess I should take a quick shower and get to cooking." Thena said, wrapping the towel around her waist.

"I have a better idea...why don't we take a shower together, you know...to save time, and then I'll help you make that salad." Mason winked.

"Gee that's so thoughtful of you." Thena teased, leading the way.

Chapter Twelve

Eliza opened the silver locket hanging from a chain around her neck that housed a hidden timepiece. Squeezing the sides back together between her thumb and index finger, she sighed heavily. Adara was more than an hour late. Once again, her niece was proving herself unworthy of the title about to be bestowed upon her. Not since Mercy, who made history accusing George Burroughs of witchcraft had there been a Lewis descendent more aligned with the five elements. Born on the eve of a full moon, bearing a birthmark that could only be interpreted as the sign of a pentacle, Adara had spent her entire childhood and adolescence preparing for the year of her initiation. Now twenty-five, it was finally time for her to step into the role the Goddess herself had chosen for her.

The ringing of the door chimes announced entry into the shop and Eliza peered through the beaded curtains to confirm Adara's arrival. Preparing herself for the confrontation, she moved to the table, dropping into her usual chair. Eliza took a deep cleansing breath, praying to the Goddess to give her patience as Adara sauntered into the room as if she didn't have a care in the world.

"Hi. Auntie...sorry I'm late." Giving her Aunt a quick peck on the cheek, she took the seat opposite her.

While Eliza prepared herself for another lecture, Adara chomped on bubble gum, blowing bubbles and sucking them back into her mouth.

"I don't think you're ready. Adara. Perhaps I was mistaken about your role in our circle."

"I'm sorry…please. Auntie…I've been waiting so long." Adara pleaded, sitting up straight and reaching her arms across the table to place her hands on top of her aunt's.

Eliza sighed, "When you were born your mother asked me to take you under my wing. She always believed you were destined for great things and she knew I was capable of helping you get there. Perhaps I should have insisted you forgo the usual rituals of a teenager and had you concentrate more on the circle."

"I don't want to disappoint you, Auntie, I'm just nervous. Having fun with my friends is just a way to blow off steam. I promise I won't let you down. Just tell me what to do."

Eliza stared into her niece's eyes, finding only truth in her words.

"Very well. I've prepared the possession spell for you as well as a mixture of herbs that should make her more susceptible to opening up her mind. She must be completely relaxed for it to work. It's up to you to find a way to get her away from the others long enough to perform the spell."

Placing a small packet of herbs in Adara's hands along with the handwritten spell, Eliza rose from her chair, signifying the end of the meeting. Promising her aunt she wouldn't let her down, Adara left the shop, clutching the tools of her trade in the palm of her hand. Pedaling her bike off the main road to a more secluded spot, Adara laid her bike down behind a cluster of bushes and made her way into a small wooded area she frequented whenever she wanted to be alone.

Taking the handwritten note out of the pouch slung over her shoulder and across her midriff, she read the spell.

"Transport my essence into this vessel
let her succumb to my commands,
permit her mind and body to become free
make her only listen to my demands."

Shoving the paper back into the pouch before sitting down on the rotting remains of a fallen tree, Adara rested her face into the palm of her hands. Wishing she had as much confidence in herself as she had led her Aunt to believe, she prayed to the Goddess for strength. Lifting her skirt to reveal the birthmark etched into her upper thigh, she traced the outline of the pentacle with her finger. Again reminded of the many times she had doubted her significance amongst the circle of her coven, she looked upon the symbol in an attempt to see it for anything other than it appeared to be. Like so many other times before, she was unable to see beyond what she had been led to believe her whole life.

Rising from the damp wood and brushing herself off, she walked the path hoping to think of some way to get Thena alone. Obviously she would need to enlist Autumn in order to complete her mission, though in what capacity she wasn't sure. By the time she made it back to her bike, she was no clearer on the plan than she had been an hour before. It wasn't until she pedaled into the driveway of the cottage she shared with Victor that an idea popped into her head.

With the stage set and the plan in motion, Adara smiled, pleased with the fact she had thought it up on her own without the help of her Aunt or Autumn to lean on. Leaving Autumn in the dark would make her suggestion seem even more spontaneous and she didn't need to worry about her missing any cues.

Armed with a tray of margaritas for the ladies, she made her way out of the cottage to join the others who were gathered around the grill. Placing the tray on the bottom step of the porch, she grabbed two of the glasses, handing one to Autumn and the other to Thena before returning for her own. Having earlier infused the packet of herbs with a lime, Adara had placed slices of the tainted fruit into a glass, making sure it was different from the other two so as not to mix it up with hers or Autumns. Confident that each time she refreshed her drink, the limes would continue to release small doses of the mixture until she gradually became intoxicated.

Keeping a continued watch on her prey, Adara mingled with the others as they ate and drank. From their vantage point, they could clearly see the crowd gathering for the bonfire. Offering to braid Thena's hair, Adara ran inside to collect a brush and elastics, returning with the pitcher to refill each of their glasses. While the men disappeared into the cottage to get high, the women stayed outside. Autumn sat cross-legged across from Thena, who sat in similar fashion, while Adara knelt behind her slowing brushing her hair in a relaxing, unhurried rhythm.

"I bought the cutest bathing suit today." Autumn announced. "It's a one-piece with a high cut and circles cut out of the sides. I can't wait to wear it."

"What color is it?" Thena asked in a drowsy voice.

"It's red and it ties around the neck. I bought it for practically nothing because the seam needed to be repaired." She giggled, winking.

"Let me guess." Adara spoke up, "You took it into the dressing room and gave the seam a little tug?"

"Anyway…when I showed it to the clerk she offered to take twenty-five percent off the already marked down forty percent sale. I couldn't pass on the deal. Now I just have to go to the fabric store to pick up some thread to repair it."

Slowly blending Thena's hair into a fishtail braid, Adara noticed she seemed to be feeling the effects of the herbs as she unconsciously began to sway. Rising from the blanket and pulling a wobbly Thena with her, Adara suggested they make their way over to the bonfire, leaving the men behind. Too groggy to protest, Thena allowed Adara to lead her while Autumn skipped along beside them. Pushing her way through the crowd of noisy spectators circling the fire, Adara stopped when she reached the front of the assembly, dropping down and bringing Thena with her to sit on a large rock several feet from the fire. Adara looked around her in search of Autumn who seemed to have been swallowed up by the crowd.

While Thena starred into the fire, clearly mesmerized by the flames and the hundreds of voices around her, Adara began to softly whisper the words of the spell.

"Transport my essence into this vessel
let her succumb to my commands,
permit her mind and body to become free
make her only listen to my demands."

Repeating the verse over and over, she continued to scan the crowd while also keeping a watchful eye on

Thena. Not until she saw Mason approach did she stop, hoping enough time had passed for the spell to take effect.

"There you are. Why didn't you wait for the rest of us?" Mason asked, kneeling down next to Thena.

Oblivious to his presence, Thena continued to stare into the fire.

Adara laughed nervously."I think someone's had a little too much to drink." She lied, nodding toward Thena.

"I guess so." Mason agreed, pulling Thena up from the rock. "I think it's time to get you home, what do you say?"

Rather than respond to Mason, Thena looked to Adara for direction.

"I think that's a good idea. You get some rest Sweetie. I'll stop by tomorrow and return your bowl."

Thena nodded, unable to speak in her current condition. Stepping out of the crowd, Adara watched as Mason led Thena back down the beach in the direction of her cottage. Pleased that she had completed her task without the assistance of others, Adara headed back to Victor and Bryce who were sipping beer on the porch.

"Where are the others?" Victor asked, looking past her.

"Mason took Thena home, she was a little wasted. I think Autumn's still at the bonfire, I lost her in the crowd."

"I guess I better go find her before she hurts herself." Bryce laughed, stepping off the porch and handing his bottle to Adara.

While Victor took the remaining food back into the cottage, Adara collected the tray of glasses, careful to toss the tainted limes into the grill before heading inside herself.

Mason helped Thena out of her clothes and into a nightshirt before tucking her into bed. Certain she would be in no condition for company when she woke the next morning, he left her alone, locking the door on his way out. Unable to remain focused, Thena quickly feel into a deep sleep.

The following morning she awoke to a splitting headache and waves of nausea so powerful they brought her to her knees. Resting her head on the cold porcelain of the toilet, she took deep breaths in an attempt to calm her stomach. Ultimately, she lost the battle and vomited up the bile remaining in her stomach. Groaning, she flushed the toilet and pulled herself up off the floor to splash cold water on her face. Uncertain how much she'd actually drank the previous night, Thena struggled to recall the events leading up to her current condition. Looking at her pasty face in the mirror she noticed for the first time that her hair was braided in a manner she was unfamiliar with and immediately knew she must have blacked out at some point. Not only did she not remember someone braiding her hair, but she had no recollection of when she returned home or changing into her pajamas. Certain Mason had something to do with seeing her safely home, she returned to her bed hopeful a couple more hours of sleep would improve her condition.

Unfortunately, her head was pounding so badly she was unable to fall back to sleep and she slowly rose, making her way to the kitchen where she popped a couple pieces of bread into the toaster and poured herself a glass of juice. Reaching into her bag to retrieve a bottle of aspirin, she nearly jumped out of her skin when Adara knocked on the door.

"Morning, sleepy head." She cheerfully called through the door.

Thena opened the door, squinting to keep the sunlight from blinding her.

"What are you doing up and about so early?" Thena asked, popping a couple pills into her mouth and washing them down with a big gulp of orange juice.

"Well most of us don't sleep until noon. I knew you had a lot to drink last night, but I figured you'd be up by now."

"Noon?" Thena glanced at the clock on the stove, confirming that it was in fact a few minutes past noon. "How much did I drink last night anyway?"

"I wasn't keeping track, but you went down pretty hard. What's the last thing you remember?" Adara questioned her casually.

"I don't know…I remember going over to your place and I remember eating…I guess that's it."

"Wow, you might want to take it easy. You don't remember me braiding your hair or going over to the bonfire?"

Thena shook her head. "Not at all. Damn, girl, what was in those margaritas anyway?"

Adara laughed. "Just the usual. Autumn and I are fine, I guess you're just a lightweight."

"Well I guess I'll have to keep that in mind." Making her way over to the toaster, she pulled the hot slices out and placed them on a plate. "What brings you here anyway?"

Adara held up her bowl. "I told you last night I would bring back your bowl. I guess you don't remember."

"I guess not…thanks." Thena sat down and rubbed her forehead.

"Okay well I'm off to the grocery store. Can I pick you up anything?"

"No thanks." Thena muttered before biting off a small piece of dry toast and struggling to get it down.

"Okay Sweetie. You take care. You might want to stay in tonight." Adara suggested.

"Yes, Mom." Thena responded sarcastically.

Hopping on her bicycle, Adara made her way into town, anxious to share the success of her spell with her aunt. When she arrived, however, her mousy clerk Micha informed her that Eliza was in the middle of a reading with a handful of elderly women and had instructed her that she was not to be disturbed. Disappointed, Adara decided to head over to the coffee shop.

As usual the shop was nearly filled to capacity with tourists taking a break from shopping to local students drinking iced coffee while accessing the shops WiFi connection. Nodding hello to several regulars she recognized, Adara made her way to the counter to order herself a cup of coffee and a muffin. An hour later, she left the shop and returned to Mystical Treasures.

With her reading completed and her afternoon free, Eliza invited her niece into the back room, eager to learn the results of her assignment. As Adara excitedly detailed her success and the flawless way everything had fallen into place, Eliza nodded her pleasure while maintaining a stoic façade. With her recap complete, Adara sat nervously as her Aunt quietly digested the information. Disappointed that her Aunt wasn't beaming with pride and smothering her with compliments, Adara dropped her eyes to her hands, which she nervously folded and refolded in her lap.

"Well, I have to admit I'm a bit surprised. I had expected you to fail in your mission."

Adara looked up, hopeful she was about to receive the praise she so desperately wanted.

"We mustn't get too cocky though. Just because you managed to administer the herbs and make her susceptible to the spell, doesn't mean it actually worked. We will need to test her allegiance in order to be certain."

"What did you have in mind?"

"I think you should invite her to join you and Autumn for a reading. You mentioned she wasn't into that sort of thing so she ought to decline the offer. That is, unless she is under the spell."

Adara agreed and rose to leave.

"Adara...don't forget...we need her to be a willing participant in order to complete the circle. If she has any reservations at all, it could destroy everything we've worked for and there won't be enough time to find a replacement before the next full moon."

"I understand...I won't let you down." Adara promised.

Chapter Thirteen

While the residents of Wells Beach continued to enjoy a carefree summer, Adara cautiously avoided pressuring Thena, allowing time to pass before testing the waters.

When Mason announced he had to return to Boston to finalize a deal and would be gone for a couple of days, Adara used the opportunity to suggest the reading.

The six of them were enjoying a relaxing evening on the beach while Victor strummed on his guitar when Mason made the announcement.

"I'm going to be gone a couple of days and I'm expecting the meetings to go well into the night. I was hoping you all could look after Shane for me while I'm gone. I hate to leave him cooped up in my apartment by himself for so long."

Thena spoke up first. "I would love for him to stay with me."

"Are you sure?" Mason asked.

"Yes, he's like family, he probably won't even realize you're gone." Thena winked.

"Gee thanks."

As the men wandered inside to get more beer, Adara spoke up.

"Since Mason will be gone, I was thinking us girls could do something together."

"What did you have in mind?" Thena asked, scratching Shane's belly.

"It's been a while since I've had my cards read, why don't the three of us go down to my Aunt's shop for a reading and then maybe some shopping. We can make a day of it...lunch, the works."

Autumn perked up immediately. "I'm in."

Thena on the other hand seemed less thrilled at the suggestion.

"What do you say, Thena?"

"Yeah, I guess...I mean, I'm not really into that kind of stuff, but I guess there's no harm in it."

Although it wasn't quite the response she was hoping for, she had agreed and Adara was certain that her acceptance was proof of her submission. Satisfied, she relaxed a bit, giving her mind a rest from the constant "what ifs". Thena, on the other hand, contemplated whether or not she should actually go through with the plan, wondering if it might be possible to bow out at the last minute.

By the time they called it a night and headed back toward their own cottages, Mason was convinced Thena's mind was elsewhere.

"You seem a little distracted tonight. Anything you'd like to talk about?"

Thena shrugged not sure how to put her worries into words.

"Sometimes it helps just to talk things out. Did I say something to upset you?" Mason asked scanning his memory for any inappropriate comments he might have made over the course of the evening.

"No, nothing like that. Adara invited me to join her and Autumn for a reading."

"As in cards?" Mason asked.

"Yeah…I guess there's no harm in it. It's not like any of that stuff is real. I don't know…it just makes me a little uncomfortable."

"So just say no." Mason suggested.

"I kind of already accepted the invitation. I just wonder if there's any way for me to get out of it at the last minute. I don't want to hurt their feelings, but it just gives me the creeps. The whole thing with her Aunt peering through the door at me the first time I went to the shop still has me a little nervous."

"I think you should go with your instincts. If you're afraid of hurting their feelings just go. Like you said, it's not like it's real even if they think it is. Just think of it like playing with a Ouija Board. We all did that when we were kids even though we knew it wasn't real. Have fun with it. If you start to feel uncomfortable, just tell them you changed your mind."

"I guess you're right. What's the worst that could happen?"

A haunting look passed over his eyes, too quickly for Thena to detect it. Although he was confident she was too strong-willed to be victimized by anyone, especially a couple of locals, he wasn't as certain they weren't above using her.

The following morning Mason dropped off Shane before heading back to Boston instructing Thena not to spoil the dog.

"I'll make no such promise." Thena replied, shaking her head and smothering the dog with kisses.

Rolling his eyes, Mason gave Thena one last kiss before telling her to try to behave herself while he was gone.

"Again, I make no promises." Thena teased, returning the kiss and walking him out to his car with Shane in her arms.

Watching as he backed out of the driveway and disappeared around the bend with a honk of his horn, Thena sighed, realizing once again how close she was growing to her neighbor. It was moments like this that made the thought of summer's end simply too painful to think about. On the other hand, it wasn't like they hadn't discussed how they might be able to alternate weekends and holidays at each other's homes, something that certainly sounded plausible on the surface but Thena knew could only last so long before they would have to make a decision.

Putting such thoughts behind her, Thena carried Shane back into her cottage where she poured water into one bowl and emptied a scoop of dog food into the other. She had more than four hours before Adara and Autumn were scheduled to pick her up so she showered, dressed and cleaned the cottage, hoping to distract her mind of the anxiety building inside her. After thoroughly cleaning the bathroom, she moved into the main room of the cottage where she stripped her bed and changed the sheets before folding it back into the couch. While Shane watched from his bed with interest, she dusted the sparse furniture and swept the floors before mopping. By the time she reached the kitchen he was softly snoring, content in his new surroundings. Rather than disturb him with clanking dishes, Thena poured herself a cup of coffee and brought it out on the porch.

As she sipped her coffee she watched in amusement as a young mother chased a toddler on the beach. Allowing the little girl enough room to think she couldn't be caught, the mother would stop and pretend to catch her breath each time the toddler would stumble to allow her time to get back up again. The girl shrieked with laughter as the mother continually chanted, "I'm gonna get you". Eventually exhausted, the toddler stopped and ran into her mother's arms and was rewarded with a big hug and kiss.

A sudden gust of wind swept across the sand, blowing over a couple of beach umbrellas and sending their owners racing after them. Looking up to the sky, Thena noticed that the previously calm sky with puffy white clouds had changed and seemed to indicate a storm on the horizon. As the clouds moved quickly by, the waves intensified and she could now hear the lifeguard's whistles as he motioned for swimmers to head for shore.

Heading inside, Thena went about the cottage closing windows in preparation of the impending storm. Deciding she had better take Shane out to relieve himself before it started to rain, she strapped on the leash just as Adara knocked on the screen door.

"Good Morning."

"Good Morning. I'm all ready; I just want to take Shane out before we leave. Come on in."

Stepping aside to allow the two women to enter, she told them to make themselves at home and pulled a reluctant Shane down onto the sand. More interested in sniffing a dead fish than relieving himself, Thena urged him back inside, hoping he would be able to control himself until she returned.

When she returned to the cottage the two women were discussing where they might go for lunch, considering the weather might not be agreeable to outdoor seating. Suggesting a quaint little Irish pub and restaurant in town, Thena proposed they follow lunch with a stroll through some of the town's lesser known antique shops. With the women in agreement they headed out with Autumn at the wheel.

As they pulled into the parking lot of the plaza that held Mystical Treasures, Thena's earlier anxiety returned. Although she put on a pleasant front, she was aware both Autumn and Adara sensed her apprehension.

"You're not nervous, are you?" Adara teased.

"No…well, a little I guess. I've never done anything like this before." Thena admitted.

"Oh, it will be fun…I promise. My aunt has been doing this for years. She will only tell you what you want to hear. If you only want to know about certain aspects of your life she will direct the reading toward that."

Comforted by Adara's promise, Thena took a deep breath. "Okay…I can do this."

Holding her by the hand, Adara led the way into the shop where the same clerk Thena recognized from her previous visit greeted them.

"Eliza's ready for you, go on in." Micha motioned, avoiding eye contact with Thena.

Without acknowledging the clerk, Adara stepped inside the beaded doorway, pulling Thena behind her. Bringing up the rear, Autumn stepped inside, immediately planting herself on the sofa. After a brief introduction, Adara volunteered to go first and Thena gratefully joined Autumn to watch from a distance.

"Is there anything in particular you want me to concentrate on?" Eliza asked as she shuffled the tarot cards in her hands.

"I would love to know whether or not Victor will ever pop the question." Adara asked, turning to wink at the women who smiled in response.

"Very well." Eliza responded, giving the cards to Adara for one more shuffle before asking her to cut the cards. Five cards were then laid out in a horseshoe spread and Adara was asked to select a card.

Although the reading was nonspecific as to the person Adara would marry, her aunt advised her that she did see marriage in her near future. Noting change brought on by an outside force causing the stars to align in her favor, Eliza advised her that good things were coming her way if she continued on her destined path.

Pleased with her reading, Adara rose from the chair opposite her Aunt. "Who wants to go next?" She asked, looking from Autumn to Thena.

Anxious to get it over with, Thena volunteered. Once again, Eliza asked whether she wanted an open reading or a question reading. Without wanting to disclose too much information to her friends concerning her relationship with Mason, she asked whether she would remain in Vermont or whether she would move. After shuffling the cards and splitting the deck, Thena waited for Eliza to instruct her on what to do next.

"Go ahead and select a card." Eliza instructed.

Thena hesitated only briefly before selecting a card and Eliza turned it over to reveal the "Ten of Swords". A knowing look passed over Eliza's face, too brief for Thena to interpret before it disappeared. After a moment's pause Eliza advised her that her future was unclear and that circumstances not yet in place would determine the outcome. Too vague to either rattle or excite her, Thena left the chair relieved and yet somehow disappointed by the reading. Autumn chose an open reading and was rewarded by several positive responses to her cards regarding marriage, children and career.

By the time they left the shop it was nearly noon and the women were anxious to eat and discuss their own interpretations of the cards. Ordering several appetizers to share and a pitcher of beer, Adara opened the conversation.

"Well I for one am excited that I may actually see a ring on this finger in the near future. Perhaps I can encourage him by a romantic candlelit dinner on the beach."

"I believe your aunt mentioned an outside force, not your personal orchestration to manipulate him into proposing." Autumn reprimanded.

"Whatever...all I know is if I wait for him to get around to it on his own, I might be thirty before it happens."

"God forbid." Thena mocked, "At that age you might need a wheelchair to get you down the aisle."

Autumn giggled and was rewarded with a firm smack to the arm by Adara. While they ate their lunch, the women discussed the latest fashion trends and whether or not Autumn should cut her hair. Lifting her thick auburn locks off her shoulders, she tucked it inside the back of her shirt to show the others what it might look like.

"I don't know," Adara admitted, sitting back to examine her friend at a distance, "your hair is kind of curly. If you cut it short it might spring up like clown hair. Oh course, if that's the look you're going for, then by all means."

"I hate you." Autumn spat, pulling her hair out of her shirt.

"You could take off four or five inches and have your stylist put in some layers." Thena suggested.

Autumn nodded, smacking Adara in the arm. "See now that's helpful."

Adara flinched from the sting of the hit and rubbed her arm. "Whatever...do what makes you happy. I for one don't plan on cutting my hair. I like it long, that way I have tons of options for styling it."

Directing the conversation to a less hostile subject matter, Thena questioned the women on what they liked to look for when they went antiquing. While Adara admitted she preferred to concentrate on vintage jewelry and clothing that she could work into her modern wardrobe, Autumn detailed her love of the Victorian era. Describing her extensive collection of dinnerware in various floral patterns, she shared her desire to collect as many pieces as she could possibly find before moving on to silverware.

Somewhat surprised by her enthusiasm for her collection, Thena considered whether or not she may have misjudged at least Autumn. While Adara's interest seemed more superficial, having more to do with her self-image than the pieces themselves, Autumn seemed to have a real passion for the Victorian era and the beauty of the pieces.

"What about you?" Autumn asked.

"Oh I love anything to do with horses. I mainly collect figurines, but I've also bought paintings and books. That reminds me...I meant to ask you...is Prudence Putnam any relation to you?"

Autumn seemed to be caught off guard, stumbling with her words.

"I...um...Prudence you said? I'm not sure. Why do you ask?"

"The other day when we went to the bookshop I picked up a couple of books that had a stamp on the inside that said they were from the library of Prudence Putnam. I thought someone had mentioned that your last name was

Putnam so I was wondering if she might be an ancestor of yours."

"Oh…" Autumn let out a breath that could only be interpreted as relief; "She might be, I'm not sure. It's a fairly common name around here, but I suppose we're all related in some way."

Adara cleared her throat. "Well what do you guys say…shall we hit the road?"

Adara's sudden desire to get going couldn't have been a more obvious attempt to change the subject and Thena made a mental note to readdress the subject at a later time. It was obvious that Adara was the alpha dog in the friendship, leading Autumn around on a short lease. Seemingly oblivious to the control Adara had over her, Autumn shrugged.

"Whatever you guys want to do is fine by me. Do you have any places in mind?"

While they waited for the waitress to return with their check, the women took turns suggesting locations where they might find items for each of their collections. Heading up Route 1 in the direction of Kennebunkport, the trio avoided the more popular shops for their lesser-known counterparts. Pulling off the main road onto a long dirt driveway, which led to an old barn, long ago converted to an antique shop, the women peered out the windows with excitement at the abundance of goods spilling out of the old barn. Rusty plow heads, a turn of the century wooden washing machine and an antique rot iron bed frame were amongst several other large items scattered near the barn doors.

Seated just outside the barn on a weathered wooden spindle chair, was an elderly man donning a straw hat and a dirty pair of bib overalls. As they got out of the car, he nodded hello before wiping his sweaty brow with a handkerchief.

"You ladies let me know if you need help with anything." He muttered, giving them a glimpse of his rotting teeth.

When they were well inside the barn and out of earshot Adara turned to the other women.

"Ew...did you see his teeth?" She shivered, in disgust.

"Adara, that's not nice. He probably can't afford to go to the dentist." Autumn scolded her friend.

Adara shrugged it off, unwilling to be shamed by her friend. Ignoring the comment, Thena distanced herself from the other two, feigning interest in a collection of old postcards. Splitting off, the women went in search of their various items of interest, meeting up occasionally to show off their finds. Nearly an hour later, they gathered at the front of the barn, advising the old man they were done shopping and ready to check out. Grabbing an old cane leaning against the barn, he slowly raised from his chair in obvious discomfort, making his way on shaky legs to the makeshift counter where he wrapped their items in old newspaper before depositing them into burlap sacks.

"You have quite the inventory here, how long have you been collecting?" Thena asked, curious as to how someone like him managed to get into the business of selling antiques.

"Why, thank you, dear. Let me see...well I guess it's been about thirty years now. In my younger days I went to a lot of flea markets and yard sales and I had a pretty good collection of my own, but then when the family started dying off and I inherited a couple of farms I decided to turn the old barn into an antique shop rather than make a quick buck at an estate sale. It pays the bills and gives me something to do."

Thena smiled warmly. "That's wonderful. Have you ever thought of advertising? There's no sign at the end of the driveway. If you aren't from around here, people probably wouldn't even know you were here."

"No...it's just the way I like it. I get a pretty steady flow of folks by word of mouth. Just enough to keep the heat and lights on, as they say."

Thena had to admire the old man who seemed to be doing what he loved without trying to get rich in the process. His prices were reasonable, if not under what other shops in the area were charging and he seemed to be working the place on his own. Anxious to move on, Adara nudged Thena in the back. Thanking him, Thena followed the women back to the car.

"I thought you'd never stop talking to him. How could you stand there without staring at his teeth?" Shivering again to emphasize her point, Adara shifted in her seat to look at Thena.

"Oh my God, Adara, get over it." Autumn snapped.

"If you look beyond people's physical appearances, you might find you'd be surprised at what they have to offer." Thena commented, leaving Adara defeated and annoyed.

Returning her focus to the front seat, Adara instructed Autumn to head north where there was a tiny shop called The Victorian Attic. True to its name, the shop was in the attic of an old Victorian home that was accessible by way of an outside staircase with a separate entrance. Catering to just the sort of things both Adara and Autumn collected, the shop was a step back in time. The shopkeeper was dressed in period clothing and spoke as if she just stepped out of an

Emily Brontë novel. Fascinated by the unexpected performance, Thena engaged the woman in conversation while
her friends browsed the shelves and display cases.

Adara shrieked with delight when she stumbled upon
a small basket filled with hairpins, brooches and period but-
tons. Gathering several items, she placed them on the glass
counter, advising the shopkeeper that she was making a pile
for herself. Moving across the room, she browsed through
an old armoire stocked with period clothing.

Autumn quietly examined the shops collection of tea-
cups and saucers as well as a beautifully engraved silver
platter. Placing a set of four cups and saucers on the tray
she brought it to the counter to purchase. While Thena absently looked around, not really interested in anything but
curious all the same; she listened to the shopkeeper recommend another shop that was likely to have additional
pieces from the set.

It was nearly five o'clock when the women returned to
the beach, Autumn's trunk loaded with the spoils of their
shopping excursion. Although Adara invited her to join
them for burgers on the grill, Thena declined, exhausted
from the day and looking forward to a quiet night with
Shane. After taking the anxious dog for a walk on the
beach and refreshing his bowls, she tossed a salad and
brought it out on the porch to eat while she watched the
calming waves and the sun slowly set with Shane at her
feet. She was contemplating what to do next when she
heard her cell phone ring. Collecting her dirty dishes, she
made her way inside just in time to catch the last ring.

"Hello?"

"Thena…its Celeste."

"Oh hi, this is a surprise. What's up?" Thena asked,
suddenly nervous something may have happened to Mason.

"I know Mason is here in Boston so I thought I'd give you a call to make sure you're okay."

"Careful, Celeste, you're becoming more and more like my mother every day. Of course I'm okay, why wouldn't I be?"

In all the years Thena had been renting from the Parrish's she had never heard from Celeste as many times as she had this season and she wondered whether or not her mother had put her up to it knowing if she called herself it would only annoy Thena.

"It's just that Mason mentioned to Clay that you were having your cards read today by Eliza Lewis." Celeste paused, clearly at a loss for words.

"I'm surprised he even mentioned it. I was kind of nervous about going, but he convinced me it might be fun."

"Was it? Fun, that is."

"I don't know if fun is the right word, but it was harmless. You know how those things go…they give you vague answers that could apply to anyone and can be interpreted a hundred different ways depending on how gullible you are. She seems a little eccentric, but that's not surprising. Her niece is a little odd herself. Do you know the family?"

Celeste hesitated briefly. "Let me just say it might be wise to keep your distance. I had no idea when you mentioned you had become friends with a couple of locals that you were referring to Lewis."

"Is that a bad thing?" Thena pressed, wondering what she might have gotten herself into.

"I really can't say for certain, but the family has a reputation around Wells for being involved in some things that might be considered dark. There's a reason they have kept the family name despite several marriages and few sons to carry on the name. They like people to know exactly who they are."

"And who exactly are they?" Thena asked in a near whisper. Suddenly nervous she made her way to the cottage door, looking up and down the beach to assure herself she was alone before shutting and locking the door.

"There have been rumors going back centuries that the Lewis family dabbled in black magic. Of course, as far as I know it's all speculation and there was never any real proof or witnesses to their so-called practices. Still, it might be wise to keep your distance or at the very least be aware."

Thena laughed, partly because the thought of modern day witches seemed so ridiculous and partly because she was afraid to admit it might be exactly the reason she felt so nervous around Eliza.

"Well, I don't know that I believe in any of that stuff, but as far as Adara and Autumn are concerned; the two of them are harmless. Other than being a little too free with their bodies and smoking a little too much weed, they don't seem the type."

Describing the ritual that took place at the fundraiser, Thena acknowledged that the two women did seem to be a part of some sort of Community Theater, but as far as it being dark or sinister in nature; she disagreed.

"Well you're a smart girl and I trust your judgment. Just promise me you'll be careful and avoid any situations that might seem even a little bit odd."

Assuring Celeste she would keep an eye out, she stopped short of making a joke of it all and upsetting her friend and landlord. After all, she knew she was only looking out for her and she did appreciate that.

Chapter Fourteen

Mason returned from Boston exhausted, but also anxious to share his success with the one person that was constantly on his mind while he was away. Armed with a bouquet of assorted wild flowers he had purchased at a farm stand on the drive in and a bottle of champagne given to him by Clay after they had finalized the deal; Mason made a beeline for Thena's cottage, taking the steps two at a time.

With music softly playing on the radio, neither Thena nor Shane had heard his car pull into the driveway and they both jumped when he knocked at the screen door. Jumping off the sofa where he had been curled up next to Thena, who was reading a book; Shane ran toward the door barking.

"Hey, boy...did you miss me?" Mason called, turning the knob and opening the door just as Thena approached.

"Hey, welcome home, I didn't expect you back so early."

Swooping her into his arms, Mason gave her a warm passionate kiss before letting her go and handing her the flowers.

"They're beautiful, thank you. So tell me...does this mean the trip was a success?" She asked, pointing to the champagne bottle.

Squatting down to pick up Shane, who was eagerly jumping up and down to get his master's attention, Mason smiled broadly.

"Not only was it a success, but the deal's been signed and I am now free the remainder of the summer. No more trips back to Boston."

"That's wonderful. Clay must be thrilled." Making her way over to the sink, she filled a glass pitcher with water and placed the arrangement of flowers inside.

"He was more than thrilled. This puts us more than a month ahead of schedule. We had anticipated the investors would drag their feet at least a couple more weeks, but apparently they wanted to get moving as much as we did."

"So how would you like to celebrate?" Thena asked, certain she knew what his response would be.

To her surprise he informed her he had already made reservations at The White Barn Inn, a renowned five-star restaurant in Kennebunkport. Shocked, Thena stood speechless by the romantic gesture. Not only was the restaurant someplace she never envisioned herself dining at, but the fact that he had been able to secure a reservation and wanted to bring her there spoke volumes of the seriousness of their relationship. If she had any doubts before as to whether or not this was to be a long-term relationship, he had put them to rest with this one grand gesture.

Amused by her response, Mason watched as she went from stunned silence to a frantic search for the perfect dress to wear. Placing the champagne in the refrigerator to enjoy later, he followed her to the closet, wrapping his arms around her waist from behind and kissing her neck.

"Whatever you decide will be perfect. I'm going to go next door and take a shower and get Shane settled in. I'll come back over in about an hour."

Barely hearing his words as she thumbed through her limited summer wardrobe, Thena mumbled her agreement. Ultimately selecting her only real option, the cocktail dress she had purchased for the fundraiser; she sighed, wishing she had known ahead of time and been able to wear something he hadn't seen her in before. When he returned an hour later, freshly shaven and dressed in an amazing black suit and polished black oxford shoes, he nearly took her breath away. With his wavy dark hair slicked back and his crisp white shirt, he looked like he had just stepped out of a photo shoot for GQ. Likewise, Thena was every bit as polished in the amazing beaded cocktail dress. A single strand of pearls accentuated her long neck and her hair was pulled back into an elegant French twist. Her tanned skin was a beautiful contrast to the pale ivory dress and nude heels.

"You look amazing." Mason said, taking her by the hand and spinning her around. Offering his arm he asked, "Shall we?"

Thena smiled and nodded, speechless once again by the effect he had on her.

As they dined on pan-roasted duck breast, glazed carrots and duchess potatoes pared with a lovely pinot noir, the couple barely spoke a word. Swept away with sensory overload, both Thena and Mason quietly enjoyed the food and atmosphere while at the same time content in each other's company. Interrupted only by the occasional comment about the offerings before them and the touch of their hands across the table, the waiter had to clear his throat to gain their attention. Anxious to return to the beach, Mason asked the waiter to bring the check, allowing Thena to select a dessert to take home.

Pulling into their shared drive, Mason put the car in park and turned the key before making his way around it to help Thena out. Slightly tipsy from the wine, Thena leaned heavily on Mason as they made their way around the cottage to her front door. Putting her key in the lock, they were just about to go inside when a movement caught their attention.

Turning in its direction, both Thena and Mason stared into the distance trying to make out the figure down the beach.

Upon discovery, the woman turned and walked away until she was no longer visible to them.

"What the hell? Who was that?" Mason asked.

"I don't know…it was like she was watching us."

Not to be deterred from the romantic night he had planned, Mason brushed it off and urged Thena inside. While Thena retrieved a plate and a couple of forks for the dessert, Mason opened the champagne and poured a couple of glasses.

Outside, the mysterious woman made her way behind the darkened cottages, their occupants unaware of her presence, until she arrived in front of Thena's cottage. Slowly making her way around the perimeter, she released a trail of salt, encircling the entire cottage before once again disappearing into the night.

A heavy rainstorm during the night soaked the sand making the ring of salt invisible to the naked eye. By the time they woke it was nearly nine o'clock and Mason stumbled next door to take Shane out before he peed inside. Thena stayed in bed for a while longer, reflecting on the most romantic evening of her life.

Throwing on a short robe she had left lying on the floor next to the bed, she slowly made her way into the bathroom where she brushed her tousled hair and pulled it up into a high ponytail. Making her way to the kitchen she tossed a couple of bagels into the toaster, poured herself a glass of juice and wandered out onto the porch.

The beach was already buzzing with activity and she watched as a young mother and child collected seashells, depositing them into a plastic pail. To her left, a seagull dropped in, plucking a cookie out of a toddler's hand and causing her to burst into tears. As the mother rushed in to comfort her, handing her another treat and standing over her to protect the child from another attack, a couple of unruly boys kicked up sand as they dashed toward the water nearly knocking over the toddler and enraging the mother.

With her eyes fixed on the beach, Thena didn't see Adara as she approached the stairs and practically spilled her juice when she spoke.

"Looks like someone had a late night...I'm assuming Mason's back in town." Adara teased, plopping down in the empty rocker.

"Oh my God. Don't you know you shouldn't sneak up on people like that? You nearly gave me a heart attack." Thena scolded, placing her free hand over her heart.

Adara laughed, encouraged by Thena's obvious distraction. "I'm going to take that as a yes. Details, girl...and don't leave anything out."

Thena was about to tell her it was none of her business when Shane bonded up the steps, followed closely by Mason; sparing her from having to deny what was so obvious to everyone around them.

"Morning Adara, what trouble are you up to today?" Mason asked, certain she didn't just happen to have stopped by without some sort of ulterior motive.

Feigning innocence, it was Adara's turn to clutch her chest. "Whatever gives you the idea I'm up to trouble? Nothing could be further from the truth. I was merely stopping by to make sure you got back safely."

"Yeah I'm sure you were worried sick."

Rising from the chair while pretending her feelings were hurt, Adara headed toward the steps.

"Thena, if you're not too busy, Autumn and I are planning on going into town for lunch. You're welcome to join us." Looking at Mason she added, "You're not." Sticking out her tongue in a childish gesture, she returned her attention to Thena.

"Maybe another time...I plan on staying in today."

Winking her understanding, Adara skipped down the steps and headed down the beach toward her own cottage. Mason chuckled, taking the seat she had vacated.

"So what do you really have in mind for today?" Mason asked, assuming she was just blowing Adara off so she could spend time with him.

"Actually I was planning on heading back to Kennebunkport today. The woman from the bookstore called yesterday and left a message that she located the donation document from the Prudence Putnam estate. According to the message there are more than two dozen volumes on the list and at least half of those are still available for purchase."

"Would you like some company?" Mason offered.

"I'd love some company...who did you have in mind?"

Chapter Fifteen

With the full moon quickly approaching and a significant amount of preparation left to be done, Eliza peered out the window of her shop cursing her niece, who was more than an hour late for their rehearsal. In less than an hour, Micha would be arriving to open the shop and their window of opportunity would be lost.

As the hour of her initiation into the circle grew closer, Eliza was becoming less convinced of Adara's commitment to the craft. On the surface she appeared both willing and eager to perform the necessary sacrifice and earn her place as the fifth element in the circle, however her inconsistencies in adhering to a set schedule caused Eliza to wonder once again whether or not she was truly worthy of the position.

This wasn't the first time she had doubted her interpretation of the manual, as set forth by their ancestor's more than three hundred years in the past and she was certain it wouldn't be the last in the days leading up to the sacrifice. Years of careful planning and preparation had led her to this moment and now, when she was so close to its completion, she feared her niece might be her ultimate downfall.

Spotting the mint green bicycle approaching, Eliza unlocked the door and returned to the back room to prepare. The sound of Adara's carefree footsteps as she casually strolled toward the back room only infuriated her more.

The swoosh of the beaded curtain, alerted her to her niece's presence and she spoke without turning in her direction.

"You're late."

Adara hesitated, trying to think of an excuse.

"Don't bother trying to justify your tardiness. Punctuality is key to the sacrifice. If it isn't timed correctly, your mission will have failed and all will be lost. It won't be just me you'll have to answer to and the elders will most certainly not be as forgiving as me."

"I'm sorry...I..."

"We have work to do." Eliza interrupted. "Have you memorized the spell?"

"Yes, I've been practicing with Autumn."

"Very good and do you have a plan to ensure Thena will participate?"

"We decided to invite her and Mason to a surprise birthday party for Victor."

Eliza considered the scenario. "Victor is agreeable to the plan?"

"Actually he doesn't know. I plan on telling him we're going for a sail to celebrate the end of summer before Mason and Thena leave town."

"And if they claim to have other plans?"

"I hadn't considered that." Adara admitted, once again acknowledging she was less prepared than she thought.

"You will have to use every opportunity you can get in the next few days to complete the necessary tasks. If one attempt fails, you will need to have a backup. I don't need to remind you, the circle is depending on you."

Adara nodded, taking a deep breath and letting it out slowly.

"I invited her out to lunch today, but she declined. I think she's spending the day with Mason."

"That's fine…the more distracted the better. We don't want her to feel pressured, but at the same time, our success depends on her as much as you."

The bells on the shop door jingled, alerting them to Micha's arrival and signifying the end to their meeting. Walking her out of the back room, Eliza nodded to the clerk, who seemed intrigued by Adara's unusual presence so early in the morning. Ignoring her curious stare, Adara hugged her Aunt, wishing her a good day and disappeared out the door.

Ignoring Micha's obvious curiosity regarding her niece's increased visits to the shop, Eliza returned to the back room, where she collected any evidence of the upcoming ritual and returned the items to the safe. Giving a final look around to ascertain she hadn't forgotten anything, she picked up a box of new inventory and returned to the front of the shop.

"What's Adara up to today?" Micha asked, no longer able to contain her interest.

"She just stopped by to invite me to her boyfriend's surprise party." Eliza responded, annoyed by her prying. "I have some new items here I need you to enter into inventory. After you've entered them into the system, make a spot for them on the back shelf."

Aware that Micha was less than satisfied with her response and probably eager to get more details, Eliza turned and disappeared into the back, smiling to herself. She hadn't been gone five minutes when she heard her clerk whispering the news into her phone to whom she could only guess was someone from the old circle.

Long ago she had realized someone close to her was spreading word of activity going on inside Mystical Treasures and it was easy to arrive at the conclusion that Micha was the source. With Celeste in Boston and Annabel out of the loop, Micha was the only other disassociated member of the original circle. After the unfortunate accident leading to Ingrid's death, Eliza had attempted to salvage the fractured coven. While a few brave souls, deeply committed to the craft continued to show their allegiance, others sought to distance themselves from the coven and the atrocity of what happened that night.

After returning from Boston, Eliza had called a Sabbath in an attempt to renew the bound of the coven and to pray for Ingrid's lost soul. Fearful of retaliation for inviting Ingrid into the circle, Celeste declined to attend, accusing Eliza of putting the candidate at risk for her own selfish gain. Annabel, never having a mind of her own, attended the meeting only to announce she too was breaking ties, but would take their secrets to the grave. Bravely, or perhaps because she had no other friends, Micha had stood by Eliza and the remaining members of the coven. Although she no longer participated in the gatherings and was little more than a servant, willing to do whatever Eliza asked of her while incapable of performing her own magic, she was useful nonetheless.

Rather than get rid of the girl, as many had suggested, she decided to use her to her advantage. Leaking certain information that would work in her favor, Micha had proved to be a useful tool. As long as she didn't fear Eliza, she would continue to be an unwitting aide to the dark side.

Satisfied that she had given her enough information and time to inform her people, Eliza returned to the front to look over the schedule. With no appointments on the books, she decided to use the free time to procure the items necessary for the ritual.

"I need to step out for a couple hours, are you okay here alone?"

"Yeah, that's fine. Just in case someone comes in for a reading, do you know when you'll be back?" Micha asked nervously.

"I should be back before noon." Eliza assured her.

Micha smiled, relieved that her boss seemed unaware of her phone conversation. Had she realized she would be stepping out she simply would have waited until she was gone to make the phone call. The last thing she wanted was to become the target of her black magic.

She had been thrilled when she was entrusted to place the salt ring of protection around Thena's cottage. It was the first time she had been asked to do something so important. Although she rationalized her choosing had been more a matter of convenience than an acknowledgement of her abilities, she was nonetheless proud of her accomplishment in the task. When Thena and Mason had returned earlier than she expected and spotted her in the distance, she was fearful that she might be recognized. If she had failed in her mission the result might have been catastrophic. The fact that Eliza seemed to be proceeding undeterred could only mean Thena remained safe, protected against whatever evil she and her niece had planned.

Back at the beach, Adara rode her bicycle up Thena's driveway, anxious to invite her to the fictitious birthday party. Although Mason's car was gone, Thena's remained parked in its usual spot. Announcing her arrival, Shane barked loudly, drawing her attention to the window of Mason's cottage where she could see the terrier anxiously scratching at the window's screen. Ignoring the dog, Adara rounded the cottage and made her way up the steps to

Thena's door. Normally open to the beach with only the screen door in place, the storm door was closed indicating she was either out or didn't want to be disturbed. Disappointed, Adara didn't bother knocking, instead returning to her bicycle where she retrieved a tiny notebook and pen from the wicker basket attached to the front of the bike which she kept handy for shopping lists and notes. Jotting down a quick message inviting her and Mason to join them later for drinks, she returned to the cottage where she slipped the note under the door.

Arriving at the bookshop in Kennebunkport, Mason and Thena browsed through the shelves while the lavender-haired lady attended to several customers. When she had finally checked out the last patron, she motioned to them to approach the desk.

"I apologize for making you wait, there's a group that comes in once a month by shuttle from the elderly home and I don't like to keep them waiting."

"No problem, we're not in any rush." Thena assured her.

Reaching under the desk, the shopkeeper pulled out a stack of books bound together with twine and topped with a sticky note with Thena's name and number penned in ink.

"As you can see, I was able to locate several volumes. Feel free to look through these and see if any of them interest you. You might be interested to know that the large volume that you had previously inquired about was a part of Prudence's collection."

"Really...well that is interesting." Thena looked to Mason expecting to see the same shock on his face as she felt but was surprised by his seeming indifference to the inference the news provided. Returning her attention to the stack of books, Thena untied the bundle and sorted through the titles. Amongst the stack of a dozen books there was a vast array of subject matter. Although there were only three titles she recognized, there were half a dozen books pertaining to horticulture, a book on the history of Maine and perhaps most surprising a book of spells of Domesius. Shifting her attention back to Mason who now seemed to share her shock, they made eye contact.

"I'll take these." Thena managed to say; placing the Domesius book on top of the other three she had set aside.

"Wonderful...I'm so glad I could find them for you. If you have an interest in the occult I can recommend a couple of local shops that might appeal to you."

"Thank you but no, I don't have a personal interest, I just thought my friend might like the book."

The lavender-haired lady smiled, returning the remaining books to a cart next to the desk to put away later. While Thena fumbled through her purse in search of her wallet, Mason placed a reassuring hand on her shoulder to calm her nerves.

Once outside the shop, Thena drew a settling breath.

"You okay?" Mason asked, wrapping his arm around her waist and walking her toward the car.

"Yes...no...I don't know. It's all so strange. If it was just one book I could brush it off as mere curiosity, but two books...two is more than mild interest, don't you think?"

"I think you're reading far too much into all this. First of all, you don't even know for certain that this Prudence is even related to Autumn; second...even if she is and she was involved in some sort of black magic, it doesn't mean that Autumn is; and third, even if Autumn is into it, it's all bullshit."

"I saw the look on your face, you can't deny you were as shocked as me when you saw the title."

"Surprised maybe, but not in the same way you apparently are. Unlike you I merely find it curious that some old lady would have a book like that in her collection. Don't you think if the family were really into that kind of stuff they would have kept the book? Obviously it had no meaning to the people that donated the books."

"Yeah...I guess you're right. I don't know it just gives me the creeps."

Mason laughed. "Then why the hell did you buy the book?"

Thena looked down at the stack of books on her lap, creased her brow and then started laughing. "You have a good point there. I have no idea why I bought it, maybe to keep it out of the hands of someone that might use it for evil."

Mason reached over and squeezed her hand. "Don't worry, I'll protect you."

Changing the subject, Thena suggested they swing by Annabel's shop on their way back home so she could introduce him to her friend and invite her to join them for lunch. Anxious to meet someone who had known Thena before he met her and who might have some juicy tidbits on her previous summer flings, Mason eagerly agreed. The smirk on his face made Thena instantly regret her suggestion and she tried to back out of the plan.

"Now that I think about it, she's probably going to be too busy to join us for lunch. Maybe we should grab lunch here in Kennebunkport."

"Oh no you don't. I know exactly what you're doing." Mason waged his finger at her while keeping his eyes on the road.

"What? It's not that I don't want you to meet her, I just think now might not be a good time." Thena argued.

"Well, we'll just have to see won't we? It can't hurt to stop by and ask. That is...unless there's something you don't want her to tell me."

"She doesn't...that is...I have nothing to hide. I'm a good girl." Thena folded her arms across her chest and stiffened her back, turning her attention to the scenery passing by her window.

"Um hmm...we'll see. It seems to me you might be a little weary of what she might reveal. Perhaps you're not the angel you pretend to be."

Thena ignored his taunts, which only made her appear guilty. Mason chuckled to himself imagining all sorts of antics she was likely to have gotten herself involved in. In his experience, the more innocent they appeared, the more devious they were.

As it turned out, the shop was swamped with a tour bus full of shoppers and Annabel only had time for a brief introduction before her customers descended upon her and she was forced to walk away. Promising to call her later, Thena led the way out of the shop relieved that she had avoided any uncomfortable questioning on Mason's part.

Somewhat disappointed, Mason suggested they head over to Billy's for some take out that they could bring back to the beach. Not unlike Annabel's shop, Billy's was swarming with tourists and they had to wait in line for nearly an hour before placing their order to go. By the time they made it back to the beach, opting to eat at Mason's so he could let Shane out, it was nearly two o'clock. After a leisurely lunch, followed by an afternoon nap, Thena made her way over to her own cottage to change for a late day swim. With the stack of books in one hand and her key in the other, she opened the door, walking over the note Adara had left without noticing it. It wasn't until she had changed and was heading back out that she spotted the piece of paper and picked it up to examine it.

Tossing the note in the trash, she continued on her way next door. Mason was waiting on his porch, dressed in a pair of board shorts and struggling to keep Shane from running off.

"Here she is, boy...relax." Mason patted the dog. "I thought I was going to have to go in without you, he's anxious to get out there."

"Sorry, I stopped to read a note Adara left under my door. She invited us over for drinks later."

Mason nodded, stepping off the porch and letting go of Shane's collar. Racing ahead of his owner, Shane headed out into the surf zigzagging back in forth from the sand to the water in an attempt to catch the waves. Taking Thena by the hand, Mason strolled casually toward the water, testing its temperature first with his toes before lifting her up and carrying her into waist deep water. Shockingly cold, the water lapped at her bottom as Mason struggled to keep her above the surface.

"Oh my God...it's freezing." Thena cried out.

A sly look passed over Mason's face too quickly for Thena to react and before she knew it, Mason had tossed her into the frigid waters and swam away. Laughing as she struggled to catch her breath and chase after him, Mason dove under the surface, popping up several feet away. Quickly adjusting to the temperature, Thena sped after him, latching onto his foot and yanking him backwards. While the couple took turns besting the other, Shane playfully ran back and forth on the shore.

By the time the trio returned to the sand, nearly all the beachgoers had gone for the day and only a handful of residents remained scattered up and down the shore. In the distance, they could hear the familiar sound of Victor's guitar and Mason suggested they shower, dress and join their friends. Although she would have preferred a quiet evening alone with Mason, Thena agreed.

It didn't take long to realize their beach friends were under the influence when Autumn rose to greet them and nearly stumbled into the fire pit. Bryce reached up and grabbed her just in the nick of time, pulling her backwards and sending them both sprawling onto the sand. Adara roared with laughter as Autumn attempted to right herself without exposing her backside, which appeared to be naked beneath her flimsy cotton sundress. Conscious of the failed attempt, Autumn struggled to hide her embarrassment. Always the perfect gentleman, Mason pretended not to notice the reveal, instead commenting on Victor's musical talent.

"Thena and I could hear you playing from our end of the beach. You continue to impress me, brother."

Victor ignored Adara's childish laughter at her friend's expense and thanked Mason for the compliment.

"You two should come down to the coffee shop to hear a set." He suggested. "I can give you a copy of my schedule."

"That would be great." Mason nodded, looking to Thena who shared his enthusiasm.

While Mason and Victor discussed their favorite artists, Adara nudged Thena, motioning for her to follow her into the cottage.

Curious as to what she might be up to now, Thena nodded and rose. "Be right back." She assured Mason.

Following Adara into the cottage, Thena wasn't sure what to expect. Checking to make sure they hadn't been followed, Adara pulled her into the sitting area.

"I'm going to have a surprise birthday party for Victor on the twenty-first and I wanted to make sure you and Mason will be there. It's going to be out on Fisherman's Cove."

"That sounds wonderful. I'll be here through the end of the month so you can count me in for sure. I'll check with Mason, but as far as I know, unless he needs to go back to Boston; I'm sure he'll go as well."

"Great, I'm only planning on a couple dozen people at most. It will be an evening event. I had to get special permission to get exclusive access and that wasn't going to happen during the day. I've arranged to rent a boat for the evening and all Victor knows is that the six of us are going to spend the evening sailing. He thinks it's an end of the summer celebration. Once we've set sail, my Aunt is going to see to everything else. I've arranged for a clambake and we have permission for a bonfire."

"Wow that's amazing, you've set the bar pretty high for the rest of us."

Adara laughed. "Okay well let's grab a joint and get back out there before he suspects something."

Chapter Sixteen

With less than three weeks until the summer's end and dreading the day she would have to say goodbye, at least temporarily, to Mason; Thena vowed to make the most of their time together. Avoiding the party scene at the other end of the beach, they spent lazy days lying in bed talking and enjoying each other's company. Most days they didn't leave the cottage until well after noon, only to stroll on the beach with Shane or grab a bite to eat in town. Absorbing the town's unique history they visited all the tourist spots including the local museums and parks.

Although she had been vacationing in the area for as long as she could remember, her family never strayed far from the beach, restaurants and coastal shops. It was the first time she had ever truly explored the town and she was thrilled to be able to share it with Mason.

While both Autumn and Adara relentlessly invited them to join the foursome for dinner and drinks, they managed to keep them at bay with one excuse or another. Although she shrugged it off, it was becoming obvious that Adara was becoming frustrated by their continued refusals. Having declined an invitation five days in a row, she climbed the steps to Thena's cottage determined not to leave without either an explanation or an agreement to attend a gathering they had planned for the evening.

Taking a deep breath and straightening her back, Adara rapped firmly on the screen door. She could hear the shower running inside the cottage and was about to let herself in when Thena approached the door wearing only an oversized t-shirt and her hair pulled back in a sloppy ponytail.

"Did I wake you?" Adara asked, looking her up and down.

"No, I've been up a while. I was just waiting for Mason to get out of the shower so I could get in there. What's up?"

Since Thena didn't offer, Adara pulled the door open and stepped into the kitchen.

"We're having a cookout tonight and I want you guys to come." Holding her hand up to stop Thena, who was clearly about to refuse, she continued. "You've been making excuses for a week now and I'm not leaving until you agree to come over."

Thena sighed, "I'm sorry…it's not that we didn't want to hang out, it's just that we wanted to spend as much time alone as we could before the end of the summer."

"Is that all? Why didn't you just say that? I've been racking my brain trying to figure out what we might have done to upset you two. You're a really bad liar, just so you know."

Thena rang her hands nervously. "I know I'm sorry…I should have said something. I just didn't want to hurt your feelings. We will definitely come over tonight. What time? What should we bring?"

"Seven o'clock, we've got everything covered."

"Are you sure? I can make a salad or something."

"Just come."

Without waiting for a response, Adara turned and walked back out the door, letting the screen door slam shut behind her just as Mason exited the bathroom.

"Who was that?" He asked as he toweled dry.

"It was Adara. She insisted we come over tonight. She wasn't going to take no for an answer so I agreed."

"That's fine...I've been feeling kind of guilty blowing them off."

"Me too...anyway...I'm going to jump in the shower then I was thinking we could drive over to Annabel's and see if she can join us for lunch today."

"Sounds good, I'll take Shane out and fill his bowls."

Less than an hour later they pulled into the parking lot of Annabel's shop and Thena was thrilled to see only her friend's car in the lot. Through the window of the shop, she could see her friend moving about. As they entered, she peered over a shelf and smiled.

"Hey you must have read my mind. I was just going to call you and see if you wanted to join me for lunch." Approaching the couple she gave Thena a quick hug before shaking Mason's hand.

"Great, that's exactly why we're here. Where would you like to go?"

"I've been craving pizza, how about Varano's?"

"Sounds good." Thena agreed, waiting while her friend gathered her bag and locked the door, placing a sign in the window that she would be back at one o'clock.

While they ate, Thena filled her friend in on their latest adventures exploring the town.

"I can't believe you've never done that before. I just assumed your parents dragged you through that stuff when you were a kid."

"I know, right? I'm kind of glad they didn't, I wouldn't have appreciated it as much back then. Besides it was nice to share the experience with Mason." She said, squeezing his hand.

Winking in response, Mason, who had remained quiet until now, asked Annabel whether or not there was any interesting architecture in the area they should explore.

"Nothing comes to mind, but then again, I've lived here all my life so what might be interesting to you would just seem normal to me. It sounds to me like you've already been to the old schoolhouses and museums. You might want to head out toward Kennebunkport."

"Actually...we've been out there a few times." Unsure whether or not she had mentioned it before, Thena recounted her trips to the unique bookshop.

A look of unease passed over Annabel's face and even Mason, who had previously been skeptical about the whole thing, couldn't help but feel a chill run up his spine. Glancing at the time on her cell phone, Annabel unconvincingly explained that she needed to get back to the shop.

"I didn't realize how late it was, I hate to cut this short, but I really do need to get back to the store."

Although Mason nodded, raising his hand to signal they were ready for the check, Thena wasn't buying it.

"Annabel? What is it? I know you too well to know when you're sidestepping. What aren't you telling us?"

Annabel looked from Thena to Mason and back to her phone again before responding.

"Just be careful...it's better to be safe than sorry. You're a smart girl, let your intuition guide you."

The trio sat in awkward silence while they waited for the waitress to return with the check. While Annabel carefully avoided eye contact with her friend, Thena stared out the window, her mind reeling with questions. Mason cleared his throat, drawing their attention back to him.

"Are you ladies ready to go?" Mason asked, stepping aside to allow Thena and Annabel to pass before him.

Both women mumbled a "yes" and "thank you", before rising and heading out the door. On the drive back to the antique shop, Annabel attempted to lighten the mood by suggesting they might want to check out a performance at the Booth Theater in Oqunquit. Promising she would look into it, Thena thanked her friend halfheartedly without turning in her seat to speak to her. Uncomfortable by the sudden change in mood, Mason kept his eyes on the road.

After returning Annabel to her shop and promising she would be in touch before she left at the end of the month, Thena drew a deep breath.

"Well that wasn't awkward at all." Mason whispered sarcastically.

"I'm so sorry you had to endure that. I don't know what to make of her comments. She's always been such a free spirit. It's not like her to be wary of anyone or anything."

"Well if you ask me...I think this whole town is a little off. Everyone seems to walk around on eggshells, worried that they might say or do something to provoke some sort of voodoo. Like I keep saying...it's all a bunch of hogwash."

"I know you're right and I completely agree with you..."

"I sense a but coming."

"But...it still makes me uneasy." Thena admitted.

"You know you could always come right out and ask them. The night of the fundraiser Bryce was pretty forthcoming about the performance. It doesn't seem like they're trying to hide anything. Don't you think if there was anything to it they would keep it behind closed doors and not flaunt it in front of the whole town?"

"I guess you're right, I'm probably just searching for something that isn't there. My mother always said I have an overactive imagination."

To get her mind off things, Mason suggested they change and head out to the nature reserve to do some hiking. Grateful for the distraction, Thena quickly agreed, suggesting they bring a camera in case they spotted any interesting wildlife. With only a few short weeks until the end of summer, she was determined to explore as much of the town as she could. Having the company of Mason allowed her to discover things she never would have, spending the summer alone. While her previous summers had been spent sunbathing, shopping and hanging out with friends at the local pubs, this summer had been filled with surprises she never thought possible in the tiny town.

Dressed in a comfortable t-shirt and a pair of Capri leggings, Thena sat on her porch steps tying her sneakers while she watched Mason attempt to drag Shane away from the shore. The look of determination on his face was hysterical and she couldn't help but laugh when the terrier slipped out of his collar and sent Mason, who was pulling on his leash, sprawling in the wet sand. Furious, he scooped up the dog and stomped toward the cottage, ignoring the laughter from several onlookers. With his shorts soaked and sand covering his shirt where Shane innocently clung on, Mason had no choice but to change again.

When he finally emerged from the cottage, minus the dog, the look of annoyance on his face sent Thena; who had managed to regain her composure, into another fit of laughter.

"I'm sorry, but that was priceless." She apologized.

"Glad you enjoyed it. That mutt will be the death of me you wait and see."

"Oh, you know you love him. He was just trying to chase the waves, the poor thing spends more time inside than out, it's only fair that he gets to have some fun."

"I don't mind him having fun, but does it have to be at my expense? That was downright humiliating. Did you hear all those people laugh?"

"No I must have missed that, I was laughing too hard."

Ignoring the goading, Mason made his way around to the driver's side of the car purposely forcing her to open her own door as payback for her unsupportive attitude. The gesture did not go unnoticed and Thena bit her lip in an attempt to keep from laughing.

For being peak season, the trails were unusually desolate and they looked forward to a peaceful walk without having to maneuver around large groups of hikers. The unusual heavy rainfall had increased the population of insects beyond what was normal for August and they were only two miles into the hike when they decided to turn around. Covered in mosquito bites and annoyed by a constant swarm of flying insects around their heads, it suddenly became clear why they were the only two on the trail.

"I can't take it anymore." Mason announced.

"Oh thank God, I was wondering how long you were going to punish me for laughing at you before."

"That would only make sense if I was immune to these annoying parasites. Let's go back to the beach and take a swim. Maybe the salt water will counteract these bites."

Thena happily agreed, stepping up her pace to keep up with Mason who was practically running to get back to the car. Determined to salvage the so far dreadful day, Thena chose her most revealing bikini in hopes of making things up to Mason. His reaction was exactly the response she was hoping for and she had to struggle to get him out of the cottage and into the water.

"I think you should wear that all the time. What have you been saving it for?" Mason teased, walking a few steps behind her to admire the view.

Ignoring his comments, she sprinted for the water, shrieking as he caught her and pulled her into the surf. For nearly an hour they played, riding the waves, swimming and clinging onto each other. By the time they finally headed for the shore, it was nearly five o'clock and the beach was mostly deserted. With almost two hours to spare before they were invited to meet the others, they showered and laid down for a nap, even allowing Shane to nestle between them.

Adara watched the couple from inside her cottage as they rolled in the surf. With Victor down at the coffee shop, she was free to strategize without his constant interruptions. Although he was aware of her affiliation with the coven, he never asked any questions, leading her to believe he preferred to be left in the dark.

She had secretly been watching the couple for the past week trying to determine whether or not they appeared to have any kind of schedule. Although Mason seemed to take Shane out at approximately the same time each day, his personal schedule seemed to vary. While they spent most of their time at Thena's bungalow, he occasionally returned to his own to shower and change.

Making her way down the beach toward their cottages, Adara kept her head down, avoiding speaking to any of the other residents who might engage her in conversation. She needed to make the trek as quickly as possible and avoid the possibility that they might recognize her voice outside their window. Silently making her way up the steps to Thena's cottage, she peered through the screen door. The faint sound of the fans oscillating was only interrupted by the occasional snore from Mason. Glancing back to the beach to make sure no one was watching, Adara crept over to the picture window to confirm that they were both napping and that Shane was with them. Satisfied, she made her way back down the steps and over to Mason's cottage.

Not surprisingly, she found his door unlocked and quickly stepped inside before she was seen. Uncertain whether or not Mason would be called away for work the night of the ritual, Eliza had suggested she come up with a plan to make certain he was unable to attend. The only solution Adara could come up with was to make sure he was too sick to attend, but figuring out how to make him sick without infecting Thena was proving to be difficult.

Rummaging through his refrigerator and cupboards she was unable to locate anything he alone might consume. Frustrated, she spent another ten minutes snooping around before exiting the cottage and returning back home by way of the road rather than risk being spotted on the beach. With no other options, it appeared she would have to wait until the day of the ritual and somehow administer a powerful dose of food poisoning.

Returning to the cottage just as Victor was arriving home from the coffee shop he greeted her with a wary eye.

"Where are you coming from?" He asked, giving her an accusing look.

"I was just out for a walk."

Although he didn't challenge her, it was obvious by his demeanor that he suspected she was up to no good. Early on in their relationship, Adara had made it clear she answered to no man. While she adored his free spirit and uncomplicated attitude, her first priority was the coven and no one, not even Victor; would stand in her way of achieving her goal. Not that he had ever attempted to intervene. Unlike Bryce who constantly ridiculed Autumn for her beliefs, Victor turned a blind eye to the craft. Each time she thought she had convinced Autumn of the importance of their mission, Bryce sought to undermine her. Several times she had tried unsuccessfully to persuade Autumn to end the relationship, even going as far as to cast a spell of doubt upon her. Whether the spell was inadequate or she simply wasn't powerful enough to convince her, Adara wasn't certain, but the relationship remained intact.

While Victor made the beef patties and lit the charcoal, Adara tossed a salad and transferred the potato salad she had bought at the grocery store into a bowl. Autumn and Bryce arrived first carrying a cooler full of beer and hard lemonade. Bryce opened a bottle and handed it to Victor while Adara dragged Autumn inside.

"What's up?" Autumn asked as she stumbled over a pillow.

"I wanted to talk to you before Mason and Thena arrived. We need to find out whether or not he plans on going back to Boston next week without being obvious. If not, I need to figure out how to make sure he doesn't come to the ritual."

"Why don't we just ask him if he's coming? You're over thinking again. Just tell him you're trying to get a head count."

Adara considered the suggestion. "Yeah...I guess... ugh I can't wait until all this is behind me. It's all I think about."

"Well relax, we can only control so much. We have to trust the circle."

Adara nodded, unconvinced but confident at the same time that the sacrifice would seal her fate. If she didn't need to rely on so many others to fall in line, she would feel better, but the truth of the matter was that the actions of at least a half of dozen individuals would determine the success or failure of the ritual.

Hearing the arrival of their guests, Adara and Autumn returned to the beach where Bryce, who was well into his second beer was attempting to entertain Thena and Mason with a joke they had all heard him tell at least a couple times before. Both Thena and Mason listened politely, laughing at the appropriate times, while Adara and Autumn stood behind him making faces.

Victor announced the burgers were ready and they gathered around a folding table to fix their plates. Adara used the distraction to approach the topic before they were all too intoxicated to think clearly.

"So is everyone as excited as me to go sailing next week?"

"It sounds awesome, I've never been on a sailboat." Thena responded.

"How about you, Mason?" Adara pressed.

"I actually sail quite a bit back in Boston. My boss has a pretty nice boat and he likes to invite prospective investors and myself out for a sail. I've actually gotten quite good at tacking if I do say so myself."

"That's wonderful, so maybe you can teach us all a thing or two when we go out?"

"Careful, Adara, you're going to give him a big head." Thena teased.

Concealed behind the half wall of the porch, Annabel listened in on the conversation, careful to remain out of sight while still close enough to hear what was being said. When Celeste has first contacted her, voicing her concerns regarding Thena's safety; she had laughed it off as nothing more than the overactive imagination of a bored housewife. When Thena herself brought up her feelings of unease, however, she couldn't ignore the possibility that the coven was planning something big.

Of course there had been rumors around town for ages that Eliza was attempting to pick up where they had left off, but it seemed to be nothing more than idle gossip by a bunch of religious fanatics. The so-called Christians had gone as far as to address the town council, demanding they officially ban the practice of witchcraft in their community. The counsel, which was almost entirely made up of descendents of the town's original witches, quickly put an end to the matter stating it was the right of the citizens of Wells to practice whatever religious beliefs they wanted, backing it up with the First Amendment. With no legal foot to stand on, the vocal group was forced to back down, fearful of retaliation by the so-called witches.

As far as Annabel had been concerned it was much ado about nothing and she mostly tried to stay out of it. She was neither involved with the fanatics, being a non-practicing Catholic, or the coven. As a member of the business community, she felt it was in her best interest to simply keep her mouth shut.

From what she could gather from the conversation on the beach, the group was planning an outing the following week. Nothing about what was being said seemed suspicious to her, but then again, she really wasn't sure what she was listening for. Satisfied with Thena's safety for the night, she crept back to the street and walked the short distance to where she had parked her car. When she returned home there was an anxious voicemail waiting for her from Celeste. Knowing she would continue calling until she heard back from her, she picked up the phone to call.

Assuring Celeste that, not only was Thena safe, but that she had actually spoken to her earlier in the day and advised her let her intuition guide her, Annabel relayed the conversation she had overheard. While Celeste had to admit it didn't sound like anything on the surface, her recent call from Micha had her on edge.

"We need to find out when this supposed surprise party is going to take place and when they're going sailing. Why don't you give her a call tomorrow and ask her if she has any plans for next week. Tell her you'd like to get together again before she leaves town."

"Actually I was planning on doing that anyway. I didn't like how we left things today. It was really awkward."

"Great, give me a call after you talk to her."

Annabel promised to call, again stating her opinion that she needed to get a hobby. While Annabel enjoyed the single life and the fact that she didn't have any children to worry about, it was no secret that Celeste had longed for a child since the day she married Clayton. Perhaps because they had no children of their own and because she was old enough to be Thena's mother, she had taken on the role, at least from her perspective. Not only did she rent her the cottage well below the standard, but when the cottage next door became available she had talked Clayton into buying it in an attempt to find her a suitable mate. The minute Annabel met Mason; she knew right away that Celeste had a hand in selecting him. He was nothing if not a younger version of Clayton. The fact that he worked under her husband only sweetened the pot. Yes, Celeste was the puppet master and Thena and Mason were her puppets. If she had to guess, she would bet she already had them registered for china patterns.

Pouring herself a glass of wine, Annabel turned on the TV and made her way to the bathroom for a hot bath to relax away the stress of the day.

Chapter Seventeen

With the night of her initiation rapidly approaching, Adara focused her energy on preparing herself both physically and spiritually. Under the guidance of her Aunt, the coven's High Priestess, she memorized the key elements of the ritual using Autumn in place of the real sacrifice.

Despite the fact that she committed the words and motions to memory, Eliza reminded her of the likelihood of the inevitable setback in an otherwise perfect ritual. Certain elements were beyond even her control. An unpredicted storm, for example, might prevent them from performing the sacrifice outside, forcing them to come up with an alternative location. Although a full moon was a prerequisite to the success of the ritual, it wasn't necessary for the ceremony to be performed outside. There was also the matter of ensuring Mason's incapacitation should he plan to attend the fictitious surprise party. In that regard, Adara planned a pre-sail luncheon complete with tainted seafood specifically marked for his consumption. If she calculated the dosage correctly, it should result in an acute bout of food poisoning, forcing him to bow out of their plans. There was a slight chance that Thena would want to stay behind to tend to her ailing boyfriend, but more than likely, Mason would insist she go as planned.

Finally, and most importantly there was the Celeste factor. Despite months of preparation and purposely-leaked information, Eliza was still uncertain as to whether she would ruin their opportunity or inadvertently play into its success. For as long as she could remember, Celeste had been unpredictable. As far back as the sixth grade, when their bodies were changing and they were becoming young women, Celeste had scoffed at the suggestion she use her menstrual blood as part of a love spell. Disgusted by the very suggestion, she had broken all ties with Eliza and her friends, but not before revealing their secrets to the entire class. It had taken Eliza years to recover from the embarrassment she had caused her, not to mention the damage to her reputation.

Later, when their paths crossed again in high school, they mended fences, each acknowledging their faults and agreeing to put the past in the past. Eliza had spent the last two decades painstakingly preparing for this year. Every book she read, every chart she analyzed and every card she read told her that this was the year of her making. With each sacrifice she drew ever closer to obtaining the ultimate power her ancestors had fought so hard for. There was no telling what she might be capable of once the circle was complete. Now, with only one ritual remaining, she could practically taste the energy flowing through her blood.

More than once she had questioned her interpretation of her research in respect to Adara's significance to the circle. Her gut told her the girl was not worthy of such a vital role and her gut was usually right. As High Priestess she relied heavily on instinct and if history told her anything, it was to never trust anything to chance. It was for this very reason she had insisting on personally mentoring Adara through the initiation faze. Normally such matters would be handled by a teacher of the craft or another member of the coven.

Not since the early days of witchcraft had a coven bloodied their hands with human sacrifice. Her desire to separate herself from today's pathetic interpretation of the craft in order to obtain a higher power was Eliza's chief goal. She had been taught by the best, while aspiring to surpass those before her. Only with great loss were there profound rewards. Her leadership had resulted in the loss of several original members of the coven who believed she had let the power go to her head and was becoming too dangerous, especially when Ingrid was accidently killed during her initiation into the coven. While some left, others, who sought a more traditional based coven; took advantage of the openings by securing a position in a coven they would otherwise never had an opportunity to be a part of. Too afraid of what she might be capable of, the former members kept the coven's secrets, never revealing the group's mission.

Tasked with finding an alternative location in case of inclement weather, Adara rode the back roads of Wells in search of a secluded site where the ritual could take place without the possibility of someone stumbling upon them. Doing her best impression of a summer tourist, she loaded the basket on her bicycle with a camera, bottled water and a map of surrounding area. Making her way quickly across Route 1 onto Route 9, she stopped for a water break. Consulting her map she determined the most deserted location would likely be on 9A and carried on accordingly.

There were only a handful of individuals, mostly farmers; who lived amongst the thick vegetation that seemed to go on for miles and was just as deep. If she had been driving by in a car, she might have missed several small dirt roads leading into the woods, however the occasional incline of the road and the fact that she was growing tired, slowed down her pace enough that she was easily able to make out the entry of an otherwise hidden path. Steering onto the dirt path, she made her way down the winding road for approximately a quarter of a mile before she located an abandoned barn.

Despite the fact that it appeared as though a gust of wind could knock it down at any minute, the barn was ideal for what they had in mind. Hopping off her bicycle, Adara made her way inside the dilapidated structure, brushing away cobwebs and swatting flies. The smell of rotting wood and moldy hay permeated the air. As she shuffled her way to the center of the barn, a couple of large rats scurried by. Although large sections of the roof were missing, leaving gaping holes that filtered in sunlight; enough of the structure was covered to provide protection in the event of a storm. It wasn't pretty by any means, with rusty tools and the carcasses of feral cats in various stages of decomposition scattered about, but then again...it didn't need to be. The isolation of the structure was beyond reproach and she smiled broadly at her luck in finding it.

Hopping back on her bike, she made her way back to the main road, stopping briefly to tie a purple ribbon from her hair onto a tree branch to mark the spot. She would need to return with a more visible means of locating the path in the dark, but for now it would suffice.

Rather than return home, Adara rode her bike into town, where she stopped off at Mystical Treasures. Perched behind the counter, Micha perked up when she saw Adara enter. Sweaty and disheveled, Adara slowly made her way toward the back, nodding a greeting to the meddlesome clerk.

"Oh my, you look like you've just run a marathon." Micha commented.

"I was just out for a bike ride. Is my aunt here?" She inquired, peering toward the beaded curtains.

"She's doing a reading but she should be done shortly. Can I get you something to drink?"

"Thanks but I think I'll just head home. I need a shower in the worst way. Can you just tell her I stopped by?"

"Oh course...would you like to leave her a message?"

"No, I just stopped by to say hi. Thanks anyway."

Adara turned to leave when Micha stepped out from behind the counter.

"So I understand you're planning a surprise party for Victor." She pressed.

Adara's immediate thought was to tell her it was none of her business and to stop being such a snoop, but she put a smile on her face and turned around.

"Yes, just a few close friends and family." Adara wondered if she was looking for an invite.

"That sounds lovely. Are you having it out at the beach?"

"I considered that, but it would be too difficult to keep it a secret there. We decided to go out to Fisherman's Cove."

Adara could practically see Micha's wheels turning as she mulled over the information.

"Well if you need any help setting up or anything just let me know." She offered casually.

"Thanks...I'll keep that in mind."

Turning once again, Adara quickly made her way to the door before Micha could say another word. As soon as the door closed behind her, Adara burst into laughter. How that woman didn't see how transparent she was, was beyond her. If it was up to her, she would put her in her place once and for all, but Eliza constantly reminded her that she was a necessary component in the success of their plan. Exhausted, she returned to the beach to shower and change.

The scent of her eucalyptus body wash combined with the steam from the hot shower was enough to soothe her tired muscles. Unaccustomed to such lengthy excursions, she was certain to pay the price and anticipated being sore for days. By now she expected Micha had informed her aunt that she had stopped by so she dressed and poured herself a cup of tea to await further instruction. Nearly thirty minutes later there was a knock at the door.

Carrying a large brown bag and a leather pouch slung over her shoulder, Eliza entered the cottage. Dressed in a Bohemian style gypsy skirt in multiple colors and patterns, topped with a bright yellow pheasant blouse, she looked like the quintessential hippie. As always, her wiry gray hair was pulled up in a sloppy bun atop her head, adding to the bag lady effect. Accessing her Aunt, Adara understood why Eliza's appearance frightened strangers.

Relieving her of the bag, which Adara placed on the small kitchen table, she offered her aunt a cup of tea. Accepting the offer, Eliza immediately began removing items from the bag.

"What is all that for?" Adara asked, looking over her shoulder while she poured the tea.

"I brought you some influences to use in the upcoming days."

"Influences?" Adara returned to her Aunt's side, handing her the cup before turning her attention to the items on the table.

Amongst the items were five candles, a vial containing oil, a stone diffuser bearing the sign of the pentacle, several sheets of parchment paper as well as black ink and a quill for writing.

"I realize this is unfamiliar territory, but I promise you, it will be worth it in the end. Come...sit, let me drink my tea and I will explain everything."

Following her Aunt into the living room, Adara sat beside Eliza on the sofa, waiting patiently as she took several sips from the steaming cup.

"The items alone have no power, they are merely objects, however combined, they contain the energy to influence whoever the spell is directed at. We cannot assume that the elements alone will control the outcome of the ritual. We must take it upon ourselves to ensure the cooperation of the individuals necessary to perform the task."

Adara nodded. "So I need to do a spell using that stuff?"

"We will use the tools together. Until you complete the ritual, your powers aren't strong enough alone, but together we will achieve our goal."

Taking the final sip of her tea, Eliza placed the cup down on the table and rose, taking Adara by the hand. One at a time she lit each candle, tipping them to spill wax onto the table and then pressing the base of the candles into the wax. In the center of the candles she placed the stone diffuser, which she filled with the oil before lighting the tea candle below to heat the oil. Dipping her finger into the oil, she drew a circle around the outside of the candles. Adara could now see that the candles were specifically placed at points representing the five points of the star depicting a pentacle. As she watched in silence, Eliza tore a small piece of parchment from a large sheet and dipped the quill into the ink before handing it to her.

"What do I do?" Adara asked nervously.

"In your own words, write a spell to influence Thena to cooperate." Eliza instructed.

Adara held the quill over the parchment, her mind a complete blank. Sensing her nervousness, Eliza stepped back.

"Take your time, there is no rush. Let your mind guide you, I will step outside. Come and get me when you're done."

Nodding nervously, Adara watched as her Aunt stepped out of the cottage, leaving her alone to complete the task. Taking a deep breath, she closed her eyes and allowed her mind to wander. As she concentrated on her breathing, the words miraculously spilled forward. Whether it was by divine intervention on the part of her ancestors or instinctual, she couldn't be certain, but once she began writing, the words simply flowed.

> My requests my desires I give onto you
> To obey and be willing in friendship be true
> No distraction or illness shall keep you from coming
> When the moon is full and the demons are summoning.

Satisfied, Adara set down the quill and called to Eliza. Returning to her side, Eliza read the parchment. "If I had any doubts before, I no longer do. You have the gift, Adara."

Taken aback by her aunt's compliment, she was speechless. She couldn't recall when if ever her aunt had shown, not only pleasure, but pride in anything she had done.

"I expected to be waiting long into the night. I barely had time to rest my weary bones. Now we have only to collect a piece of her hair to complete the spell."

Adara jumped up, running to the bathroom and returning with her brush. "I braided her hair the other night. I'm sure there must be a few strands in my brush."

Eliza smiled her approval as she watched Adara pick through the bristles and pull out a long strand of Thena's dark hair. Handing it to her Aunt, Adara anxiously looked on as she examined the lock.

"You are certain this belongs to her?" She asked.

"Yes, besides from myself, she's the only person I've used it on."

"Bring me a bowl." Eliza instructed.

Placing the strand of hair into the bowl, Eliza reached into her leather pouch and retrieved a small vial filled with herbs, which she poured on top of the hair. Next she placed the hand-written spell inside the bowl before handing Adara a box of matches. Accepting the matches, Adara opened the box and removed a single match before closing it shut.

"Do I need to read the spell out loud before I burn it?" She asked.

"If you like, but it's not necessary." Eliza responded.

Taking a deep breath, Adara struck the match, watching it burn for a moment before dropping it into the bowl. The smell of burning hair was masked by the fragrant scent of the herbs. Adara watched in silence as the parchment burned. Long after the flames died down, the aroma of lavender, sage and various other herbs she couldn't identify remained and it wasn't until Eliza rose from the table that she came out of her trance.

"Is that it? Do I need to do something with the ashes?"

"Once they've cooled down you will need to make sure she consumes them. I would suggest you add them to cookie dough and bake her a batch. It's okay if Mason consumes them, only Thena will be affected by their power."

Without another word, Eliza collected her belonging and headed out the door, leaving Adara to her task.

Chapter Eighteen

Amongst the three of them, Micha's position allowed her the best opportunity to obtain useful information and both Annabel and Celeste relied greatly on her. Before she had secured the position at Mystical Treasures, Celeste depended solely on Annabel's connections with the business community as well as any overheard conversations inside her own establishment. Was it not for the wagging tongues of Wells senior citizens, they might not be aware of half of what went on behind the closed doors and dimly lit rooms of some of the town's most notable families.

What had seemed to be nothing more than a group of curious teenagers with a passion for the unknown had become something all together more sinister over the last two decades. While the majority of the town's population consisted of transplants seeking a leisure existence outside the hustle and bustle of city life, there remained a solid basis derived from the original settlers; a handful of whom had ties to the town's wicked past. While most of the town's residents chose to turn a blind eye to the evidence, others were more vocal.

In the early 90s a small group of religious fanatics had made it their mission to rid the community of all things Wiccan but in doing so had merely alienated themselves from the population. If the majority wasn't willing to acknowledge the coven existed, they certainly didn't want to associate themselves with any group whose mission it was to call attention to those who might be involved. Eventually, the group disbanded, but not before they suffered the wrath of the coven.

During their brief crusade, several members found their pets slaughtered, their tires slashed and rocks thrown through their windows. Despite reporting the crimes to the authorities, little was done to investigate the offenses and rather than continue to live their lives looking over their shoulders, they threw in the towel. While some sold their property and left town, those that remained kept to themselves hoping as time passed their involvement in the group would be forgotten.

Both Celeste and Annabel were aware of the coven's existence, having once been a part of it. While neither was involved in any overt plan to expose the coven, they did have concerns about the safety of those that might fall victim to the group. Living in Boston, Celeste relied on Annabel to keep watch over the community and the safety of their loved ones. Although neither believed in magical powers, they knew firsthand the lengths Eliza would go to in order to achieve the power she felt she was entitled to. It was only recently that Micha had joined their mission, when her cousin had failed to return from an out of state trip to visit friends. If it wasn't for the fact that several known members of the coven had been out of town at the same time, she might not have connected them to her disappearance. Nearly two weeks later, after an exhaustive search that turned up little if anything, her body had washed ashore with the markings of a ritualistic killing. With abrasions to her wrists and ankles, it appeared as though she had been bond. On her bloated belly was the mark of a pentacle etched into her skin. Her autopsy revealed the cause of death was a stab to her chest.

Micha had been working for Eliza for nearly a year when her cousin's death occurred and had overheard plans being made for a ritual out of town. Never had she envisioned her cousin being the sacrifice they had alluded to. Eliza had gone and returned before the family was aware anything was wrong. When it became obvious that something was amiss and she hadn't just neglected to call home, Micha's somber mood and erratic behavior had prompted Eliza to ask her what was the matter. When Micha explained that her cousin was missing, the look on Eliza's face spoke volumes. If she didn't realize there was a connection to her assistant before, she certainly did then and her look of concern quickly changed to panic.

It was then that Micha reached out to her former friend and sister of the coven Annabel.

Devastated that a life had been taken, despite her efforts to monitor the coven's activity, Annabel felt it was her responsibility to ensure the safety of her former friend. Protecting the woman was going to be difficult given her position under the watchful eye of Eliza. Relinquishing her position was out of the question. If Eliza suspected for a moment that Micha might have figured out that she and her coven were responsible for her cousin's death, she would likely be their next victim. After several days of consideration and conversations with Celeste, it was decided that she would continue to work alongside Eliza, providing them with information only someone on the inside would be privy to. As long as she continued to work for her, showing her the same respect as she had before her cousin's death, there was no reason for Eliza to suspect she knew the truth.

Now that it appeared something was about to transpire on the eve of the next full moon, Celeste and Annabel were relying on Micha's position to provide them with the information crucial to preventing another death. From Boston, Celeste concentrated on research, reading everything she could get her hands on in respect to ritualistic killing.

Because the cases were unsolved, the media left out critical information connecting the crimes, making it difficult to track them. From what she pieced together, it appeared there had been four ritualistic killings since the beginning of the year. The first was the murder of a young woman in Hartford, Connecticut whose body was found in an abandoned church. The second, unfortunately, was the body of Micha's cousin located on the beach in Hampton, New Hampshire. A month later, in Pownal, Vermont a young woman was found hanging from a tree in the center of town. Finally and perhaps most revealing was the body of a woman atop the grave of Wells own, George Burroughs in Salem, Massachusetts. It was then that Celeste put the others on alert.

"From what I can surmise, it appears as though they're using the elements of the pentacle to draw power. The church represents spirit, the ocean represents water, the hanging would be air and the grave is earth. If that were the case, the final element would be fire. My guess would be a bonfire or maybe a torched abandoned building."

"But if Eliza's coven is responsible, why spread them across New England?" Micha questioned.

"I don't know." Celeste admitted. "Maybe to keep the attention away from Wells."

"Or because each of those towns have a history with witchcraft." Annabel chimed in.

"Now that you mention it...and if that's it, the next logical location would be Wells."

Figuring out what the coven was up to was easy compared to figuring out what to do about it. Going to the local police was out of the question. If they contacted the state police it was unlikely they would be taken seriously and if word were to get back to Wells, one of them might become the next target. It was imperative they keep whatever information they gathered to themselves.

Although Annabel wasn't as concerned as Celeste seemed to be, she had agreed to keep a watchful eye out for anything sinister that might be going on. Now, tasked with the added responsibility of watching over Thena, she wondered if perhaps Celeste wasn't reading too much into things. While it did appear that Eliza's group might be involved in the death of Micha's cousin or at least been present during the ritual, that didn't mean Eliza was responsible of the other deaths. Unlike Celeste, whose childhood had been scarred by the actions of a vengeful Eliza, Annabel's dealings with the younger version had been less traumatic, that is until the fateful night of Ingrid's death. Still, they were young and foolish when that had happened and she wasn't convinced Eliza was the same person as she was so many years ago.

By all accounts she was an upstanding citizen in the small community. A business owner and respected member of the council, Eliza was at least partially responsible for several of the town's charities. Not only did she organize and oversee the annual food drive, but she donated substantial funds toward the building of the town's animal shelter. She had singlehandedly taken on the teacher's union when they threatened to strike, turning the tables and shaming them into volunteering their time to after-school activities in exchange for renewing their contract. Not only did the settlement guarantee the continuation of the athletic department, but it also gave the town another year to figure out where to secure the funds for the next pay raise.

If it weren't for the fact that all the murders appeared to align with Celeste's theory and the evidence seemed to point to Eliza, Annabel would never have made the connection. While the press seemed to suggest the deaths might be the work of a deranged individual, they didn't go as far as to label them as satanic, though they expressed concerns over "ritualistic elements". Each community appeared to have their own theory as to who might be responsible for the death of their young women. Only Celeste seemed to have made the connection of the placement of the bodies to the points of the pentacle.

Weary from lack of sleep and vivid nightmares, Annabel awoke to the sound of rain pounding against her tin roof. Sighing, she dragged herself out of bed only to stub her toe on the foot of her nightstand. Rapidly firing off every curse word she could think of, she limped her way into the bathroom where she examined her throbbing toe. Not surprisingly, the nail of her big toe was already beginning to turn purple.

Hobbling back into the bedroom, she drew the curtain aside to assess the strength of the storm. While the rain continued to come down heavy, she could see street traffic was already starting to pick up. Sighing she realized it would be impractical to simply return to bed when weather like this always meant increased sales. Being the sole proprietor of the antique shop had its drawbacks and days like this reminded her just how difficult it could sometimes be. The upside of course were the six months of the year that she scaled back her hours and only opened on the weekends, leaving her weekdays free to catch up on everything she pushed aside during the busy season.

Gingerly making her way over to the bedroom closet, she selected an emerald green maxi dress and a pair of flip-flops. Taking her time, she undressed carefully, avoiding touching her sensitive toe. Having taken a bath the night before, she simply washed her face and brushed her teeth and hair. A glance at the clock on her nightstand confirmed she was already running late.

When she arrived at the shop she had barely enough time to turn on the lights and settle in before customers began to arrive. A steady flow of patrons gave her little occasion to sit, let alone pamper her injured toe. Having skipped breakfast and more importantly her usual coffee break, she was both exhausted and famished. Normally the shop would completely empty out by noon and she could take a leisurely lunch. Today, however a trickle of shoppers continued to drop in until she finally closed the door at one, placing a sign in the window indicating she would be back in an hour.

Hoping she wasn't too late, Annabel phoned Thena to invite her to join her for lunch.

"I'm so glad you called. I was just saying to Mason your shop was probably crazy today."

"You can't even imagine. So what do you say? Stutesy's Pub?" Annabel suggested.

"Sounds great, I'll meet you there."

It seemed they weren't the only ones with that idea and they had to wait nearly thirty minutes to be seated. While they waited, Annabel used the opportunity to find out what Thena's plans were for her final week in town.

"Ugh, I don't even want to think about it. This summer has just flown by. It seems like I just got here."

"Have you and Mason talked about what happens once you return to Vermont?"

"I've been kind of avoiding the subject. He suggested we alternate weekends at each other's places but to be honest, I'm not sure that would work in the long term."

"You're afraid he'll get tired of having to drive so far?"

"I'm afraid I'll get tired of it."

"All the more reason to make the most of the time you have left before you go back. You should plan something romantic."

"I don't know...we have plans to go sailing with some friends, that could be romantic. Although that's going to be followed up with a surprise birthday party for one of the guys so that kind of ruins the mood."

"Oh, anyone I know?" Annabel pressed.

"I've mentioned him before...Victor. He lives with Adara Lewis. They work at the coffee shop in town."

"Oh yes, Eliza's niece. Well that ought to be interesting." Annabel laughed, hoping to sound casually amused.

"Well anyway, I know your time is precious, but I hope the three of us can get together for dinner before you leave."

"Absolutely, let me talk to Mason and we'll figure out what night works best for all of us."

By the time they were finally seated and ate lunch it was nearly three o'clock and Annabel returned to the shop only to turn off the lights and close out the register before heading to the emergency room to get her toe checked out. On her way to the hospital, she called Celeste to confirm what Micha had already told them.

Chapter Nineteen

Carrying a plate of warm chocolate chip cookies, Adara picked her way across the beach toward Thena's bungalow ever mindful of the flock of seagulls ready to swoop down and pluck them from her grasp. Keeping her eyes focused on the sky, she sidestepped her way past sunbathers and children playing in the sand occasionally stumbling over obstacles beyond her vision. As she approached the cottage, Thena pulled up in her beat up Volkswagen. Adara attributed the timing to be a sign from the Goddess that her destiny was clear.

"Thena, hey…your timing is perfect. I just made a batch of cookies and I thought I'd bring you over some."

"Wow thanks, they look yummy. Can I offer you a drink?" Thena opened the door, stepping aside to allow Adara to enter first.

"Sounds great, I'm absolutely parched. I don't usually bake in the summer, but I had a craving for chocolate."

Grabbing a couple of lemonades from the refrigerator, Thena handed one to Adara before reaching over to the plate and selecting a cookie.

"Shall we take these out on the porch?" She suggested.

"Sounds perfect." Adara agreed, placing the plate on the counter.

"Aren't you going to have one?" Thena asked.

"I probably shouldn't…I've been sampling in between batches. Oh what the hell…one more won't kill me."

While they ate their cookies and sipped hard lemonade, Adara fabricated details about the upcoming surprise party.

"Do you have a backup plan in case it rains?"

"Not really," she lied, "I'm crossing my fingers that doesn't happen."

"You might want to give it some thought. You could always set up some canopies just in case."

"I suppose… I guess I'll just wait until the date gets closer and if it looks like there's a good chance the weather won't cooperate I'll plan accordingly."

Thena smiled, "I wish I was as carefree as you. I over think everything. I've never been the go with the flow type of person. If it were me, I'd have a backup plan and a backup for the backup."

"Believe me, you're better off being prepared. My aunt is always…" Adara caught herself, "oh no…I think I left the oven on. I better go check." Jumping up she hurried toward the steps. "Thanks for the lemonade, I'll catch you later."

As Thena watched in stunned disbelief, Adara ran in the direction of her cottage, knocking over empty beach chairs, sandcastles and everything else in her path without stopping to apologize or help those affected by her irrational behavior. In her shock, Thena hadn't heard Mason approach and she practically jumped out of her seat when he spoke.

"What the hell was that all about?" He asked, following her line of vision down the beach as Adara disappeared into her cottage.

"Oh my God, don't you know it's not polite to sneak up on people?"

Mason leaned in to give her a kiss.

"Sorry about that, I heard you pull in while I was in the shower. I didn't realize you had company."

"She came by to bring us some cookies. They're on the counter...go ahead and grab one, there's lemonade in the fridge."

While Mason disappeared into the cottage, Shane settled in on Thena's lap, rolling over so she could scratch his belly. Mason returned with a handful of cookies and a bottle of lemonade and sat down beside her.

"So why did she run off like that? She practically took that toddler down and didn't even stop to make sure she was okay."

Thena returned her attention to Adara's cottage.

"I'm not really sure. She started to say something about her aunt and then stopped midsentence and said she left her stove on and ran off. By the way she took off you would have thought the place was on fire."

Mason merely shook his head, stuffing another cookie into his mouth. Returning her attention to him, Thena scowled.

"You might want to slow down a bit, I think there's more cookie on your shirt than in your mouth."

Back at her cottage, Adara cursed herself for being so careless. Understanding once again why her aunt was constantly at wits end with her, she tidied up the kitchen in hopes of settling her frayed nerves. If she didn't get it together and quickly she would lose her one chance at fulfilling the destiny bestowed upon her. All she could hope for at this point was that Thena bought her lame excuse for running off and didn't suspect she was up to no good. If she bowed out of the invitation at this late date, there was no way they could get a replacement in time.

She was so caught up in the drama she created she hadn't even noticed Victor sitting on the couch and nearly dropped an arm full of dishes when he spoke up.

"What are you up to Adara?"

"Jesus, Vic, would it have killed you to announce yourself when I walked in the door instead of sitting there spying on me like some kind of creep?"

"You didn't answer my question. What are you up to?"

"I'm not up to anything. I made a batch of cookies and I brought some over to Thena."

"Yeah that doesn't seem suspicious at all."

"What is it you're suggesting? Please...enlighten me."

"Well let me see...I've known you for what...eight months now? In all that time I've never seen you bake anything. Hell, I didn't even know you knew how to turn on the oven. Call me skeptical if you will, but it seems a little out of character."

"So I don't bake that often...so what. I had a craving for chocolate chip cookies and I made too many. I thought maybe Thena and Mason would like some."

"So where's the rest?"

"Rest? What rest?"

"You said you made too many so you brought some over to them. So where's the rest?"

Adara stood frozen, scrambling to think of some kind of defense. Her aunt was right...she was an idiot. It hadn't even occurred to her to leave a handful at home, she simply loaded them all onto a plate and brought them down the beach.

"Don't strain yourself, Adara. Whatever you say will just be a lie."

Shaking his head, Victor walked out, letting the screen door slam shut behind him. In a rare moment of weakness, Adara burst into tears. Perhaps her aunt was right, maybe she wasn't ready. Maybe she wasn't deserving of the title she was about to receive. Every time she tried to do something on her own she screwed it up. If Victor didn't even buy her sincerity, how could she expect Thena to buy it?

Plopping down on the couch she cried until her tears ran dry. A half an hour later, with her face puffy and eyes swollen, she took a deep breath and forced herself up from the couch. Making her way to the bathroom, she stripped off her clothes and stepped into a hot shower, determined not to let her emotions get the best of her.

While Autumn and Bryce constantly argued about her involvement in the craft, this was the first time Victor had vocalized his displeasure. While he didn't come right out and say what his suspicions were, she could only assume he put two and two together and knew the cookies had something to do with a spell. For the life of her, Adara couldn't understand why either one of them would care one way or another. It wasn't like they used their magic against them. If that were the case, Autumn would most certainly have a ring on her finger by now.

By the time she emerged from the bathroom, freshly showered and ready to face the world, Victor had returned from wherever it was he had taken off to.

"I'm sorry...I had no right to confront you like that." He apologized.

"It's okay, and you're wrong. You have every right to question my motives. The truth is I made the cookies as a practice run. I didn't want you to see them because I didn't want you to ask me any questions. Now that you know, I'll tell you the truth. I've been planning a surprise birthday party for you."

"My birthday isn't until next month."

"I know, but by then our friends will be gone. I wanted to do it while everyone was still here."

"I don't know what to say. I feel like an ass."

"Just promise me you won't let on that you know. It was supposed to take place after the sail. The less you know the better. I don't want to spoil it for everyone else."

"Oh course...I really am sorry."

Adara found it difficult to hide her satisfaction of once again succeeding in being deceptive. Her aunt would be proud of how easy it was becoming to cover her tracks. Victor hung his head in apparent shame as he made his way to the bathroom to shower. Once out of sight, Adara did a little victory dance before realizing she now had another hurdle to contend with.

Although the ritual was her primary focus, she had spent some time considering how to distract the men. It would be easy enough to see that Victor was scheduled to perform at the coffee house that evening but convincing Bryce to join him while the women went off on their own might be difficult. Bryce wasn't exactly a social butterfly. It was hard enough to get him off the beach when they planned something as a group. The likelihood of him being willing to sit alone at the coffee shop to listen to Victor's set was slim to none. He was much more likely to want to tag along with the girls. There was also the possibility that after sailing for a couple of hours, Victor wouldn't feel like performing.

Ultimately, Adara had decided she would wait until the day of the ritual to suggest that the guys go out for a boy's night while the girls did their own thing. As long as no plans were discussed in front of Thena, she had nothing to worry about.

Now that Victor expected a party, the triumph she immediately felt was short-lived. By the time Victor stepped out of the shower, she was in full-blown panic mode. Avoiding another uncomfortable conversation, Adara announced she was heading out to pick up some take-out for dinner. Once outside the cottage, she hopped on her bicycle and made a beeline for Mystical Treasures. She was nearly halfway there when it dawned on her that she could use the same method to incapacitate Victor and Bryce as she was planning on for Mason.

Changing direction she headed toward her favorite thinking spot to work out the details. An experienced witch would simply cast a spell on the men to ensure their debilitation. She, however was still a novice and unsure of her capabilities. She couldn't risk failure. No, her only option was to make certain all three of the men ingested the same concoction, making certain they wouldn't interfere with the ritual. Rather than her previous plan to poison Mason's food, she decided she would purchase a mini keg of beer for the men while preparing a separate mixture for the girls.

Satisfied that her plan was foolproof, she got back on her bike and headed in the direction of the local sub shop. By the time she returned to the bungalow, Victor was well into his third beer and eager to put their little spat behind them. Confident she had avoided a near disaster, Adara showed her gratitude as only a woman was able to do.

Chapter Twenty

Celeste was now more convinced than ever that her greatest fear was coming to fruition. Not only was she certain that Eliza had a hand in the deaths of the four innocent young women, but she believed Thena might be her next and final victim. What better way to complete the circle than to sacrifice the woman Celeste had come to think of as a daughter? It would be the ultimate revenge.

It hadn't taken too much consideration, especially after the death of Micha's cousin, to figure out that all the victims were somehow related to the original members of Eliza's coven. While the others had been less obvious, perhaps by design, she had only to contact the former members to confirm her suspicions. Despite her attempts to persuade them to join forces, none of the others wanted to get involved.

Micha was the only one willing to assist in her investigation and even then, only by disclosing pertinent information. She refused to dirty her hands by engaging in any activity that might put her at personal risk.

With neither Celeste nor Annabel having children of their own and no family on the east coast, the next logical victim was Thena. Celeste had considered refusing to rent to Thena, at least for this summer or until she was certain she was either wrong about Eliza or the final sacrifice had been chosen, but she couldn't think of any way to refuse her that wouldn't hurt her feelings. When the Millers had offered to sell their cottage next door, the most logical thing to do was to rent to someone she could trust to look after Thena.

Despite all of her precautions, Eliza was still able to worm her way in by way of her niece. Now, with the full moon only days away, there was little she could do without implicating herself in Ingrid's death. How many years would they have to suffer the consequences of bringing the young woman into their coven? It wasn't as if they could have foreseen the accident. Now, even after all these years, Eliza was still punishing those who turned their backs on her following the horrific event and at the center of her vengeance was the person solely responsible for introducing Ingrid to the coven...Celeste.

In those days they were merely girls, not experienced enough to imagine the potential dangers of the craft. Growing up in Wells, they had all heard the accounts of George Burroughs and his supernatural abilities. Eliza's own ancestor Mercy Lewis had been one of those responsible for pointing the finger and accusing him of witchcraft. When Eliza uncovered a trunk in her grandmother's attic containing journals belonging to Mercy, she had come to realize it was she, not George, that was involved in the craft. Having stumbled upon Mercy and her friend Ann Putnam in the woods performing a spell, he had threatened to expose them. Unfortunately for him, he didn't act quickly enough and they turned the tables, accusing him first. After the Salem Witch Trials, Mercy moved to Boston where she continued to hone her craft, chronicling both her successes and failures.

With those journals in hand, Eliza set about to reclaim her destiny. After spending countless hours studying and tweaking Mercy's work, she recruited several young women in the community to participate in the secret society. Her closest friends were placed in positions of power with her at the helm as the High Priestess. In the early days of the coven Eliza focused her supposed powers on love and healing spells, however as she gained confidence she leaned toward darker magic with a concentration on revenge.

As she continued to delve deeper into Mercy's journals she was convinced they needed to form an inner circle within the coven, calling upon the elements in order to achieve a higher level of power. While Mercy's instructions called for the sacrifice of innocent lives, Eliza was certain they could achieve their goal without such drastic measures. Convincing those closest to her in the coven, they had begun the initiations. Celeste, followed by Annabel and Micha were confirmed into the circle representing water, fire and earth. It was Celeste that had suggested Ingrid to represent Air and it was her duty to prepare her for the initiation. A single mother, struggling to make ends meet while attending college, Ingrid had formed an instant bond with Celeste. Ingrid was only sixteen when she found herself pregnant and alone. Instead of supporting her, her parents had thrown her out of the house and she was forced to rely on the compassion of others and low paying jobs to support herself and her son. She had finally settled in the town of Wells where a childless couple took pity on her and welcomed her and her son into their home. Offering her childcare, she was able to get her GED and eventually go onto college.

In preparation for the initiation, Celeste was tasked with teaching Ingrid the basics of the craft. Because she worked part-time and attended classes, the only time she had available was in the evening. For nearly three months they had prepared for the ritual while Eliza continually reminded her that failure was not an option. While Celeste thought little of Eliza's idle threats, should Ingrid change her mind and back out at the last minute, she did value her friendships with the other members of the circle and didn't want to disappoint them.

The night of the ritual Celeste was beaming with pride. Ingrid was everything she had hoped for and then some. With the others already in place she had driven out to the motel to pick her up and prepare her for the ceremony. She had expected Ingrid to be nervous, but she seemed more confident in herself than ever. Perhaps it was that confidence or her eagerness to please that had lead to her unfortunate death. While the past candidates had nervously clung to their sponsors for both support and assurance, Ingrid had chosen to stand alone. Without the hands of her sister witches upon her body to steady her she had been unable to maintain her balance and when she was startled by the sudden roar of the fire as the dripping oil fueled the blaze, she had fallen backwards and was immediately and grotesquely engulfed by the flames.

To this day the vision of her friend's beautiful face, mutilated by the flames, was seared into her memory. The sound of her cries, drowned out only by those of her son would forever be branded into her nightmares.

Unwilling to stand by while Eliza once again attempted to achieve greatness at the risk of others, Celeste vowed to end her quest once and for all. Picking up the phone, she called Annabel, making arrangements to stay at her place for the next couple of days. Normally she wouldn't go to Wells until the official end of summer when she would prepare the cottage for the winter months. Convincing

Clay she needed more time was easy, seeing that they now had two properties to maintain. While it wasn't unusual that she go it alone, she crossed her fingers that he didn't volunteer to join her. Now all she had to do was come up with an excuse that would seem plausible to Thena, who was certain to question why she would choose to stay with Annabel rather than wait a few days until her own place was free.

On a hunch, she searched the Internet for anything that might be going on in or near Wells in the upcoming week and stumbled upon a private auction scheduled to take place in the nearby town of Ogunquit. Since it was by invitation only, she could easily convince Thena she was attending without the risk of her wanting to tag along. Satisfied, she called Thena to inform her she would be in town and suggest they meet for dinner. One way or another she was going to attend the fictitious birthday party or at the very least find out where it was going to be.

"I can't wait to see you, when do you expect to arrive?"

"I have a few things to do tomorrow morning before I head out so I'm not sure exactly when I'll get in." Celeste lied.

"Are you sure you don't want to stay here at the cottage? I can always stay over at Mason's."

"Oh really? Wouldn't that be a bit uncomfortable, what with you two just being friends and all?"

"Whatever...you were bound to find out sooner or later if you didn't already know. Besides, don't even try to pretend it wasn't your intention all along to set us up. You showed your hand a long time ago."

"I'll admit no such thing. Anyway...I'm actually looking forward to spending some time with Annabel so I think

I'll stick to the original plan. I do want to get together while I'm in town though so will you be free for dinner?"

"We can do dinner Tuesday night if that works for you. We have plans Wednesday."

"Actually the auction is Tuesday afternoon and I'm not certain how late it will run. I guess we could play it by ear. What do you have planned Wednesday?"

"It's a birthday party for one of our beach friends."

"Oh well perhaps we can hook up before that if Tuesday doesn't work out."

"Actually we have plans to go sailing before the party, that is, if the weather cooperates. The last I heard it's supposed to rain so the whole thing might be a wash."

"Well you have my cell number. Just give me a call once you've confirmed your plans."

Although she had expected to feel some sense of relief at having spoken to Thena, Celeste was more anxious than ever. Her entire plan was based on the knowledge that the ritual was taking place out in the open where she could easily intervene. If Eliza was forced to alter her plans there was no telling where it might take place. With her hands shaking, Celeste quickly phoned Annabel to discuss the latest developments.

"Don't panic...Eliza is too smart to overlook the possibility of inclement weather. My guess is there's a backup plan. I'll give Micha a call and see if she's heard anything. If not, it will be easy enough for me to tail Adara and see where she goes. You know as well as I do there are preparations to be made beforehand. Eliza won't trust just anyone to prepare the alter and she certainly won't do it herself."

By the time they hung up, Annabel had talked Celeste off the ledge and she was once again confident she had what it would take to put an end to the coven once and for all. While she packed a bag she couldn't help but think about Ingrid. What would have become of her, whether they still would be friends and most of all how differently her son's life might have been.

Chapter Twenty-One

Adara awoke with the anxiety of a Kindergartner on the first day of school. With less than forty hours separating her from perhaps the most significant event of her life, every nerve in her body was on fire. Despite the intense humidity that saturated the cottage, clinging to every surface she touched, the hair on her arms stood up, electrifying her senses. Looking over at Victor, who's even breathing was interrupted only by an occasional snore; she drew from his calm peaceful slumber.

Stepping outside, she invited the salty air into her lungs, breathing deeply and exhaling slowly. Wearing only an oversized t-shirt, she stepped onto the cool sand and made her way toward the shore. Other than an early morning jogger at the other end of the beach, she was completely alone. Although she would normally be thrilled by the rare opportunity to enjoy the quiet luxury, she felt somehow overwhelmed by loneliness and vulnerability. The elements that were key to the power of her craft had a way of making her feel both invincible and insignificant at the same time.

As if sensing her inner turmoil, Victor woke suddenly with an overwhelming feeling of foreboding. Calling out her name, he waited for a response before climbing out of bed and searching the small cottage. Wearing only a pair of boxer briefs, he stepped out onto the screened-in porch just in time to see Adara step into the water. Fearful that she might be sleepwalking, he ran as fast as he could in her direction, cringing as the cold water lapped at his legs.

"Adara!" He yelled.

Turning at the sound of his voice, Adara looked at him with confusion.

"Vic? What's the matter?"

As he battled the persistent waves to approach her, she could see the panic in his eyes.

"What are you doing out here? I thought you were sleepwalking."

Adara shook her head and rolled her eyes.

"Since when do I sleepwalk? It's hot as hell, I was just going for a swim to cool off."

Frustrated by her lack of common sense and furious that he was waist deep in the frigid water with only his underwear on, he muttered what could only be interpreted as a curse under his breath and stormed off toward the shore.

"Vic...wait...I'm sorry." Adara struggled to keep pace with his aggravated step.

Ignoring her he made his way up the beach in a near jog allowing the screen door to slam behind him and disappearing into the cottage. Her confusion very quickly turned to anger as she followed him inside.

"Hey! Look I said I was sorry. I thought you were sleeping. What was I supposed to do, wake you up to tell you I was going for a swim? Don't blame me because you're disappointed that you didn't turn out to be my knight in shining armor."

"Is that what you think? You think I ran out there to save you for a pat on the back and recognition for my bravery? I did it because I love you and I thought you were in danger. Jesus, Adara! Just when I think you might be a human being like the rest of us, not the self-centered bitch you want everyone else to believe you are, you turn around and say something that makes me wonder why I fell in love with you in the first place."

"Is that so? Well if that's the way you feel then maybe I should just cancel the party. God forbid I do anything that might make me appear weak. I wouldn't want anyone thinking I have feelings for you."

Adara struggled to keep her voice from shaking or showing any sign of weakness as the lump in her throat threatened to choke her.

"Yeah, why don't you do that. I'm pretty sure it was just a sham anyway."

"What the hell is that supposed to mean?"

"Don't get all indignant with me, I'm not as stupid as you think I am. I know very well this so-called birthday party was just a cover for some stupid Wicca ritual. I'd have to be an idiot not to see what you and Autumn have been up to. Let me guess...you've decided to induct Thena into your little circle. Well I've got news for you Adara...she's way too smart to get involved with the likes of you."

Pulling on a pair of blue jeans and a wrinkled t-shirt, Victor grabbed his sandals and walked out the door leaving Adara speechless with her mouth hanging open. Torn between a fit of rage and an overwhelming urge to burst into tears, Adara grabbed the closest thing next to her; a ceramic vessel containing a bundle of herbs, and threw it across the room where it shattered into a hundred pieces. Overwhelmed, she ran back into the bedroom and threw herself onto the rumpled bed before giving in to her emotions and allowing the tears to flow with the force of a tidal wave.

For nearly fifteen minutes she cried, burying her face into Victor's pillow where the smell of his shampoo lingered. How had an innocent swim erupted into such cruelty? If she was being honest with herself, perhaps they had been skating around the issue of her craft for far too long. Rather than avoiding the subject and keeping her activities a secret, maybe she should have confided in him. If she hadn't seen how Bryce had reacted to Autumn's involvement with the coven she might have been more apt to share her own contributions, but seeing how he ridiculed her, making a laughing stock of the very fact that she believed in the craft; she had refused to share her own experiences with Victor.

Now, only hours before the most important day of her life, she may have blown her opportunity and lost him forever. What if he was so angry he exposed her true plan to Thena and Mason? What if he outed her to those in the community who up until now only speculated about her involvement with her aunt and the coven? More importantly, what if her aunt found out that she might have just blown their one chance at completely the circle and obtaining the power she had worked toward her whole life?

Something inside her shifted, whether it was her inability to accept defeat or something beyond this realm she couldn't be certain, but she rose from the bed, stripped off her wet t-shirt and made her way to shower, determined not to let Victor or anything else come between her and her destiny. By the time she emerged she was more determined than ever to complete the circle and she knew exactly what she had to do to make it happen. Although it was only a little past eight, she made her way over to Autumn's cottage, eager to put her plan in motion. Surprisingly, she found her friend already up and outside where she was attempting to keep cool under a large umbrella.

"Good Morning." Autumn called from beneath the brim. "I couldn't help but overhear your argument with Victor this morning. Are you okay?"

Adara sighed, plopping down next to her friend. "You heard that huh? So I guess you know that he stormed off."

"Do you think he'll apologize and go along with the original plan?"

"I'm not going to count on it. In fact, the way I look at it, he might actually have done me a favor."

"How so?" Autumn asked, suddenly perking up.

"I'm going to beat him to the punch. I'm going to tell Thena we had a big fight and that the sail and the party are off. Then I'm going to suggest a girl's night and we can take her out to the old barn."

"What about Celeste?"

"Let me worry about Celeste. If I know Micha, she's reporting everything she hears back to her. All I have to do is go to my aunt's shop and make sure she overhears the plan."

Autumn nodded, "What do you need me to do?"

"I'm going to need a ride out to the old barn, we need to make sure the road is clearly marked so everyone can find it at night."

"What if Victor has a change of heart and insists we stick to the original plan?"

"That's not going to happen. I could see it in his eyes. Whatever he might have felt for me, and I truly believe it was love; changed in an instant. It was like watching a light turn on. Suddenly everything that he had been holding in exploded. There's no way of coming back from that. My guess is he'll keep his distance until all this is over and then he'll come back to collect his things and leave for good."

"I'm so sorry Adara. I know how much you love him."

"Thank you, but I believe it's all part of the Goddess' plan. Perhaps I'm destined to be alone like my aunt."

Chapter Twenty-Two

Before heading out to the barn, Autumn and Adara made a quick stop at Thena's to inform her of recent developments, leaving out the most telling details.

"I don't know what to say Adara. I'm so sorry. Maybe he just woke up on the wrong side of the bed. Let him cool his heels for a bit, I'm sure he'll come around. I wouldn't cancel anything until he's had time to think."

"I appreciate your concern, but I've known Vic long enough to know whatever we might have had is over. My guess is he'll hold up somewhere until you all leave town and then he'll come back for his stuff and go. He'll probably head back to Boston where his family is."

"Are you sure you're going to be up for a girl's night out? We could always have Bryce and Mason do something and we could hang here?"

"I'm sure...besides, I have just the place in mind. We can get as wild as we want and no one will bother us."

"Geez...exactly what did you have in mind?" Thena asked nervously.

"Just leave the details to me. I promise...you won't be disappointed."

With that, the two women headed off, leaving Thena standing on her porch scratching her head. She was still trying to sort it all out when Mason came up behind her and wrapped his arms around her waist.

"What was all that about?" He asked, dipping his head down to kiss her neck.

"Apparently Victor and Adara had a big fight and he stormed off. She's canceling the party. She seems to think it's the end of the relationship."

"That's too bad. Although I have to admit…I always thought they were an odd match."

"Really? How so?"

"I don't know…he's so laid back and she seems kind of high maintenance. Not in the material sense of the word, but personality-wise."

"Hmmm, I never really thought about it. My guess is he's just out walking it off and will come back, but Adara seems to be convinced it's over. Either way, she wants to do a girl's night out. Lord only knows what she has planned"

Mason laughed. "Knowing Adara she's going to perform some sort of spell and put a curse on him."

"Well if that's the case, perhaps you should keep an eye on him and make sure he doesn't start walking on all fours or sprout hideous lesions all over his face so no woman will ever find him attractive."

For the next several minutes, while they walked Shane on the beach, they discussed the possible results of Adara's fury until their sides hurt from laughter. By the time they returned to the cottage they both agreed whatever she had planned for him, it wouldn't be good.

It took Adara longer than she expected to locate the purple ribbon she had tied to the branch to mark the spot of the old road. Several heavy rain and windstorms had practically torn the ribbon to pieces and only a thin strip remained tied to the branch. Autumn was forced to drive up and down the road at least half a dozen times before Adara finally spotted it. Together they worked to cleared away enough of the brush to make it possible for cars to pass through. Next she used a couple of pieces of string to secure the reflectors she had removed from her bicycle to the trees on either side of the old road to mark the spot. As they drove slowly down the road, Adara got out several times to clear away brush that made the road too narrow for passage until they finally reached the old barn.

"Wow, you weren't kidding. This place is perfect."

"Right? I wish we had found this sooner. I think we should make this our official meeting place. All it needs is a little work."

Making their way inside they were immediately struck by the overwhelming stench of moldy hay and rotting carcasses. Since her original discovery of the barn there were at least three more dead cats in varying stages of decomposition.

"Ew...what are we supposed to do with those?" Autumn asked, holding one hand over her nose and mouth while pointing out the obvious with her other.

"Don't worry, I brought a couple of trash bags and some gloves. I'll take care of them, you figure out what we can use for an altar."

Relieved, Autumn picked her way across the floor of the barn, carefully avoiding looking at the rotting flesh of the feral animals. By the time Adara retrieved the supplies from the car and returned, Autumn had managed to uncover a fairly decent stash of hay that had been protected from the elements by a green tarp or what remained of it after the rats had chewed up large sections to make their nests. Flipping the bundles over, she found that the underside was completely dry. Dragging the bundles into the center of the barn, she folded the tarp and placed it on top of the bundles.

While Adara went about collecting the dead cats and tossing them into a large trash bag, Autumn explored the exterior of the barn. Behind the barn, partially hidden in the overgrown brush, she located several pieces of lumber. One at a time, she dragged the heavy planks around the building and into the barn where she laid them on top of the bundles of hay to make a stable altar. Next the women swept the floor of the barn using a couple of rusty rakes they found hanging from nails against the back wall. As they swept they uncovered dozens of dead mice as well as a few live ones that scurried off into the far corners of the barn. Satisfied, they headed back to town to inform Eliza of the change of plans and collect the tools necessary for the ritual.

Although she had expected Eliza to scold her for having put the ritual at risk by fighting with Victor, she hadn't predicted the response she got. Anticipating a tongue lashing, Adara instructed Autumn to distract Micha while she met with her in private behind the beaded curtains. Adara braced herself for Eliza's wrath.

"Auntie? There's been a change in plans." Adara twisted her hands waiting for Eliza's response.

"Has there? Enlighten me."

"Vic called me out this morning. He knew the party was just a front for some kind of ritual. He didn't say exactly what he thought was going on, but I gathered he thought we were going to initiate Thena into the coven. Anyway, I got the jump on him and told Thena the party was canceled. I told her that I wanted to have a girls night out instead."

"Did she buy it?"

"I think so. She agreed to join Autumn and me."

Adara waited nervously as her aunt paced the floor. The fact that she wasn't screaming at her seemed to indicate she might not be as upset as Adara had anticipated.

"How did you leave things with Victor?"

"He stormed out. My guess is he'll lay low until Mason and Thena leave town and then he'll come back for his stuff. I'm fairly certain things are over between us."

"How can you be so sure? The last thing we need is him interfering with the ritual."

"It was the look in his eyes. I've never seen such hatred. It was as if he couldn't stomach looking at me." Adara struggled to keep her voice steady.

"Don't let your love for the man distract you from what's important. We've come too far to be sidetracked now. Does he know about the barn?"

"No…and he won't find out. Autumn and I just came from there. We marked the entrance and prepared the altar."

"Very well…follow my lead."

Eliza led the way through the curtains into the store front stopping within earshot of Autumn and Micha where she began filling a basket with candles, herbs and scented oils.

"What else do you think you'll need for Victor's party?"

"I'm not sure, what do you think? Since it's going to be inside now instead of out on the beach we're going to need more candles for light."

Adara could see Micha's ears perk up with the announcement of the change in plans.

"Oh no…is it going to rain tomorrow night? What are you going to do?"

Eliza played her part effortlessly; giving Micha a look that said, "mind your own business".

"Don't you have inventory to tend to, Micha?" Eliza suggested reminding her of her place.

"Yes, of course." Micha scurried off, far enough away to appear as though she was working while still remaining within earshot.

In a raised whisper, Eliza continued the conversation.

"So tell me again, where exactly is this barn?"

"It's off of 9A, we marked the entrance with a couple of reflectors. It should be easy enough for everyone to find. Will you let everyone know the change of plans or should I do that?" Adara asked.

"I'll take care of informing the others. You two go on and finish the preparations. Stop by the museum on your way out, I'll let Ramona know you're coming. She'll give you a half dozen hooks and lanterns to place around the barn for light."

Adara nodded, sneaking a look at Micha who was clearly taking mental notes of their conversation. Thanking Eliza for the supplies, Adara followed by Autumn, made their way out to the parking lot where they placed the basket of supplies into Autumn's trunk before heading off to the museum. The gravel had barely settled in the parking lot when Micha asked Eliza if it would be all right for her to take an early lunch.

"I suppose but be back her by noon. I have a lot to do today and I need you to man the shop."

Micha agreed wasting no time collecting her pocketbook from behind the counter and rushing out the door.

"Stupid woman." Eliza muttered under her breath.

Taking advantage of the empty shop, Eliza phoned each member of coven beginning with Ramona. By the time Adara and Autumn arrived at the museum, the lanterns and hooks had been gathered and were waiting to be picked up.

Micha immediately made her way to Annabel's shop to inform her of the latest developments.

"I wasn't privy to the reason behind the change of plans, all I know is they're meeting at some old barn off 9A. I can't risk Autumn or Adara spotting my car out there so either you or Celeste are going to have to figure out exactly where it is."

"I agree. Now get back to the shop and make sure you act as though today is no different than any other day. It's imperative Eliza doesn't suspect your allegiance to us."

Micha agreed, taking a deep breath and heading toward the door.

"Oh, and Micha…watch your back."

Micha hesitated, looking back at her friend long enough to nod her understanding before disappearing through the door. Annabel watched as Micha returned to her car and backed out of the parking lot and onto the road, carefully considering their next move. Like Micha, she couldn't risk closing the shop early and tracking the girls out to the old barn. Eliza was certain to be watching her every move.

Picking up the phone, she called Celeste, informing her of the latest developments and suggesting she give the girls a head start and make sure the coast was clear before she checked out the location. Celeste wasted no time gathering her GPS as well as a camera to document the layout. Because she wasn't certain how far off 9A the barn was located, she parked her car just off route 9 where Sanford Road met N. Berwick Road, realizing the girls would most likely come back that way. With only a vague description of the car they were driving to identify them, Celeste crossed her fingers that it would be enough.

Nearly an hour and a half passed with only a half-dozen cars passing by and she was just about to chance it, assuming they had been quicker than expected and left before she got there, when a vehicle matching the description sped by with two young girls inside. Waiting only long enough for them to disappear around the bend, Celeste started her car and headed in the direction of route 9A. With no traffic to speak of, she was able to drive slow enough to spot the reflectors Annabel told her would mark the entrance to the old road. Noting the coordinates for later reference, she slowly made her way down the narrow road until she arrived at the old barn.

Fearful the girls might return unexpectedly, she pulled her car around to the backside of the barn, noting several missing boards, which made it impossible to hide. She found it shocking that the old barn still stood given the rotting timber and structural deficiencies. Moving quickly and leaving her engine running, she snapped pictures of the exterior of the barn on all four sides. Making her way inside she found exactly what she expected. Hanging lanterns were placed at the four corners of the barn as well as either side of the makeshift altar. Bales of hay topped with planks of wood served as the altar. Beyond the altar were several more bales of hay, stacked one on top the other and covered with a purple cloth stamped in gold with large pentacle. Laid out atop the cloth were candles, salt, incense, a bowl of water or perhaps oil, a chalice and a ceremonial dagger.

Celeste's hands shook as she raised her hands to snap a picture of the instruments. Not since that horrific night in Salem had she seen such a display and seeing it now brought back a flood of memories she was ill prepared for. As if witnessing the gruesome scene once again, she was overcome with nausea. Rushing outside, she dropped to her knees where she chocked up the contents of her stomach. Waves of heat caused her to sweat profusely followed by chills that shook her to the bone. Bracing herself against the unstable siding of the barn, she rose to her feet, carefully checking her balance before making her way back to her car.

Inside the car, she threw it in drive before cranking up the AC and making her way back down the narrow road and away from the painful past. For the first time since she became aware of Eliza's plan, she wondered if perhaps she was in over her head. If the mere sight of the tools of the craft made her react so strongly, how could she possibly protect Thena? She had to make a conscious effort to pass by Annabel's shop and go directly to her home without stopping. Every nerve in her body told her to put an end to this madness before another life was lost.

The obvious solution was to warn Thena she was in danger, convince her not to go, but how could she do that without disclosing her past involvement? If she merely suggested Eliza was dangerous, perhaps unstable; Thena was likely to think she was being ridiculous and ignore her warning. Clearly Thena believed Eliza's niece was odd, but dangerous? No...she would never accept the notion she was dangerous. Even if she did somehow manage to save Thena, who would take her place? Micha? Annabel? No...she couldn't risk it. She couldn't risk losing another friend or even have the blood of an innocent on her hands.

The only answer was to expose the coven once and for all and put an end to their deadly reign of terror.

Chapter Twenty-Three

Walking away would have been the smartest thing to do. Every instinct in his body told him so. Hell, not just walk...run...run until his lung bleed, until every muscle in his body was exhausted...until the soles of his feet resembled ground beef. There was only one problem...he loved her. Despite her involvement with the coven, despite her willingness to sacrifice another for her own selfish gain...he loved her.

It hadn't been his intention. Hell...if he was being honest with himself, she was merely a necessary means to get inside. He had done his research, planned his attack, spent countless mind-numbing hours listening to her self-glorification. He had bit his tongue when every fiber of his being wanted to scream out. He wanted to confide in her, tell her it was the craft that had taken his mother from him. Describe the horrifying sight of her burning flesh, the coppery-metallic smell once the flesh melts away and the bodily fluids are exposed. He wanted to explain how even to this day the smell of pork on the grill triggered flashbacks of that horrific night.

So many times he was on the verge of telling her his true identity, but somewhere inside him that scared boy still existed. What if she revealed his secret to her aunt? What if the council decided it was too risky to keep him around? No...he valued his life too much to risk being exposed. So he kept his mouth shut…watched from the sidelines as four young women were snuffed out. Perhaps it was because he hadn't known the women, or the fact that he couldn't be certain of the coven's involvement that he hadn't stepped forward until now. His gut told him they were. His gut told him she might even have witnessed the sacrifices, but his love for her convinced him only a heartless monster could watch an innocent die and he refused to believe she was capable of that. Despite all her flaws, and he admitted she had many; he was certain of her love. It was impossible for a heartless monster to love anyone other than themselves.

He had spent nearly three years in a psychiatric hospital following his mother's death. During that time he had little memory of the events leading up to his commitment. He remembered his mother of course, even the trip to Salem, but beyond that he had simply woken up one day in a hospital room that he shared with three other boys. At first he was scared but he held back the tears he was too embarrassed to shed in front of the other boys. He peered out of squinted eyes across the room where the boys sat on the floor playing a game of cards. Finally, when one of the nurses came in to announce it was time for them to play outside, he asked for a drink of water. Even at his young age he saw the look of fear in her eyes, though he had no idea why at the time. He couldn't have known the doctors feared what he might be capable of, having witnessed such horrors at such an early age. He wasn't privy to the fact the nursing staff gathered each night discussing whether or not it might be better for him and everyone else if he remained in a drug induced coma.

As the weeks and months passed he came out of his shell. Although he was required to talk to a doctor every day, they eventually stopped asking him about the night he appeared to have no memory of. While his days were filled with activities designed to soothe his tortured mind, his nights were empty and lonely. Nearly every night he awoke from nightmares he could never recall but left him soaked in sweat and occasionally urine. Eventually, for sake of the others, he was placed in a private room. Although the nightmares continued, he was somehow able to control them enough that the staff was no longer aware he suffered. Eventually his memories of that horrible night came back and he grieved in silence, afraid to share the painful event with anyone else.

Finally, he was moved to Boston's Home For Little Wanderers where he lived until his emancipation at the age of sixteen. From there he took on several menial jobs, taking shelter wherever he could until he was finally taken in by an elderly pub owner with no family of his own. Under his direction and firm hand, he learned the necessary skills to survive in the real and often cruel world. Despite his obvious Irish heritage, his guardian wisely insisted he change his name to protect him from those that might wish to do him harm. It was then that he became known as Victor Rodrigues, son of Filipe Rodrigues.

With no funds of his own and few prospects, Victor remained a loyal and grateful son to his stern but loving father. When Filipe finally passed away from too many years of hard drinking and heavy smoking, Victor grabbed his few belongings and whatever cash he could find on the premises and headed for Wells. Although he assumed the old man had left him an inheritance, he cared little for material things. Rather than be saddled to a less than prosperous business that offered him little in the way of life, he took the one thing that had ever brought him peace…his guitar, and headed out of town.

Having learned the instrument during his days at the Little Wanderers, Filipe had encouraged him to share his gifts with others. During those years he had developed a following of sorts amongst the young people of the south side. While he tended bar at Filipe's during the week, Saturday nights he played his guitar and sang at the various watering holes scattered about town.

Although he had been satisfied to put the past behind him and get on with his life during his time with Filipe, once again alone in the world, his thoughts returned to his painful past and he vowed to avenge his mother's death. The only thing he had from his childhood was his birth certificate, which indicated he was born in Wells, although he remembered nothing of his time there. Unfamiliar with the town or what opportunities if any awaited him once he got there, he purchased a traveler's guide at the train station.

With no direct routes, he was forced to make multiple stops along the way giving him ample opportunity to consider his options. It was only by happenstance that weary from travel, he walked into the coffee shop for a much-needed dose of caffeine as well as a bite to eat. Much later he would convince himself that he was guided there by his mother's restless spirit.

With the help of a beautiful barista, who turned out to be none other than Adara, he was introduced to one of the waiters' who was looking for a roommate. With enough money to get by, he was able to survive on the money he made playing guitar and singing.

Now, only hours away from the opportunity he had been waiting for all these years, he was forced to choose between the woman he loved and the retribution he longed for. He had watched from a safe distance as Adara, along with Autumn had made their way down the beach to Thena's bungalow and back again only to take off in Autumn's car. When he was certain they wouldn't return, he made his way down the beach where Bryce was working, repairing some of the dune fencing that had been destroyed during the hurricane. After briefly explaining he and Adara had argued, he asked if he could borrow his motorcycle for a couple of days.

"I just need to get out of town for a day or two. I promise, I'll take good care of her."

"No problem, bro, do what you need to do."

"Thanks, buddy...oh and please don't mention it to the girls. I don't want Adara tracking me down."

"You got it."

Certain Adara was headed to her aunt's shop, Victor rode the bike into town, pulling into the plaza where he watched from a safe distance. He had nearly given up hope when they pulled into the parking lot and made a beeline for Mystical Treasures. Ten minutes later they were off again and he followed at a safe distance. After a brief stop at the museum where they collected a bunch of hooks and lanterns, they headed out to route 9 and eventually 9A where they seemingly disappeared. He continued on for a while until it was obvious they had given him the slip or pulled off somewhere. Furious he might have lost them, he turned around taking it slower on the return.

He might have missed the entrance again if he hadn't spotted a car coming out of a narrow dirt road hidden amongst the trees and surrounding brush. Uncertain who she was, he continued to follow at a safe distance until she turned onto route 9 before turning around and heading back. This time he clearly spotted the reflectors marking the entrance to the old road and turned onto it. As soon as he spotted the old barn he knew he was in the right place. Cutting the engine, he pulled off his helmet and made his way into the barn.

The familiar setup of the altar flooded him with emotion and he had to steady himself to keep his panic at bay. Everything, down to the position of the items on the pentagram, was exactly as he remembered them from his childhood. Suddenly he was back in his living room, hidden from sight as the pretty lady and his mother whispered words he could neither hear nor understand. A current of electricity ran up the back of his neck causing him to stumble and he reached for the wall to steady himself. Panic threatened to cripple him as he struggled to calm his emotions. Taking a deep breath, he made his way along the wall of the barn to a bale of rotting hay where he sat down placing his folded arms on top of his knees and rested his head in his lap.

Although he had spent years waiting for this day, now that it was here, he was ill prepared. While he had gone over the actions he would take time and time again, he hadn't taken his emotions into consideration. What if he froze? What if the sight of the ritual drove him over the edge or rendered him incapable of reacting at all? He could still smell his mother's burning flesh, still hear her tortured screams before the flames melted her vocal cords. No...he wouldn't let her death go un-avenged. He would make certain those responsible for her death paid for their crimes and make sure future generations didn't continue the practice.

Chapter Twenty-Four

Celeste had just returned to Annabel's and was about to jump in the shower to wash away the stench of the old barn when her cell phone rang. On edge from her earlier expedition, she was relieved to see Thena's name on the screen of her phone.

"Hey, Sweetie, I'm glad you called. The auction got done early, are you still free for dinner?"

"Actually that's why I was calling. Mason suggested The White Barn Inn…our treat of course."

"I'm not sure I packed anything appropriate for such a fancy restaurant, I'll have to see if Annabel has anything in her closet that I can borrow. Can I give you a call back?"

"Sure…Mason made a reservation for seven so we have plenty of time to change plans."

Under normal circumstances, Celeste would have used the unexpected invitation as an excuse to go shopping, but considering where she was and the likelihood she might run into a member of the coven or even worse, Eliza, she was forced to stay indoors and off the radar. Phoning Annabel, she conveyed her findings in regards to the reason for her visit before asking permission to go through her things in an attempt to find something to wear to dinner.

"Oh course, you don't even have to ask. My house is your house. It's actually a good idea to dine out of town. You're less likely to run into one of Eliza's minions. Just do me a favor and leave your phone on in case I need to call you."

More relaxed after sharing her findings with Annabel, Celeste sorted through her friend's somewhat disorganized closet for something to wear. Selecting half a dozen dresses she deemed appropriate, she tried each one on before settling on a midnight blue satin cocktail dress. Luckily she had packed a pair of basic black pumps, a staple in any woman's wardrobe; although she acknowledged an open-toe would have been more suitable. Before heading into the shower she made a quick call to Thena to confirm she was good for the original plan.

Out at the beach things were unusually quiet and Thena couldn't help but wonder whether or not Victor had returned. Sensing her concern, Mason tried to distract her suggesting they take Shane for a walk.

"I'm sure they'll work things out."

"You're probably right but I still feel bad for them."

"From what you said, it doesn't sound like Adara was too broken up about it."

"On the surface no, but I'm sure her attitude was only a cover to hide her true feelings. I guarantee you…by the time we get together tomorrow night, after she's had a couple of drinks and time to think about things, the floodgates are going to open up."

Mason shook his head, "Women…I don't get you."

"What's to get?"

"Men say what they have to say and they're done with it. You women stew over things for days, building things up and reading stuff into our words that were neither said nor intended. I actually feel kind of bad for the guy. If I know Adara, and I think I do, her type anyway…she's going to make him pay for ruining her plans and not just once."

"Whatever…from the sound of it, he was the one who overreacted, not Adara. Besides, for all we know they've already made up and the party's back on."

Mason shook his head, holding his hands up in defeat. Although the plan was a leisurely stroll down the beach and back again, Shane had other plans and they spent nearly an hour chasing him in and out of the water. By the time they got him settled in for the night, they barely had time to shower and dress before it was time to pick up Celeste. Once again, Thena wished she had packed at least a couple of cocktail dresses. Despite Mason's insistence that he would never grow tired of seeing her in the stunning ivory piece, she vowed to burn it rather than ever wear it again.

Down the beach, Adara watched the happy couple emerge from Thena's cottage, dressed for an evening out. She envied the uncomplicated nature of their relationship. The fact that they appeared to look beyond the complexities of their soon-to-be long distance romance and enjoy the time they had left. She was never the type to be content in the here and now. She was always looking forward to something better. It was never enough that Victor was by her side, that she had the love a good man. She needed more than that. Perhaps she shouldn't have been surprised that he walked away, that he turned his back on her at such an important time in her life. Was she so self-centered that she hadn't seen it coming or was he simply choosing this time to drive his point home?

Angry that she didn't have him to comfort her frayed nerves and stroke her ego on the night before her initiation, she vowed to make him pay. Tomorrow she would change the lock on the door…make it impossible for him to retrieve his belonging without confronting her. If he wasn't convinced before of the powers the coven possessed now, he would be by the time she was done with him. No one humiliated her the way he had and got away with it, she would make certain of it.

Dressed in the borrowed midnight blue cocktail dress, which complimented her hourglass figure; Celeste anxiously paced the floor waiting for Mason and Thena to arrive. Despite the weight of world on her shoulders she was excited to see the pair together as a couple. She wanted nothing more than to see the two of them, both of whom she thought of as her own, happy and in love. When she heard the car pull into the driveway, she grabbed her evening bag and headed for the door, too restless to adhere to formalities and invite them in for a drink. They had barely emerged from the car when she stepped out onto the porch.

Mason whistled his approval as Thena rushed to greet her. "Celeste you look absolutely stunning."

"Why thank you, you're not too shabby yourself. Let me get a look at you." Wrestling out of her hug Celeste held Thena at arm's length. "What a beautiful dress."

"If you like it you can have it. I've about worn it out this summer."

Mason stepped in to kiss Celeste on the cheek. "Clay's a lucky man. You look amazing."

Suggesting both women sit in the back seat so they could catch up, Mason played chauffer on their way to Kennebunkport, smiling into the rearview mirror in response to their endless chatter. By the time they arrived at the restaurant they had covered everything from the unexpected hurricane to newest shops in town and everything in between. Mason simply shook his head wondering how it was women were able to keep their lips closed at all considering the force by which the flood of gossip came pouring out of their mouths. The look of wonder must have been evident on his face because when they finally stopped talking long enough to get out of the car, they both looked at him with confusion before saying "What?", simultaneously.

Despite their reservation, they had to wait nearly twenty minutes before being seated so Celeste spent the time filling Mason in on the latest developments in regards to the project he was working on with Clayton. Completely ignorant on the subject, Thena feigned interest while nursing a glass of chardonnay. When they were finally seated and their glasses had been refilled, Mason proposed a toast.

"Here's to the first of what I hope will be many more evenings spent in the company of the two most beautiful women I've ever had the luxury of knowing."

While Thena rolled her eyes, Celeste nodded her approval.

"I told you, Thena…he's a keeper."

"So…tell us about the auction." Thena insisted, eager to change the subject.

"There's not much to tell, the few items that interested me went well above my price range. Luckily they came up early in the auction and I wasn't forced to waste the entire day waiting only to be disappointed."

"I've always wanted to go to an auction. I probably wouldn't buy anything, but it would be fun to watch." Thena admitted.

Celeste felt slightly guilty about the lie and hoped that they didn't ask too many questions.

"Well I'll tell you what…the next time I hear of one coming up, we'll go together. You're welcome to join us too, Mason."

While they dined Mason entertained the ladies with incriminating stories of his youth, leaving little to the imagination and plenty of room for interpretation. If he was to be believed he was somewhat of a cad while at the same time the very definition of a hero. By the end of the evening both Celeste and Thena were holding their sides in laughter and begging him to stop. It was nearly midnight when they dropped Celeste off at Annabel's house. Both Mason and Thena walked her to the door.

"Thank you again for such a lovely evening. If your plans fall through tomorrow night, give me a call."

Back on the beach, Adara had called it an early night, bowing out of an invitation from Bryce and Autumn to order pizza and watch a movie. Although Bryce was ignorant to the fact Adara was hurting, Autumn sensed the change in her friend. While she had seen Adara through a number of relationships and breakups both good and bad, none had affected her the way this one had. Adara had a system of moving on akin to the five stages of mourning. First she would deny that the relationship was over, even going so far as to invite him to go away for a romantic weekend. Next she would lash out in anger usually at the expense of his most prized possession, slashing his tires, keying the side of his car and once nearly burning the guy's home to the ground, insisting it was an accident. If that didn't work she would bargain, promising to change whatever was causing the conflict in the relationship, namely herself. When all that failed she would fall into a deep depression, isolating herself from those that loved her most until finally she accepted the failure of the relationship and moved on. It was textbook really, all Autumn had to do was ride it out and wait until she arrived at the final step so she could be there to pick up the pieces of her broken heart and encourage her to try again.

This time however...she had blown right past denial directly to anger and that scared the hell out of her. If she didn't follow her usual path, there was no telling what she was capable of. Although she tried to convince herself the ritual was taking precedence to everything else, she couldn't help but be afraid for Victor. Terrified that his life might be in danger, Autumn tried to convince Bryce to track him down and warn him, but he refused to get involved. Unwilling to give up, Autumn had spent the better part of the afternoon after dropping Adara off, searching his usual hangouts. The fact that no one had seen him gave her even more cause for concern. What if Adara had somehow tracked him down herself and hurt him... possibly killed him? She considered going to Eliza, but she scared her more than Adara did. If Eliza thought Autumn had failed in her duty to protect her sister of the coven, she might become their next victim.

As for Adara, she focused her energy on the one thing she could always count on...her magic.

Chapter Twenty-Five

As the quaint little town of Wells slept, the skies opened up, drenching the coast and everything within its reach. Perhaps a sign of things to come, the rising sun was veiled by an abundance of dark gray clouds. Those that slept remained unaware of the storm's intensity, while Adara drew from its strength. Fueled by adrenaline and the hatred she felt toward her former lover, she exhausted every spell in her arsenal in an attempt to draw him out.

Spending the majority of his time on the beach when not performing at the coffee shop, his friendships were limited to a handful of mutual acquaintances. Having quickly eliminated each of their homes as a place to hang out, she assumed he would return when the storm moved in. Although the storm continued to intensify, he failed to return home, only infuriating her more. Had he simply come home begging for her forgiveness, she might have been willing to put the whole mess behind her, but his insistence in prolonging her suffering turned her heartbreak into rage, fueling the fire. Now as the sun rose in the distance, any chance at reconciliation was lost.

The anger that had kept her from sleep continued to eat at her brain, making it impossible to think of anything else. In less than six hours, her aunt would be knocking at her door, ready to begin preparations for the sacrifice. Physically exhausted, she made her way into the bathroom hoping a hot shower might ease the tension in her weary body. Bracing her hands against the shower walls, she dropped her head forward, allowing the hot water to penetrate her stiff neck. As the tension slowly melted away it was replaced by the sadness she had worked so hard to avoid. Dropping to the floor of the shower, she drew her knees up to her chest, wrapping her arms around her legs and resting her head on her knees. The vulnerability she felt at being alone and naked on the floor of her shower broke down the barrier she had fought so hard to build. An unexpected wave of emotion burst forward in a flood of tears and painful sobs.

Somehow she managed to lift herself up from the floor and exit the shower, stopping long enough to wrap her hair and body in towels before making her way to the empty bed. Once again she was forced to acknowledge Victor's absence as she wrapped her arms around his cool pillow and breathed in his lingering scent. It wasn't until she heard the persistent knocking at the door that she realized she had actually succumbed to her exhaustion and fallen asleep. Sitting up, she glanced at the clock, confirming what she already suspected…it was nearly noon.

Anticipating Eliza's wrath, Adara jumped out of bed and threw on a nearby robe before heading for the door. Luckily it was Autumn, not Eliza who was anxiously waiting at her doorstep.

"Are you okay? I've been knocking for like five minutes. I was about to go get Bryce to break down the door."

"Sorry, I was up all night, I guess I finally fell asleep. What are you doing here anyway?"

"I thought you might need help getting ready before your aunt arrives. I can see I was right."

Too exhausted to argue, Adara allowed Autumn to drag her back into the bedroom where she plopped her down on the bed before heading in the direction of her closet.

"Since it's raining, you should probably forgo your usual peasant skirt and stick to jeans and a t-shirt. Throw these on while I get your brush and elastics for your hair."

Tossing the clothes on the bed, Autumn disappeared into the bathroom, returning just as Adara was pulling on a pair of colorful socks. Still damp from being wrapped in a towel, her hair was a tangled mess and Autumn was still trying to brush it out when Eliza arrived. With a look of frustration and anger prominently displayed on her face, Eliza brushed by the women without a word and moved toward the small kitchen table. Adara and Autumn exchanged a nervous glance at each other before following their leader into the kitchen.

"I'm sorry I'm not ready yet...I was up all night preparing." Adara lied.

Eliza ignored her niece's obvious lie and began to unload the contents of her leather satchel. As they looked on in silence, Eliza opened several vials, emptying their contents into a glass beaker. Finally she opened a bottle of hard lemonade and made her way to the sink where she poured nearly three quarters of the liquid down the drain. Returning to the table, she poured the contents of the beaker into the bottle before recapping it.

"You will need to make sure she drinks all of this before you head out to the barn."

"What is it?"

"It's a combination of herbs and over-the-counter sleep aides. It shouldn't take more than an hour to render her completely unconscious."

Adara held the bottle up to the light, examining the contents.

"She won't be able to taste the difference?"

"No...the herbs should enhance the citrus flavor if anything. Now, I have a few things to take care of. When you've finished primping, meet me at the museum. From there we'll gather the others to perform a strengthening bond to enhance our powers and prepare for the sacrifice."

A note of disapproval was evident in her voice and it hit Adara like a slap to the face. Biting her tongue, she nodded, lowering her eyes to the ground as her aunt passed by her and out the door. Once out of earshot she drew a sigh of relief.

"I'll be so glad when this is all behind us and I've finally gained her respect. She treats me like an unwanted stepchild. I'm tired of swallowing my pride and shutting my mouth."

Autumn sensed her friend's fragile state of mind. "Take a deep breath Adara. Like you said, it's nearly over. Once the ritual is behind us, it's clear sailing from here on out. Now sit...let me finish braiding your hair."

Adara nodded, though her mind was still unsettled with emotions ranging from her wounded pride to the rage that threatened to boil over.

By now Eliza was not only aware Celeste was in town, she was having her movements carefully monitored. While a few of the original members of the coven remained unconvinced of her mission to destroy them and expose their involvement in the recent murders, the majority agreed it was not worth the risk to ignore the possibility. Those that were skeptical argued that it was impossible for her to expose them without implicating herself in Ingrid's unfortunate death. Eliza had listened to each member, discounting those opinions that didn't reflect her own and moving for a majority ruling. Once again, Eliza reminded the group they were free to walk away from the sisterhood at any time without fear of retribution. As comforting as that sounded, few believed it to be true.

Returning to her shop, Eliza informed Micha she had errands to run outside of the shop and required her to hold down the fort. Although she would normally press for details, Micha sensed her boss was not in the mood for probing questions, so she merely assured her she was up for the task. After retrieving a box from the back room, Eliza departed without another word. Micha watched her get in her car and drive away before picking up the phone and calling Celeste.

"She just took off. She didn't say where she was going, only that she had errands to do. I was afraid to ask when she planned to return."

"That's fine, thank you Micha. The less you're involved the better. I don't want anyone risking their lives over this."

"Are you sure you want to do this alone? What if she sees you?"

"Don't worry…I'll be careful. I'm only going to take pictures. I'll only step in if it looks like Thena's in danger in which case it won't matter how many of us there are. All I need to do is get evidence of the coven performing a ritual and then I'll leave it up to the authorities to go from there. That combined with the published facts of the other cases should be enough to put Eliza away for a long time."

As planned, one at a time, the thirteen members of the coven gathered at the museum to prepare for the ritual. Despite the inclement weather and overcast skies, they collectively embodied the light of a thousand stars, with their spirits high. The extraordinary ritual they were about to witness was something few witches were likely to see in their lifetime, let alone be a part of. Though each of their tasks varied in degrees of importance, no one task was any less significant than the other in respect to the outcome. Two novice members would be tasked to usher arriving vehicles onto the property, making certain all members were accounted for before the start of the ceremony. The four individuals most trusted to the High Priestess were given the title of Watchers. They would stand guard at the exterior four corners of the barn protecting the others from intruders. The ceremony itself would involve the four confirmed members representing spirit, water, air and earth as well as Adara, whose actions would confirm her as the representative of fire the fifth and final element. Traditionally, Autumn's role as Maiden or assistant to the High Priestess would lead to the assumption she was next in line should Eliza become unable to perform her duties or step down altogether, however; in this particular coven it was common knowledge Adara was being groomed for that position.

With each member of the coven accounted for and having sworn once again to uphold the sacred oath, Eliza prepared each member for their tasks. Although this was merely a dress rehearsal, they took their roles seriously. One by one they acted out their parts until all eyes were focused on Adara. Acting as the sacrifice, Autumn allowed the novices to usher her forward, passing between the elements to the makeshift altar where she was laid out and bound. Simulating a struggle, Autumn writhed back and forth, testing the ropes that bound her wrists and ankles. Satisfied her struggles were in vain, Eliza and Adara approached the altar.

"At this point Adara and I will recite the appropriate spell and she will thrust the ceremonial dagger into the sacrifice's heart. Autumn will then step forward to fill the chalice with the blood of our victim, which Adara will then drink from in order to confirm her position within the circle."

Adara took a deep breath to steady her nerves as her aunt continued to speak.

"Once the ceremony is complete, those present will secure the tools making certain no evidence is left behind. Adara and Autumn will return the barn to its original state while the novices lead the procession off the grounds. It's important that the exit be staggered so that anyone passing by doesn't witness a parade of vehicles exiting the road. You will use whatever light the moon gives off to direct you, only turning your headlights on when you're at a safe distance. When the final vehicle departs, you girls will return to the barn giving us a head start before you light the fire, burning down the barn and any evidence we were there. The firefighters will discover the body and eventually identify her so it's imperative you all have an alibi. Go out in small groups and make sure your presence is noticed."

Confirming their understanding, the women departed, ready to meet again at the midnight hour.

Chapter Twenty-Six

Just outside of town, beyond the border that separated Wells from its neighboring town of Ogunquit, Victor took shelter from the storm inside the crumbling walls of a long abandoned outbuilding. Composed of masonry indicative of the late 17th century, the walls appeared to be erected from stones unearthed from the surrounding area, perhaps during the excavation of the land to plant crops. The roof of the building was crudely fashioned out of rough lumber and tar, which appeared to have undergone multiple repairs over the years.

Perhaps originally used as a root cellar or tool shed, the crumbling walls did little to protect him from the elements, making for a restless night's sleep. Waking up in a puddle of rainwater that soaked his clothes and chilled his bones, despite the August heat, Victor stepped outside to relieve himself and survey the current weather conditions. Unfortunately it didn't appear as though the rain would let up anytime soon and it was evident he needed to return to the cottage for a change of clothes as well as the bag he had stashed away in the likelihood this day would arrive. If he left now, he was likely to arrive at the beach before Adara woke and he could watch from a distance until she left the cottage. Knowing Adara, she would insist on overseeing every detail in regards to whatever she had planned for the evening and he could easily slip in and out before she returned.

As it turned out, he had to wait much longer than expected as first Autumn, then Eliza arrived at the cottage. When the coast was finally clear, he made his way inside, even risking being caught by taking a hot shower to soothe his aching muscles. Once dressed appropriately for the inclement weather, he grabbed the backpack he had prepared nearly six months ago when it was evident Eliza was picking up where she left off, and enough food to satisfy his cravings for a day. Beyond that, if everything turned out as planned, he could return at his leisure for the rest of his belongings.

Now dressed in a pair of heavy work boots, jeans, a t-shirt and windbreaker, he got back on Bryce's bike and headed out of town to the stone hovel where he would bide his time filling his stomach and making preparations for his revenge. Emptying the contents of backpack onto the only dry surface in the crude building he could locate, he considered whether or not he was adequately prepared. Amongst the contents lay a dozen sets of zip tie handcuffs, a heavy flashlight and supply of fresh batteries, a couple of smoke bombs to use for distraction purposes along with pepper spray. While it wasn't his intent to physically harm anyone other than Eliza, he was prepared to do whatever necessary to make certain no one got in his way.

Over the past several months he had attempted to run every possible scenario through his brain, considering every potential obstacle he might encounter. Still, he was certain there were variables he hadn't thought out. The inclement weather had actually worked in his favor, moving the group to a confined area rather than outdoors where they might scatter. Amongst the contents of the backpack was a pad of paper and a pen, which he used now to map out his plan.

Back on the beach, Thena and Mason took advantage of the weather, opting to spend the day in bed. Shane, on the other hand, continued to scratch on the door until Mason was finally forced to leave the warm comfort of Thena's arms and accompany the annoying mutt out into the storm. Rather than do his business and be done with it, Shane chose to stop and snip every bit of debris that washed ashore. Despite persistently yanking on his leash to move him along, Shane stood firm, nipping at the salt water each time the tide flowed in. When he decided enough was enough, Mason bent down to scoop up the disobedient mongrel when he spotted Victor exiting the cottage he shared with Adara.

He considered calling out to him, but the look of determination on his face told him he was in no mood for small talk. Before he had a chance to reconsider, Victor disappeared around the side of the cottage and he heard the distinct roar of a motorcycle engine. His brief distraction gave Shane just enough time to squirm out of his arms and make a mad dash for the cottage, stopping at the foot of the steps long enough to pee before leaping up the stairs to the dry porch. Mason muttered a curse under his breath before heading back himself.

By the time he stepped inside the cottage, drenched to the bone, Shane was in the midst of a towel dry with the look of pure satisfaction on his little face.

"I swear to God...he deserves to be punished not pampered." Mason shook the rain out of his hair, ignoring both of them as he stormed past on his way to the shower.

"Don't pay him any mind, Shane...he's just a grumpy grump in the morning." Thena assured the dog.

By the time Mason emerged from the bathroom and joined Thena in the kitchen where she handed him a hot cup of coffee, Shane was snoring loudly from the comfort of the bed.

"Do you feel better now?" Thena asked slyly.

"I don't know who's worse...you or him. He drags me out of bed on the premise he needs to go out and when I bring him out he dilly-dallies around like he doesn't have a care in the world. Meanwhile, I'm getting soaked to the bone. Then when he decides he's had enough, he pisses on the steps, ten feet away from the door."

"You poor thing...how can I make it up to you?" Thena asked in a tone dripping with sarcasm.

"For starters you can stop rewarding him when he does something annoying."

"I was merely drying him off, I wasn't rewarding him. If you'd rather, I could let him roll around on your side of the bed soaking wet."

"Whatever...by the way, when I was out there I saw Victor."

"Really...so they're back together then?"

"I don't think so. He had a backpack and he took off on Bryce's bike. From the look on his face, I'd say things are probably over."

"That's too bad. Did you see Adara?"

"No, if she was home she didn't come outside. I'm guessing he just stopped by to pick up a few things."

"Well I guess that means I'm going to be spending the evening listening to Adara dredge up every unpleasant moment in their short relationship. I wish I could think of some way to get out of it without hurting her feelings."

Mason nodded, "Who knows…it might not be as bad as you think. After a couple of drinks she usually loosens up."

"You're probably right, still…I'd rather spend the evening with you. Which brings me to the question…what's on your agenda?"

"I hadn't really thought about it. I suppose I'll see if Bryce wants to join me at the pub for a couple drinks and a game of pool."

After a quick bite to eat, Thena headed off to the shower while Mason tidied up the kitchen. When she emerged a short time later, he was curled up next to the dog softly snoring. Smiling at the pair, she tiptoed across the room to her pocketbook where she kept her camera. Slipping back into the room, she snapped a couple shots of the sleeping beauties before grabbing a book from the shelf and making her way out to the porch.

The rain continued to come down at a steady pace, while doing little to quash the unrelenting humidity that had plagued the residents for more than a week. Other than herself, there was no one else willing to brave the elements and she took advantage of the rare quiet to submerge herself in the erotic romance novel. When Mason finally emerged from the cottage, she was nearly half way through the book and didn't notice his presence until he sat down beside her and cleared his throat.

"That must be good stuff, did you read anything you'd like to share with me?" Mason teased.

Blushing, Thena earmarked the page and closed the book, hiding the juicy scene from his curious eyes.

"I don't know about you, but I'm starving. What do you say we change and go out for some lunch?" She suggested, quickly changing the subject.

Recognizing the diversion tactic, Mason grinned, letting her know she wasn't fooling him before agreeing and making a quick run over to his own place to change. Unwilling to be betrayed twice in one day by Shane, he returned with a long leash, which he tied to the rail of the porch. Tossing a folded beach blanket on the floor of the porch, he connected the leash to Shane's collar making certain he had enough length to easily move from the blanket to the beach to relieve himself and back again. Satisfied, he refilled his water and food bowls and placed them next to the blanket. Thena looked on with pouty lips.

"What now?" Mason asked, dumbfounded by her expression.

"He was so comfortable in the bed, why is he being banished to the porch?"

"Oh for God's sake, he's a dog not an infant. He'll be fine."

Ignoring her sympathetic eyes, he took her by the hand and led her around the cottage to his waiting car.

Chapter Twenty-Seven

Adara stood watch at the bedroom window of her cottage as the storm outside intensified. Gray clouds raced across the sky, blocking out the already diminished light of the sun and casting an eerie glow on the rough surface of the water. Occasionally a bolt of lightning followed by a powerful rumble of thunder shook the cottage sending chills up her back. Her already strained nerves were stretched to their limits as a seagull came out of nowhere and smashed into the very window she was leaning up against, its empty black eyes seemingly making contact with hers for a brief moment before his lifeless body fell to the ground.

Too much to bear, Adara backed away from the window, nearly toppling over her nightstand and sending a frame; holding a picture of her and Victor, crashing to the floor where the glass shattered into pieces.

"Get it together." She whispered to herself.

Making her way into the main room of the cottage, she glanced at the clock on the wall only to once again realize she had neglected to change the batteries and for all intents and purposes time stood still, perhaps another omen of things to come. To calm her nerves, she made her way into the kitchen where she poured herself a shot of tequila, which she quickly threw back before having another. She was about to pour a third when Autumn walked through the door.

"Do you think that's a good idea?"

"Probably not, but if I don't do something I'm going to lose my nerve. This storm is only making me more nervous. What time is it anyway?"

"It's almost eight. Thena should be here any minute. Why don't you put that away and go sit down?"

Adara was about to refuse, but didn't have the energy to fight. Instead of her usual retort she twisted the cap back on the bottle and returned it to the cupboard before following Autumn into the living room.

"So have you heard anything from Victor?" Autumn asked, hoping to get her mind of the ritual.

"Not a word. Not that I expected to anyhow. At some point he'll have to come back for his stuff, but until then I imagine he's laying low waiting for me to cool off."

"You're probably right, and it's probably for the best. Once this is all over and things have had a chance to settle down who knows...maybe he will come crawling back begging for your forgiveness."

Adara shook her head, "I'm not going to hold my breath."

Before Autumn had time to respond, Thena knocked on the door before letting herself in.

"Hey...I wasn't sure whether or not you still wanted to go out considering the weather."

"A little rain isn't going to stop us from having fun. Come...sit down. I'll get us each a drink."

Adara motioned to Thena to take a seat before disappearing into the kitchen to retrieve three bottles of hard lemonade, one of which was secretly marked for Thena's consumption. While they drank, Adara suggested several options for their ladies night, letting Thena think the choice was hers, knowing full well the lemonade would render her unconscious before she had a chance to step foot out of the cottage. Practically on cue, Adara had just taken her final swig when the bottle dropped out of Thena's hand and she slumped forward, nearly falling off the couch. Autumn quickly grabbed her by the shoulders and laid her out, covering her with a blanket.

Adara smiled, "That was amazing. Eliza really knows her herbs. Let's go."

"What about her? What if she wakes up before we get back?" Autumn asked nervously.

"She won't, she'll be out for hours and if not, she'll simply assume we went out without her and go back to her own cottage."

Secure in the knowledge that things were going as planned, Adara and Autumn made their way out to the old barn, hoping to arrive before the rest of the coven. An hour earlier, Victor took the back roads by way of Ogunquit Road to Route 4 crossing over to 109 and eventually onto 9A to avoid running into Adara or one of her minions. After securing a spot close enough to see what was going on without being detected, he sat back and waited.

Almost on cue, Adara and Autumn arrived, followed shortly by Eliza who traveled alone and a car carrying two young women he was unfamiliar with. After a brief conversation with Eliza, the women walked in the direction of the hidden entrance, most likely to direct others to the location. Through a pair of binoculars, Victor watched as one by one the members of the coven arrived and took their positions.

With four watchers standing guard at the outer corners of the structure, Victor contemplated his next move. From his current position it was impossible to approach the barn without being made. Searching the grounds through his binoculars for an alternative entry point, he caught the silhouette of a woman crouched down behind a rock wall. Like himself, she appeared to be focused on securing a diversionary tactic in order to gain access to the barn. Obviously not part of the coven, he watched as she hurled a rock into the trees behind her, drawing the attention of one of the watchers who headed off in the direction to investigate.

Following her example, Victor located a rock and flung it behind him, waiting until the second guard passed by him to investigate before making a mad dash for the barn. No longer concerned about the woman's agenda, he slipped into the barn unnoticed and had just enough time to secure a hiding spot before a commotion broke out.

Unnerved by the situation, Celeste had revealed herself briefly when she stood up to investigate the sound of the second rock hitting a tree in the distance. Although she quickly returned to her crouched position behind the rock wall, it was too late. Having heard the second rock herself, the guard had turned swiftly, spotting Celeste and approaching her from behind. Despite her struggles, she was quickly apprehended and brought forward with the assistance of the second guard.

From his secure position, Victor watched as the two guards, each holding one of the woman's arms dragged her kicking and screaming into the barn where she was presented to Eliza.

"Celeste...you're just in time." Eliza motioned for the guards to set her free.

Looking around the barn frantically, Celeste's eyes returned to Eliza.

"Where's Thena? I swear...if you've done something to her, I'll kill you myself."

"Oh Celeste...you've always been a bit dramatic. I have no interest in Thena."

A brief look of confusion crossed over Celeste's face as Autumn and Adara approached her.

"Don't you see...the only way to insure you would come here was to make you think Thena was our intended sacrifice. It's always been you we wanted. It's poetic justice really. It was you who sponsored Ingrid all those years ago. It was you that brought darkness into an otherwise innocent ritual. Because of your actions I was forced to sit and wait. Wait for the years to pass by and with it any chance I had at reaping the benefits of leading the most powerful circle this town has seen in over three-hundred years."

"You're insane!" Celeste spat, struggling as Adara and Autumn dragged her closer to the altar.

"You might be right. Perhaps I am a bit crazy, but not in the way you think. Crazy for letting so many years pass without retribution. Crazy for not ending your life that night all those years ago. Anyone else would have made you pay for your actions immediately and without the courtesy of giving you an opportunity to make things right."

Celeste struggled as the women forced her arms above her head, stretching them out in opposite directions and tying them to the lantern posts at the head of the altar while two others secured her legs in similar fashion.

"It was an accident. For God's sake, Eliza, don't do this."

"There is no God, Celeste, you should know that by now and there are no accidents. We are all bound by the elements. Our destinies are written in the stars. We are merely puppets to a higher power…a power bound by spirit, water, air, earth and now fire. Your decision to bring Ingrid into our fold…to lead her onto that hilltop all those years ago, was simply an obligatory foundation to your ultimate end."

As Autumn anointed her forehead with oils, Celeste continued to squirm and tug at her binds.

"You won't get away with this. There are others that know I'm here. If I don't return they'll call the police."

"We can't be charged for a crime for which there is no evidence, Celeste. Even if your spineless friends go to the authorities with their suspicions, without a body and nothing to back up their accusations, no harm will come to us."

Victor watched in horror as the drama played out before him. Despite his original intentions to put an end to Eliza and her evil coven of witches, his body was frozen in panic. His entire being, a mirror image of the younger version that stood on that hillside so many years ago, unable to act in response to the sacrifice that was about to take place. Unlike that little boy, his screams of terror were only in his mind as he heard Adara recite the spell while raising the ceremonial dagger above her victim's chest.

"Before this coven of thirteen, amongst those which represent the elements of spirit, water, air and earth, I ask our Goddess to grant my rebirth. From this altar consent to my desire, to be reborn to represent fire. Onto you I offer in sacrifice, this woman who has betrayed us twice. Once in Salem upon a hill, one of our sisters she did kill. Then in coming here tonight, she pledged before us to make things right. Believing truth would set her free, the silencing of this trader falls on me."

There was a brief moment of silence as Adara turned to Eliza, who in turn gave a slight nod to proceed. As if by divine intervention a bolt of lightning struck the roof of the dilapidated barn causing the women to shriek with excitement. In the seconds it took for things to settle down, Victor regained his courage and bolted toward the altar. Hearing the commotion, Adara spun around, the dagger still firmly clasped between her hands as Victor lunged forward in an attempt to disarm her. As the other members of the coven stepped back in shook, both Adara and Victor fell to the floor.

It wasn't until Eliza moved in to separate the two that she realized Adara was pinned beneath his lifeless body. Motioning to Autumn to assist her, Eliza attempted to free her niece. With the help of Autumn, she finally managed to roll him off just in time to see the life drain out of his eyes. As the others, including Celeste looked on in horror; Adara stared down at the dagger protruding from Victor's chest.

"Noooooooo, Vic...no...please...I didn't mean to hurt you." Adara shook him by the shoulders.

"Adara...it's too late...he's gone." Eliza leaned forward and took Adara's chin in the palm of her hand as she forced her to look at her.

"No...he can't be. It wasn't supposed to happen this way. She was the one that was supposed to die." Adara screamed, pointing to Celeste.

"Perhaps the Goddess had other plans. It's not for us to question her choices. Perhaps someday we will understand why she chose him instead, but right now we must proceed."

"No...I can't...I won't." Adara wrapped her arms tightly around herself and rocked back and forth as she continued to stare at Victor's lifeless body.

Eliza rose, addressing the remaining members of the coven.

"Give us a moment."

One by one, the women filed out of the barn leaving only Celeste behind, still tied to the posts. When they were well out of earshot she took Adara by the arms and pulled her up.

"Now you listen to me...we have come too far not to see this through. My destiny...our destiny...is hanging in the balance. The Goddess has clearly made her choice and we must respect her wishes."

"It's not too late. child." Celeste pleaded. "You can make things right...accept the consequences of your actions. Let me go."

"Shut up, Celeste. Just because it's not your blood she will drink tonight it doesn't mean you're walking out of here."

Adara shivered, every nerve in her body strained to the limit as she looked from Eliza, to Celeste and finally to Victor lying still on the floor. Sensing her hesitation, Celeste tried again.

"Please...you don't have to do this. Let me go. Two wrongs don't make a right. What good comes from taking my life? The only thing I did wrong was not seeing that Ingrid had a proper burial. No one was to blame for her death. It was an accident. I live with the guilt of my involvement every day. Isn't that punishment enough? It's no different from what happened tonight. You didn't intend to harm this man."

"She's right." Adara responded in a barely audible whisper. "It's one thing to sacrifice in the name of our Goddess, but to kill her now would only be murder. We already have what we need."

"What then? We let her go...simply let her walk away? What's stopping her from going to the police?" Eliza challenged.

"My DNA is all over this place." Celeste reasoned. "I can't implicate you without incriminating myself. It's no different than what happened before and my silence speaks for itself. Untie me...I will stay until the ritual is complete. I'll even help you clean up."

Eliza considered her offer. "It's not up to just me. The other members will have to agree."

From the doorway Autumn spoke, "We agree...set her free and let Adara drink from the blood of our true sacrifice."

While the remaining members of the coven as well as the inner circle, returned to their original positions, Adara freed Celeste from her bonds. With the help of Eliza, Celeste and Autumn, Victor's body was transferred to the altar where Adara collected the blood of her sacrifice into a waiting chalice.

Stepping aside, Celeste watched as Adara drank from the vessel, binding their spirits forever. Next, Eliza dipped her finger into the chalice and anointed each of the five representatives of the elements.

"By the powers vested in me by the Supreme Goddess, I hereby pronounce you Spirit, Water, Air, Earth and Fire. May you rule as one under the direction of me, your High Priestess, and vow before this coven of your peers to uphold the vocation set forth by our ancestors over three-hundred years ago."

The collective group bowed in unison before their High Priestess, muttering words of gratitude.

As they had arrived, one by one the members of the coven departed, leaving behind only Adara, Autumn, Eliza and Celeste to tend to the unpleasant aftermath. No one present needed instruction as they went about collecting the tools of the ceremony and returning them to the trunk of Eliza's car. When only Victor's body and a couple of lanterns for light remained, Celeste was tasked with pouring gasoline over the corpse and setting it on fire.

"Autumn, you will stay with Celeste until his remains and this structure are reduced to a pile of ash. Make sure no evidence is left behind to indicate we were here."

Eliza took her fragile niece by the arm and escorted her out of the barn.

Chapter Twenty-Eight

It was nearly one o'clock when Eliza dropped her niece off at her cottage. To her amazement, Adara found Thena exactly where they had left her, softly snoring and unaware of the events that had taken place. Uncertain what to do with her sleeping friend; she made her way into the bathroom, where she washed away the pain and scent of the night.

Contrary to her earlier feelings of hatred toward the man who had abandoned her, now she only felt sadness over his senseless death. Why had he come there? What was it he was after? A flurry of questions distracted her from her pain, allowing her to do what needed to be done. Despite shampooing her hair twice and dousing her body in fragrant body oil, she was unable to get the smell of death out of her nose. This should have been a night of celebration. A night filled with joy at having achieved initiation into the circle, but instead it was filled with doubts and pain.

She had just finished drying off when there was a knock at her door. Grabbing the robe hanging from a hook in the bathroom, she wrapped it around her and made her way to the door.

"Mason...I was just going to give you a call." Allowing him to enter, she pointed in the direction of the couch where Thena lay unconscious. "As you can see, someone had a bit too much to drink tonight. I was going to suggest she sleep it off here and I'll send her home in the morning."

Jason laughed. "Gee, you would think a summer of partying would have made her better at handling her liquor."

"I know, right…I guess we should have kept better track of how many she had."

"Okay, well I've had a few too many myself so I can't really talk. Thanks for showing her a good time."

"No problem." Adara watched as Mason stumbling down the beach in the direction of his own cottage before locking the door and turning off the lights.

Out at the barn, Autumn and Celeste sat in uncomfortable silence as the body of Victor and the barn continued to burn. It was all Autumn could do just to hold it together. Watching as the flames engulfed the man she considered not only a friend, but the closest thing to a brother she had ever known, she silently prayed to her Goddess that he find peace in the afterlife. Celeste glanced at the young woman next to her and saw a reflection of herself in the past.

"This doesn't have to consume you. You can walk away from the coven and start fresh."

Autumn ignored her and continued to stare off into the distance.

"I know you don't know me, but I was a lot like you at your age. I went against everything I knew was right to be a part of a group. I ignored the advice of my mother who told me no good could come from my friendship with Eliza and her circle of followers. She was right…I should have listened."

Still Autumn ignored her, staring off into the fire.

"I know you don't know any other way...I know you're afraid. Afraid to go against those that are capable of atrocities like this. Afraid of leaving everyone you know behind and starting a new life. I can help you."

"I don't need your help. I'm fine just where I am. I like being a part of something this important. I like being the right-hand woman to the High Priestess. I like living on the beach and hanging out with my friends. Why would I want to leave?"

"Because somewhere inside you, you know what she's doing isn't right. Because deep down you realize she'll stop at nothing to get what she wants and it scares you to death. What happens when Eliza realizes all this power she thinks she's obtained is all in her head? What happens when she realizes none of this is real and all this pomp and circumstance is just a way to distract those that would otherwise have turned their backs on her long ago? Who do you think she'll take it out on when things don't go her way?"

Autumn turned, looking into the eyes of a woman who knew Eliza's wrath first hand.

"What is it exactly you think Eliza's planning?"

"Honestly...I don't know and that's what scares me. She's spent her whole life preparing for this moment. As far back as elementary school she dreamt of the day when she would lead the most powerful coven this town has ever seen. The problem is, unlike the rest of us who grew up to realize all those stories we heard as kids were nothing more than urban legends engineered to keep us on the straight and narrow, she used every unfortunate turn of events as validation of her beliefs. Most of us grew tired of trying to convince her otherwise and when Ingrid died we decided enough was enough. Those that were weak-minded or simply had nothing or no one else in their lives clung onto her coattails. How she's managed to keep this going is beyond me."

"I got involved through my friendship with Adara." Autumn admitted.

"I assumed as much. It's likely she used her niece to recruit new blood into her fold. The theory that an inner circle would somehow make the coven stronger was simply a way to insure renewed interest in the craft. This is a small town and word gets around. My guess is that interest was waning so she concocted the notion that an inner circle made up of the five elements of the pentacle would produce power beyond imagination. In sacrificing others for sake of initiation into the circle, she guaranteed herself a loyal following."

Autumn rose from the rock she was sitting on and began to pace. Celeste sat quietly waiting for her to digest the truth.

"I'm such an idiot. Bryce has been trying to tell me this was nonsense all along and I didn't believe him. I trusted Eliza...she's been like a second mother to me. There was nothing I wouldn't do for her or Adara. If what you're saying is true, five innocent people have died for nothing...for nothing. I don't know if I can live with that."

Celeste came to her then, wrapping her arms around her in a warm embrace.

"Don't let those responsible for their deaths go unpunished. Take it for me...your guilt will eat at you until nothing else remains. I witnessed my friend die a horrible death and couldn't do anything to stop it. Every night I see her terrified face in my dreams and wish that I could go back in time and change things. No punishment the law could sentence me to could compare to the knowledge that every night, when I lay my head on my pillow I will dream of her tortured screams."

"What can I do? How can I make things right?"

"We can make things right together. I came here tonight to secure evidence of the ritual. I intended to put together a package complete with names, faces and pictures as well as the newspaper articles pertaining to the other sacrifices. None of the agencies seem to be linking them together, which I'm sure was Eliza's plan. My original intention was to mail it anonymously, but I think we should go to a lawyer instead. We can work out an immunity deal in exchange for our testimony. We can make sure Eliza pays for her crimes."

"But what about Adara and the other women that actually performed the sacrifices?"

"That's not up to us to decide. I realize you have much more to lose...these are your friends and I'll understand if you want me to act alone."

"Can I have some time to think about it?"

"Oh course...once your decision is made there's no going back. I want you to be certain."

The barn was now fully engulfed in flames and both Autumn and Celeste prepared to leave before smoke was spotted and fire trucks began to arrive.

"How did you get here?" Autumn asked, looking around for another vehicle.

"I parked up the road, just around the corner and came in through the back way. How do you suppose he got here?" She asked, nodding toward the barn.

"My boyfriend mentioned he borrowed his bike so I'm assuming it's somewhere around here. Should we look for it?"

"It's too dark, we'll come back at daylight."

After giving Celeste a lift down the road to her car, Autumn agreed to meet her back at the barn later the next day to look for Bryce's bike and discuss whatever decision she made. Celeste returned to Annabel's house to find her anxiously waiting at the door. She was so grateful for her safe return that she grabbed her and hugged her close, forgetting the tongue-lashing she had been prepared to give her for not checking in sooner.

Likewise, Bryce was just as thankful to see Autumn and insisted she bring him up to date before retiring for a much-needed rest. Leaving out the perfunctory details of the ritual, Autumn divulged the most significant events, ending with the announcement of Victor's unfortunate passing.

Bryce rose from his position next to her on the couch and began pacing the floor in an attempt to comprehend everything he had heard. Not only had Eliza's ritual resulted in death, it the death of his best friend.

"Bryce…talk to me. Say something…anything." Autumn shook in anticipation of his response.

"I don't know what to say. I can't believe he's gone. This never should have happened."

"I'm so sorry…it wasn't supposed to happen like this."

"And how exactly was it supposed to happen, Autumn? It's one thing to sit around chanting nonsense with a bunch of hippies, but it's another thing entirely to sacrifice a human life. Did you know that was the plan? How many other sacrifices have you witnessed?"

"Please Bryce…sit down…let me explain."

"I'm not sure there's anything you can say that can convince me you're not as guilty as the rest of them. He was my best friend, for God's sake."

"I can set things right, Bryce. Celeste, the woman that was supposed to be the sacrifice, she said we can put an end to this once and for all. We can make Eliza pay for the things she's done. She said she would call a lawyer, that she would work out an immunity deal for us in exchange for our testimony."

"You didn't answer my question. How many sacrifices have you been a part of? How long has this been going on?"

"This was the only one. The others took place out of town and I wasn't involved. I never should have let Adara talk me into it. I knew things were getting out of hand; I should have listened to my gut. I just got so wrapped up in the excitement of it all, I didn't stop to think about the consequences."

"The consequences? Is that what you're worried about? How this will affect you. How about Victor or this woman Celeste? Did you ever consider the worth of their lives? Did it ever occur to you that you were taking another human's life?"

"Oh course…of course. I'm sorry…I can't begin to tell you how guilty I feel. I'll understand if you don't want to see me ever again. I'll understand if you can't find it within yourself to forgive me for my involvement. Don't you think I wish he was never there?"

"Does it really matter? If he didn't come forward to stop the sacrifice, this woman would have been killed. Would you have felt guilty then? Would you have told me what you had done then or would you simply have brushed it off as another night tossing pouches of herbs into a bonfire?"

"I don't know…honestly I didn't think Adara would actually go through with it. I know you've never been particularly fond of her. I know you think she's a bad influence…and you're right, but deep down Adara is just a frightened child, too afraid of her aunt to say no. You don't know her the way I do. She's not the spoiled, selfish person she wants everyone to see her as. That's simply a front to hide her true self. When we're alone…when it's just the two of us, she's different."

Bryce continued to pace the floor as he struggled to separate his love for Autumn from her involvement in his best friend's death. He wanted to wrap his arms around her, cradle her in his arms while they mourned the loss of a good man. Another part of him struggled to resist the urge to grab her by the shoulders and shake her until her teeth rattled and she felt the pain of his loss. Ultimately her soft sobs, composed of guilt and sorrow were his undoing and he went to her, to comfort her in her time of need. At some point her tears subsided and he laid down with her, not bothering to pull out the sofa bed.

It wasn't until the sun peaked through the blinds around noon that they woke up to face the day.

"I told Celeste I would meet her back at the barn to look for your bike and give her my answer about bringing Eliza to justice. I should probably check in on Adara before I go just to make sure she's okay."

Bryce nodded, "Would you like me to go with you? To meet Celeste, that is."

"You would do that?"

"I don't want you going alone. It could be a trap and I don't think I could handle it if anything happened to you."

"Thank you, but I don't think you need to worry. If she were going to hurt me she would have done it last night. We were alone for hours. Still, I would feel better with you at my side."

Agreeing to the plan, Bryce got dressed while Autumn made a quick visit next door to check in on Adara. Although it was evident she had been crying, she insisted she was okay and just wanted to be alone.

It was well into the afternoon when Bryce and Autumn arrived to find Celeste anxiously waiting next to the smoldering pile of rubble that was all that remained of the barn. She turned to them, but hesitated to approach until Autumn indicated it was safe by a slight nod of her head.

"I'm sorry it took us so long to get here. I had a little trouble locating the entrance without the markers. I hope we haven't kept you waiting too long."

"It's no trouble, I had nowhere else to be. Have you made your decision?"

Autumn looked at Bryce who nodded in confirmation.

"I'll do whatever needs to be done to end Eliza's reign once and for all. Even if that means I go down in the process. I simply can't live with Victor's blood on my hands."

"You're doing the right thing…we're doing the right thing. It's time we set things right."

Chapter Twenty-Nine

Thena had awoken at first light, confused as to where she was and what had happened the previous night. It took her a moment to adjust to her surroundings and thinking she was in bed she rolled over and immediately fell to the floor. Realizing she was still at Adara's she rubbed her temples and attempted to piece together her last lucid memories. Although she didn't recall having more than one drink, clearly she had much more and she stumbled to her feet and headed for the door.

Picking her way across the wet sand to her cottage she wondered whether or not she had told Mason she was spending the night down the beach and accordingly whether or not he would be furious at her for not coming home. A pounding head and upset stomach were too much to bear and she dropped to her knees just outside her cottage and vomited.

Inside she could hear the loud snores of Mason, who had evidently spent the night alone at her cottage instead of his own. Covering her sickness with a handful of wet sand, she rose slowly and climbed the steps, carefully clinging to the railing for support.

Once inside she poured herself a glass of orange juice and fumbled through her pocketbook for a bottle of Tylenol. The rattling sound of the pills awoke Shane, who jumped off the bed to greet Thena with great enthusiasm. Rewarding his affection with a treat from a box on the counter, she brushed the sand off her feet with a nearby dishcloth and joined Mason under the covers.

It wasn't until well after noon that Mason, encouraged by Shane's persistent nudging, rolled out of bed and awoke Thena in the process.

"Hey, when did you get in?" Mason asked groggily.

"I'm not sure…sometime this morning. I don't know what I did last night, but I don't remember a thing after arriving at Adara's. I'm almost afraid to find out where we went."

"You're not the only one that over-indulged. Bryce and I got pretty plastered ourselves. I stopped by Adara's on my way back, but you were sound asleep on the couch so I just left you there."

Shane tugged at the sleeve of Mason's shirt, reminding him that he needed to go out.

"Okay, boy…why don't you put on a pot of coffee and I'll make us some breakfast after I take him out."

Thena nodded, rising slowly in fear of another bout of nausea.

After a large breakfast of bacon, eggs and toast, Thena showered and headed over to Adara's to find out exactly what she had done the night before. She knocked several times on the door, but there was no response so she headed over to Autumn's assuming she was next door. Once again she knocked, peering through the picture window to the right of the door, but saw no movement inside. Returning to her own cottage she informed Mason of their unusual absence.

"They probably went off together somewhere. I'm sure they'll stop by at some point today to check on you."

"Yeah, I'm sure you're right. I guess they didn't drink as much as I apparently did."

"I'm sure they did…they're just better at it than you." Mason teased.

Normally she would have been thrilled with the rare moment of peace away from their wild friends down the beach, but anxiety over the fact she had no recollection of her actions the previous night, plagued her every thought. Unlike her, Mason was content to simply enjoy the peace and quiet. Only a handful of tourists remained as the summer was quickly coming to an end and the beach was practically deserted. Other than themselves, there were only a few stragglers quietly sunbathing and occasionally popping into the water for a quick swim to cool off.

It was nearly five o'clock when Celeste arrived unexpectedly with Bryce and Autumn in tow. By the look on the three of their faces, they were not bearing good news.

"Celeste? Autumn? I didn't know you two knew each other."

Celeste ignored the statement. "We need to talk. Can we go inside?"

Mason looked at Thena just in time to see the color drain out of her face and he grabbed her by the shoulders to steady her.

"Is everything okay, Celeste?" he asked.

"Can we go inside?" Celeste repeated.

"Of course." Thena managed to choke out in a barely audible whisper.

For more than an hour, while Mason held Thena's hand in solidarity, Celeste and Autumn relayed the events leading up to and including the previous night. Although present, Bryce remained quiet, listening to their confessions while keeping a watchful eye on Mason and Thena for their response. As for Mason and Thena, neither was prepared for what they heard, especially from Celeste.

"I tried to warn you about Eliza." Celeste was saying. "I didn't know how to convince you without revealing my own involvement, something I hoped I'd never have to do."

"I can't believe he's gone." Mason interrupted.

"I'm so sorry." Autumn cried. "I still don't know why he was there. If he had only left town…"

"What matters now is that we make things right. Autumn and I have already spoken to my attorney and she's confident we can work out an immunity deal in exchange for our testimony. We thought we owed it to you both to tell you ourselves before it goes public. We don't expect your forgiveness or understanding. What we did was wrong, none of us are innocent, but we hope by putting an end to this once and for all we can somehow move on."

"What about Adara?" Thena asked.

"She didn't intend to kill Victor, it was an accident, but she was prepared to take my life. Whether or not she would have gone through with it, we'll never know."

"Does she know what's about to happen?"

"No…and it's important she doesn't know. We've given my lawyer…our lawyer, the names of all those involved and they'll all be brought in for questioning, but until then it's important Eliza doesn't get wind of any of this. There's a number of agencies that are involved here since the sacrifices took place in five different states so it might be a few days before they get organized. Until then it's imperative we watch each other's backs."

"Thena…I just want you to know, it was never our intent to hurt you. Adara and I both love you like a sister."

Thena looked into Autumn's eyes for the first time since they'd come together and saw only genuine pain and remorse.

"I guess that should make me feel better but it doesn't. You were willing to sacrifice Celeste, a woman I think of as a second mother. You had to know it would bring me grief."

"To be honest, I was so wrapped up in the details I didn't think of much else. The friendship Adara and I have shown you was sincere. Obviously our original plan was to draw you in giving you just enough of a glimpse into our world that you would share your uneasiness with Celeste, but somehow over the course of the summer we grew quite fond of both you and Mason. If we had thought for a moment that you were in danger, we would have warned you. Even if it meant going against Eliza's wishes."

"That may be, Autumn, but you were still willing to take Celeste's life."

Autumn buried her head in her hands, unable to face those she had betrayed.

"What's important now is to set things right." Celeste reminded them. "There'll be time after all this is over to talk things out. Right now we need to act as though everything is normal. Autumn...I think you should go to Adara. She's probably grieving over Victor's loss."

Autumn nodded, unable to speak for fear of bursting into tears. With the help of Bryce, she made her way to the door, stopping at the threshold and turning to once again face her accusers.

"I truly am sorry...I hope someday you can forgive me."

Thena looked away, focusing her attention on the floor until she heard the screen door close behind them and their footsteps on the steps.

"What about you? Are you okay?" She asked. Moving away from Mason to sit next to Celeste.

"A little shaken up, but otherwise I'm okay. Don't judge Autumn too harshly. I know firsthand how easy it is to get sucked into Eliza's world. She has a way of convincing people that it's in their best interest to follow her commands. This is a small town and you're either with them or against them. It took me a long time to come to that realization. If Ingrid hadn't died that night I might still be one of her flock. I'd like to think not, but the truth is there's a real feeling of belonging within the coven. It's something that's hard to understand unless you've been a part of it yourself. It's a sisterhood that goes deeper than family. You share a common bond that encompasses not just the spiritual level, but beyond. The secrets you share bind you as one against all else and it takes over every aspect of your life."

"Even so, how do you know you can trust Autumn now?" Mason asked.

"Because I see myself in her. It's obvious she wasn't as committed to the craft as Adara. That's probably why Eliza made Autumn her right-hand. Keeping her close ensured Adara would continue to do her bidding. Eliza has never dirtied her hands personally. Like Charles Manson she sat idly by while she enlisted others to act out her dirty deeds, guaranteeing their loyalty and commitment with the knowledge that if they dared to go against her, the blood was on their hands."

"If I know Eliza, she's been grooming Adara since she was old enough to walk. She never had a choice. It was

Autumn's unfortunate luck to become friends with her and in doing so, forcing her into a role of servitude. Like I said...it's a small town. The fact that she returned to meet me today of her own free will, speaks well of her character. Whatever happens now is fate."

"I don't understand how you can be so calm about all this. Your life is hanging in the balance. What about Clay? Does he know about your past?"

"No, Mason, he doesn't, but he soon will. I'm returning to Boston tonight to tell him in person. I fear his response more than any punishment I might face through the courts. I only pray that our love for each other is strong enough to endure whatever embarrassment this may cause him. You know as well as I how fickle the investment game is. You can be on top one day and on the next investors are scrambling to distance themselves from anything associated with your name. I would certainly understand if you want to resign before this goes public."

"I would never abandon you and Clay. You're like family to me. Whatever happens; happens...we'll deal with it. People have short memories when it comes to business. There's always another headline just around the corner. Whatever happens in the short term won't affect the end game. You can let Clay know I stand behind him no matter what. Perhaps that knowledge might make it easier for him to forgive you for your involvement."

Their conversation was interrupted by the sound of a blood-curdling scream down the beach and they rushed to the door just in time to see Autumn run out of Adara's cottage and drop to her knees, followed by Bryce. Mason took off down the beach while Thena and Celeste stood frozen on the porch. While they watched anxiously, Mason briefly bent down to talk to the couple before staggering backward in response to whatever was said and looking in the direction of Adara's cottage. As quickly as he'd gone, he returned, rushing past the women in search of his cell phone. From where they stood, both Celeste and Thena clearly heard the word "suicide".

Chapter Thirty

The residents of Wells, along with Thena and Mason; grieved the loss of their loved one as Celeste slipped out of town unnoticed. Adara had left little in the way of a reason as to why she took her life, trusting those close to her needed no explanation. Rumors around town hinted to the end of her relationship with Victor being simply too much to bear. A brief note was found next to her hanging body requesting her ashes be tossed out to sea.

Autumn took her friend's death especially hard and while present at her funeral services, she appeared somewhat catatonic, requiring the assistance of Bryce to perform basic functions. Whether she was heavily sedated or going through a temporary breakdown, was difficult to say, but Eliza kept a watchful eye on her in fear she might inadvertently divulge their secrets. Mason and Thena paid their respects to Eliza and the rest of her family, careful to appear saddened by the death while not suspicious. Eliza was too distracted by the potential fallout should anyone question Victor's noticeable absence to suspect they might be privy to the real reason behind her suicide.

With a great number of the town's residents in attendance the FBI as well as the State Police moved in, rounding up the remaining members of the coven including Autumn. As the rest of the mourners stood by in stunned silence, one by one they were lead out of the funeral parlor in handcuffs to a caravan of waiting vehicles to take them to the police barracks. Eliza was the only one among the group to speak out, vowing to make them pay for disrespecting her niece's service.

As the final car drove away the remaining towns people began to depart, splitting off into groups to discuss their interpretation of the events leading up to Adara's death and what involvement the coven played. Only Bryce, Mason and Thena remained to pay respect to their fallen comrade.

"I should go...I want to be there for Autumn when she's done giving her statement." Bryce explained.

"Oh course...go. If there's anything you need you know where to find us." Thena assured him.

Bryce nodded, turning briefly for one final look at the deceased before heading out the door. Out of respect, Thena and Mason stayed until the funeral director closed the lid of the coffin and informed them the service was over.

When they exited the building Annabel was waiting for them outside.

"Celeste left without taking her things. I was hoping you could bring them back to Boston with you."

"Of course." Mason agreed. "Have you heard from her?"

"No...but I expect she'll need some time before she's ready to talk. I can't imagine how difficult it must have been to reveal a secret she's been keeping from Clay all these years."

"I've known Clay a long time...if anyone would understand it would be him. I can't imagine he would turn his back on her for something that happened before they even met, even if it might hurt his reputation." Mason insisted.

"I agree, they have a difficult road ahead of them, but if anyone can get through this it's them."

Thena stood by while Mason followed Annabel to her car, where she removed Celeste's suitcase from the trunk. How could the most unexpectedly wonderful three months of her life end so tragically? Only a week ago her biggest worry was how she would manage to get through her first week back at school without being able to come home each night to Mason's loving arms. Now all she could think about was Celeste and whether or not Autumn would recover from the loss of her best friend or choose to take the easy way out and follow her to the grave.

Mason returned to her side concerned about the faraway look in her eyes.

"Are you okay? We should probably get you something to eat. You barely touched your breakfast this morning."

"I'm not very hungry."

"Maybe not, but you still need to eat. I'll stop at Billy's on the way back to the beach and pick up some fish and chips."

Thena merely nodded, too exhausted to argue.

Later that night, Bryce stopped by to give them an update. He explained that Eliza along with four other members of the coven had been charged with the murder of four women and were being held pending trial. The remaining members were charged with the lesser crime of accessory and obstruction of justice for their part in covering up the crimes and were released on bail. As for Autumn, as Celeste had predicted, she was granted immunity in exchange for her full cooperation and future testimony and was now resting under heavy sedation.

"Is there anything we can do?" Mason offered.

"Actually there is. Victor never talked about his family so I'm not certain if he had any living relatives, but he did say he was from the Boston area. I was hoping you might be able to do a little digging when you go back. His remains...whatever is left of them anyway, have been turned over to the police and I imagine it will be some time before they release them for burial. If possible I'd like to see that his ashes are tossed out to sea along with Adara's. No matter what happened in the end, I know they loved each other."

"Oh, of course, it's the least I can do."

Mason and Thena walked Bryce out to the porch where they said their goodbyes. As they watched him disappear down the beach into the darkness, Thena realized none of their lives would ever be the same. The plans they had made for the next summer would never come to pass. Memories of the countless hours she had sat around with Adara and Autumn discussing details of weddings that would never take place would forever be an eerie reminder of what could have been. Recollections of evenings spent sitting in front of the fire, drinking hard lemonade and listening to Victor strum on the guitar would haunt her long after the salty air left her lungs and the crashing waves ceased to loll her to sleep.

Mason wrapped his arms around her trembling body, leading her back inside. Tomorrow would come too quickly, putting distance between these painful memories as well as each other. Their future was yet to be seen as well as whatever role the coven might have in deciding the fate of their loved ones. Until then...they had each other and not fire, earth, air, water nor spirit could take that away from them

~*~*~

Also by Cheryl Kennedy

<u>The Forgotten Treaty</u>

A historical action adventure romance. The introduction of the story begins in 1763. It is the end of the French and Indian War, however not every man has laid down his weapons. One group of greedy settlers takes it upon themselves to descend on a peaceful tribe of Abenaki Indians along the coast of Lake Champlain in upstate Vermont. The white men kill many of the tribe's men, women and children while one man in particular seeks out the Chief's daughter. The Chief's only daughter who is close to the end of her pregnancy runs for her life, but cannot escape the white man, who catches her when she suddenly goes into labor. After raping her and killing her newborn child he leaves her barely clinging to life. The man is hunted down by the tribe and brought back to face the Chief. A broken man, the Chief no longer has the will to fight and agrees to sign over the land to the white man, but only after he agrees to sign a treaty that the white man has no intention of honoring.

The present day story begins with the introduction of the main character Lily Moreau. Lily, who resides in Boston, Massachusetts is contacted by an estate attorney and is asked to go to Vermont for the reading of a will for a woman she does not know. Confused but intrigued, Lily, who is in her first trimester of pregnancy, decides to drive up to Vermont alone. After she is told she is the sole heir for the woman's estate, Lily decides to go to the property to try to figure out how she is connected to the deceased. Lily is befriended by a local Indian girl named Abey who stands by her while it seems that the whole town is out to get her. Fearing for her safety after several attacks on her property as well as herself, she considers leaving town, but as she discovers more and more about her ancestors, her curiosity clouds her better judgment. What is the connection between her family and the local Indian tribe? What significance does this property hold to the tribe? And to what lengths are they willing to go to get it back?

__Buried Secrets__

A charming little cottage sits on the shore of a private cove tucked between the islands of Jamestown and Newport, Rhode Island. The apparently innocent cottage conceals secrets of romance, murder, vengeance and revenge. Abandoned by its previous owners, or so it appears, what once was intended as an elderly couple's retreat becomes the back drop for nearly a half a century of one family's involvement in murder, betrayal and buried secrets.

Turning off the main street onto the rough gravel road leading to the summer cottage, Philip glanced again in his rearview mirror. Knowing she would follow him, he had loosened the bulb of one headlight enough that it would flicker on and off like a beckon, making it easy to recognize her vehicle even in the complete darkness of the back roads. As he rounded the corner he turned off his own headlights before steering his car off the road and parking it just behind the tall sea grass separating the road from the beach beyond. Smiling to himself as he watched her pass him, he lit a cigarette and settled in.

He had waited too many years for this moment, all the while suffering through countless social functions with her and her highbrow Newport friends. Never had they welcomed him into their circle, always looking at him with something between pity and amusement. He had been nothing more to her than a way to get back at her father; a game with no winner and he was the pawn. Glancing at his watch, he snuffed out the remainder of his cigarette and opened his car door. By now, he was certain, she had checked the cottage and was searching for him on the beach, hoping to catch him in the act for yet another opportunity to ridicule him. He shook his head recalling the countless times she had used his middle-class upbringing as a means by which to make herself feel superior.

It was he who had suggested they buy the property that had long been abandoned by its previous owners. All his research had led him here and he was certain that given the opportunity he would soon locate some of the missing treasure from one of the shipwrecks history recorded on the Rhode Island coast.

And so the saga begins.

<u>The Fatal Cache</u>

We've all experienced the thrill of hiding, the terror of being found. But what if no one's searching? What if no one knows you've hidden? What if you've hidden so well that you can't be found? Or better yet... what if they abandon the hunt altogether?

About our Author
Cheryl Kennedy

Born and raised in St. Albans, Vermont, Cheryl Kennedy graduated from Castleton State College where she received her degree in Communications with a concentration in Journalism. Cheryl wrote for both her high school as well as her college newspapers. While attending college, she published several poems in various anthologies. In

1983 she married her college sweetheart and moved to Rhode Island. Today Cheryl and her husband of 28 years reside in Bristol, RI. After a lengthy absence from writing while she worked and raised her two daughters, Cheryl returned to writing with the publication of a short autobiographical story The Year Off that was published earlier this year